10ᵀᴴ ANNIVERSARY

**Special thanks to our well-wishers,
who have contributed their
congratulations and support.**

"The best historicals, the best romances. Simply the best!"
—Dallas Schulze

"Bronwyn Williams was born and raised at Harlequin
Historicals. We couldn't have asked for a better home or a
more supportive family."
—Dixie Browning and Mary Williams,
w/a Bronwyn Williams

"I can't believe it's been ten years since *Private Treaty,* my
first historical novel, helped launch the Harlequin
Historicals line. What a thrill that was! And the beat goes
on...with timeless stories about men and women in love."
—Kathleen Eagle

"Nothing satisfies me as much as writing or reading a
Harlequin Historical novel. For me, Harlequin Historicals
are the ultimate escape from the problems of everyday
life."
—Ruth Ryan Langan

"As a writer and reader, I feel that the Harlequin Historicals
line always celebrates a perfect blend of history and
romance, adventure and passion, humor and sheer magic."
—Theresa Michaels

"Thank you, Harlequin Historicals, for opening up a 'window into the past' for so many happy readers."
——Suzanne Barclay

"As a one-time 'slush pile' foundling at Harlequin Historicals, I'll be forever grateful for having been rescued and published as one of the first 'March Madness' authors. Harlequin Historicals has always been *the* place for special stories, ones that blend the magic of the past with the rare miracle of love for books that readers never forget."
——Miranda Jarrett

"A rainy evening. A cup of hot chocolate. A stack of Harlequin Historicals. Absolute bliss! Happy tenth Anniversary and continued success."
——Cheryl Reavis

"Happy birthday, Harlequin Historicals! I'm proud to have been a part of your ten years of exciting historical romance."
——Elaine Barbieri

"Harlequin Historicals are charming or disarming with dashes and clashes. These past times are fast times, the gems of romances!"
——Karen Harper

the Flower
and the
Sword

Jacqueline Navin

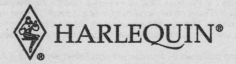

HARLEQUIN®

TORONTO • NEW YORK • LONDON
AMSTERDAM • PARIS • SYDNEY • HAMBURG
STOCKHOLM • ATHENS • TOKYO • MILAN • MADRID
PRAGUE • WARSAW • BUDAPEST • AUCKLAND

To a wonderful writer, my sister and my best friend, Mary.
To my good friends and fellow writers:
Betty, Carol, Helen, Kate, Kay, Krisann, Lorie,
Mary Anne and Peter.
And to Karen Kosztolnyik—big thanks!

ISBN 0-373-29028-4

THE FLOWER AND THE SWORD

Copyright © 1998 by Jacqueline Navin

Another voice, rich and bold, cut through the silence of the chapel.

"I am afraid she cannot marry, Father, for she already has a husband."

Lily's head shot up, and she whipped around toward the voice. That voice! It could only be...

Rogan stood directly in front of her, staring with a thunderous expression.

Rogan. Rogan was here. Alive. Impossibly, blessedly alive. Staring at her with a terrible, evil-looking smile twisting his lips. His eyes gleamed silver by the dim flames of the candles. Trust him to appear in such a shocking manner, Lily thought, so smug and poised and magnificent!

Also available from Harlequin Historicals and
JACQUELINE NAVIN

The Maiden and the Warrior (#403)

Coming soon

A Rose at Midnight (#447)

Prologue

Cornwall, England
February 1197

Lily sat perfectly still in the gathering darkness of dusk, back straight, hands folded and unmoving on her lap. She stared unblinkingly into the void of shadows crowding her chamber, blind to all the world had to offer.

Pain cradled her in its arms like an old friend, not fooled by her dry eyes and composed face.

Tomorrow she would wed a man she had met only once. A kind man with a gentle smile, whom she could never love, for all her love was dead.

She did not understand yet how all her happiness had crumbled into ashes. Or why. She was not even certain she was to blame, yet guilt ate at her soul and melded with her broken heart.

The man she loved was gone, and with him all her dreams....

Chapter One

Cornwall, England
July 1196

"My God, look at it," Andrew said to his brother. Rogan St. Cyr squinted up at the horizon.

The castle of Charolais perched on the brink of a seaside cliff, a dark sentinel standing watch over the raging surf below. Like its infamous neighbor, Tintagel, Charolais was a functional fitting together of cold, gray stone. Spartan, perhaps, but not grotesque. Rather, its awesome presence owed more to the atmosphere lent by the savage elements of its surrounding: restless sea, rolling skies and gray, barren moor that stretched as far as the eye could see.

Rogan felt a clenching deep in his gut. It had been a long time since he could last recall being nervous. Oh, a certain intensity gripped him just before battle, even after so many times, but nerve-jangling anxiety was something to which he was not accustomed.

Not for the first time, he reflected that he was not

the man for the duty awaiting him. He had no skill at diplomacy, nor did he possess a glib tongue adept at tripping over subtleties and false praise. He was a warrior—he had never been anything else—but he was also a man of honour and that was why he had come.

"I swear, my hackles are rising," Andrew muttered as they neared.

Rogan grunted and kicked his horse forward, his broad-shouldered frame moving in rhythm with the charcoal stallion. He looked completely at ease, but his eyes missed nothing as he and his men entered the gate and advanced into the lower bailey.

At Rogan's continued silence, Andrew said, "I know this duty weighs heavy on you."

Rogan finally spoke. "Not even you realize how much, brother."

As they passed through the inner gatehouse, the steep rise of the keep came into view. It was plain and unadorned, like a monolithic grave marker. The thought threw a jagged ripple up Rogan's spine.

They drew to a halt and dismounted. At Andrew's continued perusal, Rogan snapped, "Why the devil do you keep staring at me?"

"It is a sin to swear," Andrew said with a grin. Rogan finally looked at him, astonished. His younger sibling rarely took anything seriously, least of all sin—this despite the fact he was a priest.

Rogan handed the reins to one of his men and glanced about uneasily. "Garven, take the others and stay outside. Andrew, come with me."

From the huge studded door, a liveried porter eyed

him curiously. Rogan announced himself to the man, who responded with rounded eyes and a quick dash down a corridor. He and Andrew stepped inside the huge hall.

Their boots scraping across the stone floor created an echo that played a ghostly game among the vaults overhead. Rows of windows were set in elaborately arched openings, now shuttered against the late afternoon heat. Weapons hung on the limestone walls, showing the family colors emblazoned on shields and displayed boldly on banners. Several tapestries were featured, depicting battle scenes woven with care by the generations of Marshand women in order to commemorate the military prowess of their husbands and sons.

Expelling a long breath, Rogan rubbed the back of his neck. "He's rich," he said in a low voice. "He will have no trouble mounting an army."

"We are here to make certain he shall not need one," Andrew said calmly. "We shall grovel properly and offer pretty phrases to assuage his pride, and he will forgive us. Although I still say Alexander should be here to make his own apology. Let *him* beg for pardon—"

He was cut off by Rogan's derisive snort. "The idiot would make matters worse, prattling on about *love.*"

Andrew grinned. "I take it you are no great believer in true love?"

"Hardly." Rogan's handsome face was cold.

"Well, I cannot say that I either believe or disbelieve it. It has never happened to me, nor is it likely to. I am pledged to chastity and though I may be loose with my other obligations, I will not go back on a vow. Yet I must admit our colicky brother seems positively blissful with his merchant's daughter.''

"Never confuse lust and love, Andrew. Judging by the amount of time they spend in private chambers, I would say it is less an urging of the heart than an urging of a more primitive nature.'' Rogan's gaze roamed, touching on the slack, overweight knights lounging about playing chess and quaffing mead. "Alexander's mind is muddled and our family honor is at stake.''

"Agreed. And it is always you defending it.''

It was true. Although Alexander was the eldest, and had inherited the duchy and its vast estates, Rogan, the second son, shouldered the responsibility. He had hoped his four-year absence while he fought in the Holy Land would have encouraged Alexander to accept the weightier aspects of his office. As it happened, his blustering, bullheaded brother had learned nothing of tact and self-discipline. Now, less than a year after Rogan had returned from King Richard's crusade, Alex had committed the most flagrant act of disregard yet.

Rogan ran his hand through his auburn hair, ignoring the stubborn lock that fell back onto his forehead. "Where is Marshand?''

As if conjured by Rogan's impatience, a loud exclamation announced their host's arrival. Rogan swung around to face Enguerrand Marshand coming toward them. The man was short and, though not fat, had an oddly proportioned body. His hose showed almost impossibly skinny legs for such a rounded middle. Most of his hair was gone, except for a feathering of gray that wrapped around the back of his head from ear to ear. He was beaming with pleasure until he drew closer and his eyes focused on Rogan. His bushy eyebrows went down as his glance darted toward Andrew. "Where is the duke?" he said in a demanding voice.

Rogan discovered an instant dislike to this arrogant little man. "I am Rogan St. Cyr, Alexander's brother. This is my younger brother, Father Andrew."

Enguerrand did not spare the priest so much as a glance. "When I was told it was St. Cyr colors you were flying, I assumed it was the duke."

"Father?" a sharp voice demanded. Rogan had not at first noticed the woman who stood behind Enguerrand. Tall and willowy with a flawless complexion and symmetrical features, she was inarguably a beauty. Her hair was pulled back neatly in the style of the day, highlighting the prominence of her cheekbones and her pointed chin. This must be Catherine, the woman Alexander had spurned, Rogan thought. She certainly seemed of the appropriate age and he had heard tell of her comliness, though the rigid, austere perfection of this woman spoke of a coldness that faintly repelled.

"Is something amiss?" Catherine asked.

"That is why I am here," Rogan said evenly. The tension was building inside, stretching his nerves so taut he feared they would snap.

Andrew chose that moment to speak. "Perhaps we

should all sit," he said, motioning to a cluster of comfortable-looking chairs by the huge hearth.

Enguerrand was too impatient. "I want to know what is afoot. Why are you here without the duke?"

Rogan saw no point in delaying. Taking a bracing breath, he said, "He will not be coming. I am here to offer my family's formal apology and to announce that my brother is severing negotiations with you for the hand of your daughter." Rogan paused, dreading what came next. "Alexander has decided on another."

There was a short, stunned silence. "Married another?" Catherine said at last. Her lovely features contorted into a mask of outrage. "Who?"

This was the worst part. "A merchant's daughter. Her name is Carina."

"He married a merchant's daughter?" Enguerrand exclaimed shrilly.

Placing a comforting hand on the man, Andrew said, "Perhaps you would like that seat, now, I think we should—"

"Get your bloody hands off me!" Enguerrand thundered.

"Perhaps not," Andrew answered smoothly, stepping away.

"My brother has chosen his wife based on love," Rogan said without apology, surprised he could do so. His earlier apprehension was gone, and he faced Enguerrand like any opponent, only this time the parrying was with words instead of blows. Still his hand itched with longing to feel the comfort of his sword hilt. He kept it clenched to control the instinct.

"Love?" Catherine choked.

Andrew shrugged. "Who can explain that intangible emotion? It strikes even the most noble among us, and can be—"

"This is an outrage!" Enguerrand exploded. "He and I were discussing the bride-price! How much further did he think he could lead me? It is a breach of contract, a crime!"

There it was, the accusation he had feared. Rogan narrowed his eyes, ready to leap to the defense when a movement out of the corner of his eye stole his attention.

He turned, looked, then stopped.

Enguerrand's tirade faded into the background as the loveliest female Rogan had ever set eyes upon rushed forward.

She was dressed little better than a servant, in a faded gown that was much too small for her and more the worse for wear. Her hair was a riotous mass of soft ringlets that fell clear to her waist and was of the same tawny color as the noble lion he had seen many times in his travels. Her eyes, which were now wide with worry, were an impossible shade of blue. No, green. No, somewhere in between, like the color of a tropical sea.

He stood transfixed, watching her wordlessly as she came to him and sank into a deep curtsy, her head bowed. The untamed mane slid forward like a curtain, stealing his view of that beautiful face.

"Your grace," she murmured.

He was frozen for a moment. Then impulsively he reached down and touched her chin with his fingertips, tilting her head up. Those eyes fluttered open to meet his and she smiled a bashful, tentative smile.

"Lily!" Enguerrand boomed. "Get off the floor."

Confusion passed over her features. She looked about as if searching each face for an answer.

Catherine glared at her sister. "He is not the duke, you ninny. Get up! Where were you?"

"I was in the orchard," Lily explained. Hesitantly, and with a doubtful glance at Rogan, she rose to her feet.

"Where is Elspeth?"

"At chapel, I think." Lily darted another self-conscious look his way, and Rogan instinctively sensed her embarrassment at being chastised in front of him. Again an inexplicable impulse seized him and he offered a small bow. "I am Alexander's brother, Rogan." He smiled. "And you are the Lady Lily."

"Yes," she answered. Her voice was as soft as a breeze.

"I want an explanation!" Enguerrand demanded. "I wish to speak to the duke myself. For all I know this could be a trick. I've never met you two."

"It is no trick, Enguerrand," Rogan said firmly. However, he seemed to be losing his focus. The girl, Lily, was following the conversation with a mixture of bemusement and alarm, and he found the play of these emotions on her face infinitely fascinating. "You know Alexander was reluctant to make the contract final."

"He all but gave his word!" Enguerrand thundered.

It was Andrew who diffused the situation. "Well,

I must say that you are handling this with amazing self-control." This made Enguerrand's eyes bulge in astonishment. The older man was doing no such thing and knew it. Andrew continued smoothly, "I know many men, lesser men than you, Enguerrand, who would have drawn their sword and run us through without waiting for explanation. Oh, you are angry and I don't blame you. Unfortunate business, and we are all the worse off for it. You have a right to make complaint, as does your lovely daughter. But you are a man who has lofty morals, I can see, and knows the value of talking things through. Quite admirable."

Enguerrand had fallen silent and was staring at the younger St. Cyr with openmouthed shock. Andrew went on, "Of course, with the country in the state it is today, what with John aspiring to the crown and the barons in such an uproar, 'tis well that such rash behavior is beneath a man such as yourself. Why, it could mean war, and that would decimate two houses. It is hardly worth it, you will agree, but not every man would have the wisdom to see that and do what is best for his people."

Incredibly, Andrew's facetious compliments seemed to have their intended impact. Enguerrand was taken off guard and more than a bit confused, but he relaxed slightly, muttering, "Quite so. Indeed, terrible business."

For the moment, Enguerrand seemed deflated. Behind him Catherine seethed silently. Rogan exchanged glances with his brother, and Andrew flashed him a quick lift of his eyebrows in triumph.

When he turned back, Rogan saw that Lily had

witnessed his brother's irreverent gesture. Her lips compressed in a tight, controlled smile as she lowered her eyes. That simple gesture caused a sweet warmth to spread through him. With an effort, he tore his gaze away and attended his host.

Enguerrand was still disgruntled. However, he offered them sit at his table and ordered refreshments set out. Rogan inclined his head in acceptance of the offer of hospitality, relieved that, for the time being, at least, Enguerrand seemed to have calmed. Catherine, he could see, had not. Pushing aside his interest in the gentler sister, Rogan saw where his duty lay and offered the cold beauty his arm. Her eyes smoldered resentfully and then she blinked. Rogan thought he spied a flash of interest as if she had recognized something she hadn't noticed before.

Behind him, Rogan heard Andrew say, "I am neither duke nor crusading hero, but a humble priest. However, I have been told I am a pleasant enough fellow. May I?"

Lily must have taken his arm, for he heard a quiet Thank-you in response.

Rogan became uncomfortably aware that he was, of all things, envious of his younger brother.

Chapter Two

Lily Marshand had the most extraordinary sensation, of the world—the dull, familiar, unexciting, predictable world she had always known—having been turned as a whole and set askew so that everything seemed new, interesting, vibrant. Her pulse was still thrumming from when *he* had touched her, and thoughts raced wildly through her mind so quickly that each one barely had time to register before it was gone.

Rogan St. Cyr. Her mind slid over the name again and again. God's teeth, he was handsome. That he was a soldier was easy to see, both in his well-muscled frame and the fluid manner in which he moved. Only a warrior had that economy of motion. His hair was thick and a deep russet, like tarnished copper, falling in waves to curl slightly against the nape of his neck. Straight nose, square chin, strong white teeth that gleamed when he smiled. Oh, yes, he was glorious, but not just that. He had been gentle and kind, and when he had looked at her with those strange gray eyes she had seen something incomprehensible, and yet utterly exciting.

She was being wretchedly silly. He probably was like that with everyone. She had, more than likely, imagined the way his wolflike gaze had held hers and how his sensuous mouth had curved ever so slightly when their eyes first met.

Still she was deeply gratified he was not Catherine's betrothed. Or ex-betrothed, as it now stood.

Belatedly she realized Andrew was speaking to her. "I am sorry," she said, blinking away distraction. "What did you say?"

"I was merely commenting that I do not think that Rogan is very pleased with the arrangements," Andrew said. The mention of Rogan's name made Lily tense.

"Oh, what arrangements?"

"The seating arrangements. He is with Catherine trying to calm her. Tell me, does he have a chance?"

Lily immediately liked this young man, who looked to be not much older than her ten and nine years. She had hardly noticed him before, being much too overwhelmed with his imposing companion, but he was genuinely warm with laughing eyes and a gentle, oft-smiling mouth. "I must admit, Catherine can be difficult. I am certain your brother will find the right words." She couldn't resist a glance in Rogan's direction. He was speaking to Catherine, and from the look of her, Catherine was indeed thawing.

"On the contrary, my brother is usually a man of very few words." Andrew leaned forward to see for himself. "Odd, Rogan is not the most accomplished of diplomats. Well, maybe he has never tried before. Or perhaps Catherine is just succumbing to his charm. Women usually do. They find him fascinating for some reason. His looks please them, and there is his prowess on the battlefield—that is fairly legendary, if you will indulge a brother's pride. But I think the most appealing thing is he seems not to care a whit about them. For some strange reason, it attracts them all the more.''

"Really?" Lily said, hoping her interest appeared casual so Andrew would not count her among those countless besotted.

A half smile playing on his lips, Andrew said, "I hope I am not shocking you.''

"Oh, no!" Lily hurried to assure him. "Not at all.''

"Perhaps these things are not for delicate ears. I forget myself. Maybe we should change the topic.''

"Please don't,'' she exclaimed. Checking herself, she continued, "What I mean is that I rarely get to converse with guests, and I know so little about the wider world. I would be most interested to hear more.''

Andrew broke into a wide smile, "Ah, so you are curious about him, are you?''

Lily sputtered, trying to extricate herself from the trap. "Only inasmuch as he can avoid unpleasantness with Catherine. I mean, she is rather high-strung, and it would be good if your brother can persuade her with this charm of his.''

Nodding, Andrew said, "Quite so.'' But Lily sensed he was merely being kind. Her explanation had not fooled him. Andrew gave her a mischievous glance. "Well, it seems Rogan is curious about you. He keeps looking at us, and he is positively glowering. I do believe he is jealous."

Lily snapped her head around. Rogan was indeed staring at her and was not a bit embarrassed at being caught doing so. Lily blushed and looked away. Casting about for a diversion, and a safe topic upon which to converse, she said, "Why don't I tell you about the ghost of Charolais. Are you interested in such tales, Father Andrew?"

"Isn't everyone?" Andrew answered. Lily trembled so much that her hands shook as she took a draught of wine. She concentrated on keeping herself from casting any more self-incriminating looks down to the other end of the table as she began the story.

The afternoon passed into evening civilly enough, considering the circumstances. Lily's father offered the St. Cyrs lodgings for a few days until matters could be sorted out and, when Rogan accepted, Lily felt a thrill course through her limbs. He would be under the same roof for almost a sennight!

Disappointingly, he was much occupied with Catherine, who was not at all as put out as Lily would have expected. She knew her sister well and had come to fear her sister's frightful temper. However, Catherine was not displeased with the attentions of the handsome warrior. So much for indignation at having been rejected by her duke. But then, her elder sister had always been fickle.

It was the family's custom for the women to adjourn early and leave the men to their evening carouses. This Lily did reluctantly, following her sister up the great stairs to their chambers, but not before darting a quick backward glance at the man who had so completely captured her attention.

She was surprised to find his gray eyes on her once again. Pinned by that stare, she avoided colliding with Catherine only barely. Her heart hammered in her chest and her throat was dry. She whirled and sped up the stairs.

It was later in her chamber that Lily sat before her looking glass, dreamily brushing out her hair. She was far gone in fantasy, so much so that she didn't hear her door open nor the sound of gentle footfalls on the thick carpet of rushes.

"Is it true?" a small voice said into the silence.

Startled, Lily dropped her brush and whipped around. "Oh! Elspeth, you frightened me! I didn't even hear you come in."

The child was only ten and two, a beautiful cherub whose angelic face and mop of white-blond curls were an apt reflection of her sweet nature. Her eyes were clouded now, her face troubled. Lily cocked her head in curiosity. "Where have you been?"

Heavy lashes descended over the large blue orbs. "In chapel. I was saying the rosary." She sighed, a beatific smile curving her tiny bow mouth. "It was so peaceful there, I stayed and kept a vigil, like the monks do over the Holy Sacrament." This she admitted almost guiltily, as if Lily might disapprove. Lily never did, but Elspeth was a timid creature. "I missed supper. I hope Father was not angry."

"He didn't notice, so do not worry."

The frown returned. "Is it true about the duke? He is not to marry Catherine?"

Lily sighed and turned again to the mirror. "Yes, I am afraid so." She made very certain to keep her voice steady. "He sent his brothers to tell Father. Did you see them? One is a priest and the other..." What words could she find to describe Rogan?

Elspeth did not notice her falter. "Yes, I saw them. They were down in the hall when I came up, seated at the hearth."

Jumping up, Lily asked urgently, "What were they doing? Was anyone with them?"

Elspeth's puzzled expression was almost comical. "The two were by themselves, talking."

Pacing, Lily exclaimed, "Oh, I am so restless!" She looked at her sister, deciding whether or not to confide her delirious excitement. She and Elspeth shared everything, but could a child understand the tumult of feeling that had suddenly taken possession of her?

She was saved from making the decision by the appearance of Catherine at the doorway. She was pale, appearing ghoulish in the flickering light cast by the wall sconces. Lines of strain showed around her pursed mouth. "Elspeth," her clipped voice rang out. The youngest Marshand started. "We did not see you at supper."

"I was praying." Elspeth's answer was barely audible.

"And Lily," Catherine continued, leveling a shriveling gaze at her sister. "You disgraced our family with your dress and your appalling blunder."

The painful memory of mistaking Lord Rogan for the duke caught Lily off guard, though not for the sake of Catherine's censure. What had Rogan thought of the mistake? Did he think her a fool?

Catherine said, "You made an utter idiot of yourself."

Lily felt a deep flush of shame, hating herself for letting Catherine best her. She knew her hateful ploys, but that didn't make her immune.

"Sister," Elspeth said, her voice almost a whisper. "I am sorry to hear of your terrible news."

With no overt movement of a single muscle, Catherine's face transformed feature by feature into a mask of rage. Elspeth cringed, mewling a small noise that reached Lily's ear and erased her self-preoccupation with a swell of protective anger. Lily stood and went to Elspeth's side.

"Yes, little one," Catherine said, her tone clipped and cool, betraying nothing. "It seems as though I will not be wed as planned." Again, a shift so subtle it was more felt than seen. When she spoke, her eyes shone like twin blades, fierce and sharp. "But all is not lost. There are ways to turn misfortune to advantage."

Lily stepped in front of her little sister, seeing one of Catherine's moods brewing and knowing how Elspeth dreaded them. "Do not sow your mischief, Catherine. Lord Rogan is an honorable man. He has come to make amends."

Catherine gave her a withering glare. "And he will."

In a moment, she changed again, shifting her posture and giving Lily an assessing glance. By her expression, she apparently found her subject wanting. "While they are here, Lily, I do not want you embarrassing us any further. You do not seem to be able to conduct yourself properly. I think it would be wise if you kept busy in your chamber, or in the solar with the other ladies, studying your needlework."

Lily narrowed her eyes and jammed her fist on one hip. "You are not Mother, Catherine. She would never have spoken to us so. She was kind and gentle and would not have liked in the least the way you rule this castle with an iron fist. I will not have you mistreating Elspeth. And I will certainly not hide myself away simply because you dislike me."

"We shall see," she said in a brittle voice.

As Catherine turned to leave, Lily crossed her eyes and curled her top lip in an exaggerated sneer, causing Elspeth to clamp a hand over her mouth in order to stifle a gasp.

"And don't think I do not know you are making faces at me," Catherine called as she disappeared down the hall.

Collapsing onto her bed, Lily flung her head back. "Lord, she is a trial!"

Elspeth looked warily at the door, as if fearful Catherine would reappear. When she did not, she came to Lily's side and took her sister's hand.

"She frightens me."

Lily turned her head and looked lovingly at the child. "You must not let her, Elspeth."

Elspeth was still doubtful. "She has such a terrible temper. I fear what she will do now. Catherine hates to be thwarted.'' Her gaze darted to the door and she swallowed convulsively. ''Remember our rabbits?''

Lily covered her sister's hand, not able to stifle a shudder herself. When they were children, they had each been given a rabbit for a pet for the feast of Christ's Mass. Catherine's had fallen ill and died within days. She had been furious, claiming it was unfair. The next day, the other two rabbits were found dead in their pens.

''Do not think on that,'' Lily soothed. ''It was never proved that she killed those poor creatures. It could have been anyone. And even if she did do such a thing, she must certainly regret it. She has done nothing else to threaten a soul.''

''Except the servants,'' Elspeth shivered. ''Dory told me she came upon her talking to Kenneth in the kitchens, and went into a terrible fit of temper.''

Lily cut her off with a calm, steady voice. ''Catherine can be harsh, it is true, but there is a difference between anger and harm.''

The denial sounded hollow in her own ears and Elspeth seemed less than convinced. Lily added, ''Father will insure all is well.''

''With the aid of our Lord,'' Elspeth murmured.

Lily stretched the tension from her muscles. ''Of course. I am going for a walk. The night is cool, and I need some air.''

''You cannot! Catherine would be furious.''

''She will not know,'' Lily said as she scampered off the bed and flew to the door. ''And besides, I refuse to be intimidated by her silly commands. Good night, sweet sister.''

"Lily!" Elspeth whispered urgently, but she was already gone.

"I wish we were camping outside with the rest of the men instead of in this wretched place," Andrew complained. "I keep expecting Marshand to appear at any moment, screeching his pent-up fury and wielding an ax aimed for our heads!"

Rogan shrugged in studied nonchalance. "No sense sleeping out in the heat when we can enjoy the cool solace of the castle."

"'Cool solace' my arse, you have got your eye on the girl! The little flower, Lily. I saw you staring during supper."

Rogan looked back blankly. "The girl? Could you mean the very one you tried so hard to charm?"

"I was not trying to seduce her, damn it all. I was trying to be congenial."

"Admit it, you were enjoying it."

"Naturally. She is a lovely girl. Enchanting, actually. Are you going to deny that you would have traded places with me?"

A dark look came over Rogan's handsome features. "I had duty to think of."

"Is it always duty with you, Rogan?"

Rogan didn't answer. A pensive silence fell.

"You were successful, I take it," Andrew said after a space.

"Hmm?"

"I was referring to Catherine. You won her over. I thought by the end of the evening she was going to positively devour you."

"Aye," Rogan said with a hint of disgust, "she does have the look of a predator."

"She terrifies me, I am not ashamed to say. Her beauty is cold. And her eyes...they burn cold. Had you not noticed? Positively chilling. The sooner we are away, the better."

Rogan rubbed the back of his neck. "There are things to be settled here first."

"You mean the girl."

"What girl?"

"Lily, of course. Don't be so dense."

Rogan lifted a casual brow. "She seemed pleasant enough. I admit that she did not escape my notice. But you can hardly think that I would be so foolish as to allow a distraction such as her."

"Why not? Do you never think of what you want? Family obligation can be taken too seriously, you know."

"Calm yourself, Andrew. You will age before your time," Rogan said lightly. "It is hardly my habit to sniff around after virgins."

"You could not keep from staring at her all during dinner."

"Good God, brother, I am a man, and not a blind one at that. And I am not constrained to chastity as you are. I was merely appreciating the lass, for as I told you, she impressed me favorably." Rogan sighed. "Yes, it is true. She is tempting."

"And *tempted*. You were all she wanted to talk about." Andrew was not dissuaded by Rogan's impatient wave of his hand. "And not a half hour ago I saw her duck into the gardens. No doubt she walks among the scented roses—'' Andrew's voice lifted in an overly dramatic way reminiscent of a bard ''—dreaming of true love.''

''She'd make a fine companion for Alex,'' Rogan muttered. Then he raised his head. ''In the garden, you say? How long ago?''

''Not even an hour.''

Rogan stared at his brother for a long time. Then he stood up and stretched. ''I fancy myself a stroll in the garden. I have always enjoyed the outdoors just before retiring.'' He hesitated, not sure in which direction the gardens lay.

He looked expectantly at Andrew, who held up a pointed finger. ''That way,'' he said.

Chapter Three

The orchard was cool, washed in the light of a generous moon. Lily breathed in heavily of the scented air. A soft breeze stirred the branches into a crisp chorus of whispers, and the sound soothed her.

She slipped off her shoes and hiked up her skirt, then sat on the edge of the wading pool and dangled her feet into the water. Speculatively she studied the night-shrouded statue in its center. Hermes. Muscular and poised, with winged sandals and crown, he who was the messenger of the pagan gods reigned over the starless night. As a girl, Lily used to stare dreamily at the figure, making up stories in her head with him as her hero, rescuing her as he had Perseus, Odysseus and Aries but with a more romantic turn. Yet tonight, the displaced idol was only carved stone. Another stole her thoughts.

She kicked a bit to feel the water swirl around her bare legs. The pool water felt like a wonderful caress, cold against her skin yet somehow sensuous. She closed her eyes and let her head fall back. A wisp of a smile curved her lips. Just thinking of Rogan St.

Cyr set her to trembling inside. A small part of her cautioned—nagging in a voice suspiciously like Catherine's—that she should stop this foolishness at once. But it felt too wonderful, and besides, she didn't want to.

As if conjured by her thoughts, a voice, very close, said softly in her ear, "Good eve, demoiselle."

Without thinking, she jerked upright, her feet hitting the slick bottom of the shallow pool. Immediately, she felt them sliding out from under her, and just as she was about to fall, a strong arm encircled her, pulling her back up against a solid chest.

"My lady," the rich voice rumbled, "take care."

Lily caught a breath of his scent, musky and clean and completely masculine. Snapping her head around, she found herself staring up into his face, only inches from her own. His eyes, a curious shade of gray, looked down at her with a mixture of humor and concern. "Shall I help you?"

"Y-yes," she stammered, remembering herself. She pulled herself aright, slipped again, and in the end had to cling to him as she stepped out of the pool. Her gown was drenched from the knees down, making it a cumbersome weight. Standing there, soaked and embarrassed, at a terrible loss as to how to redeem herself, Lily felt perilously close to tears. "If you will excuse me," she said, making to brush past him to enter the castle. She was prevented from a graceful exit by the noisy flapping of her wet skirts. After stumbling clumsily for a few steps, she paused. *Oh, Lord,* she groaned silently, *I must look the utter fool.*

"Why are you leaving?" Rogan asked.

"I must go, I…" Why couldn't she think straight?

"You cannot go anywhere with your dress soaked as it is. It would be impossible to negotiate the stairs," he said reasonably. "Why do you not sit here and let the air dry it a bit before going inside? I think it will be much safer."

He was smiling slightly, his mouth curving in a way that made her lose what little equanimity she had left. He was not bothering to hide his amusement, but to her relief, Lily saw he was not mocking her. She sank down nervously on the carved stone bench. He sat down beside her.

"I suppose you think me rather hoydenish after such a display," she apologized.

"Nonsense," he assured her. "I found it most refreshing. After all, we all let our guard down when we are in private, which is what you thought you were."

"Well, Catherine would be furious if she knew. Not that there is ever any pleasing Catherine, but if she knew that you had seen me thus…"

Rogan's face split into a broad smile. "I assure you, my lady, your secret is safe with me."

Lily liked his smile, was a bit dazzled by it, and then looked away, uncomfortable. "Bloody embarrassing," she muttered. She had a habit of doing that, saying aloud things she was thinking before she realized it.

"What did you say?"

Immediately Lily realized her transgression. Horrified, she stammered, "I-I simply said that this is quite embarrassing—almost falling into the pool and being so wet.''

But he had heard. She could see he was trying to keep from laughing and doing a poor job of it. What must he think of her, soggy and swearing like a soldier? And why did it so desperately matter what he thought of her?

"I really should go," Lily said quickly.

"Please stay. I should enjoy the company."

"I—" She should refuse, she had sense enough left to know that much. Yet she did not move.

Her pride still smarted from her humiliating gaffes. She must find some way to compose herself. She decided to try acting like a proper hostess, as she had been taught.

"H-how do you like Charolais?" she asked politely. "Did you see the tapestries in the hall? They depict the famous battles of the Marshands. I could tell you the stories if you like."

"Perhaps some other time."

No good. Some other pleasantry, then. "Did you have an enjoyable journey? What do you think of our moors?"

Rogan apparently decided to play along and allow her to lead the conversation. "We did, though this is desolate land. It has a certain rugged beauty one would come to appreciate."

Grateful that he had settled upon a neutral topic, Lily replied, "'Tis true that the beauty of Cornwall is beloved by its natives and misunderstood by everyone else."

"It seems harsh. I wonder if it makes the people so?"

Lily did not know how to answer that. "I suppose the coast makes for a rugged life. We are closely wedded to the sea out here."

"Ah, aye, the sea. Do you love the water?"

"I love to look at it."

"Do you also love to sail? I have always enjoyed being out in the vast ocean, with blue all around."

"Heavens, no." Why did every conversation lead to questions about her? "I am afraid I was brought up quite strictly. I was never allowed to do anything like that. Much too dangerous, Father says."

"Would you like to, someday?"

Caught off guard, Lily couldn't keep the smile from her face at the prospect of such an adventure. "Oh, very much."

"Maybe you will," Rogan said, then paused. "It must be such a burden to you."

"What?"

"Always being so correct. You seem to like simpler sport. Dangling your feet in the water and the like."

Lily flushed. "You do tease me meanly by reminding me of my misbehavior."

"If that is true, I offer my sincere apology," he said. "It is just that I also find obligations tiresome. Powerful alliances and titled marriages—your family seems to be impressed with these. But not you, I'd wager."

Lily was stunned. How was it he knew her so well?

"I myself have never cared for the formality that

surrounds titles," Rogan continued. "I saw what it did to my brother. All the demands made him sullen and difficult. I suppose his recent marriage is his grand rebellion against all of it. It is better than going the way some go—becoming depraved and jaded. Privilege seems to have a corrupting influence, robbing one of the ability to appreciate something of the basic joys. And some of us, by nature, cannot abide that."

Lily nodded, allowing herself to be drawn in. "Sometimes I do wonder what it would be like to live without all of the rules and demands and just feel..."

"Free?" he supplied.

"Aye," she breathed. "It seems odd, does it not, that for all of my family's wealth, I have less to my name than my servants."

"And what freedoms do you envy your servants?"

"They work hard, indeed, my sister insures they do, for she is strict and exacting in her management. Yet, despite their burdens and lack of finery, they seem to possess a certain spontaneity, the ability to view things very clearly and without complication. Catherine says they are simple, but I wonder if they do not possess some perspective worth knowing. She says they are lawless and lusty. But they have a contentment I have never witnessed among the noble folk."

Rogan raised a brow. "Really? That's fascinating. Lawless and lusty, you say?"

"Aye," Lily said, not noticing the wicked way his mouth curled at the corners. "Sometimes I have seen them, hugging or stealing a kiss, and it seems to make them unaccountably jolly.''

"Positively shocking," Rogan commented. "And what do you think of such adventures?"

"Well, they are acceptable for servants. They are of a different sort than noble folk."

"And you, Lily? May I call you Lily?" To this, she nodded, a bit bemused but agreeing all the same. "Then, Lily, do you have cause to be jolly?"

What a strange question. "There is much that is expected of me, I suppose. I certainly have nothing to complain about. I have everything I can desire."

"How fortunate for you."

She was lying, and he knew it. She blushed, then confessed, "Well, part of the problem is that I do not know what it is I desire. Catherine always wished for a grand marriage, and Elspeth wants to go to the convent but Father is reluctant to let her. He says he will miss her, and he has been putting it off."

A short, comfortable silence stretched between them. She looked up into the heavens, alive with a host of lights winking brilliantly like a handful of diamonds strewn carelessly across black velvet. After a while, Rogan ventured, "Perhaps you will find happiness with your betrothed. Is he a man of your pleasing?"

Lily answered, "My parents promised me at birth, but he was slain in the Holy Land. I never met him. The same with Catherine. That is why Father had to find a husband for her now. He has not yet begun for me."

"What was his name? Perhaps I knew him."

"Were you on Crusade?" she gasped.

She saw his eyes darken, felt something shift between them. "Yes. I only returned last year."

"Was it glorious? What of the Saracens, are they truly barbaric heathens?" Her enthusiasm dwindled quickly at his solemn look. "I am sorry," she said. "I had not thought it would be painful to speak of."

"No, not painful really. But it was not glorious, Lily. Taking a life never is, even the life of a Saracen. It may be heresy to say this, but they are not all evil. From what I observed, they are much like us in many respects. Their religion and culture are different, and they speak a different tongue, but they love their families and would die to protect their children. Some behaved more nobly than my fellow knights." He fell silent, as if lost in some long-ago moment, then shook off the mood. "Forgive me. I do not often speak of it."

"Oh, no," she breathed, fascinated. "I do not mind at all. If ever you would like to tell me more, I would be honored."

One side of his mouth quirked up. "I shall keep that in mind."

They talked amiably until the moon began to wane and Lily was reminded of the lateness of the hour. "I should be going inside," she said reluctantly.

Rogan nodded, but did not move.

"Really, should Catherine learn I was here with you, she would be most displeased."

"Why are you so afraid of Catherine?"

Lily paused. How could she explain the subtle threat Catherine exuded? Since their mother's death, she ruled as somewhat of a tyrant at Charolais, over the servants and her sisters. Though Lily was not precisely *afraid* of her, she had a healthy dread of the trouble she could sow.

"Catherine is rather strong willed," Lily stated. "She has a way of making it distinctly uncomfortable for those who disobey her."

"I should think you would not care," Rogan observed.

True enough. It was merely an excuse for Lily's own growing feeling that she had overstepped the bounds of propriety far too much, even for her free spirit.

"Yes. But I really need to go in now."

"You seem reluctant to go," Rogan said, seeming to read her mind. Then, with a gleam in his eye, he asked, "I was intrigued by what you were saying about the servants. Being jolly. Do you remember?"

"Aye," she answered, puzzled.

"When they kiss, you said."

She blushed and lowered her eyes to her hands clasped tightly on her lap. When she looked back up, Rogan's eyes shone with a strange light, making them appear silver. He leaned slightly forward. "Have you ever been kissed?"

Lily felt as if a tankard of ice-cold ale had been splashed in her face. Her mouth dropped open in shock and her back went rigid. "That," she said with emphasis, "is a very rude question for a gently bred lord to ask a lady!"

She stood up. Her skirts were still somewhat wet, and they clung unbecomingly to her. But she was too angry to care. "I was wrong to tarry with you. Now, I really must go inside."

With that she whirled about and stomped as gracefully as she could manage to the door, which was not much with her gown flapping heavily about her legs.

Rogan had to bite his lips to keep from laughing out loud at her magnificent exit, at least until she was out of earshot. But he was soon sorry for his impulsive question. The enchantment of the garden shriveled into the shadows, deserting him and leaving the orchard lonely.

He raked his hand through his hair. Now what had made him say such a thing? he wondered.

Chapter Four

Rogan reentered the castle, relieved that Andrew was no longer about. He was not in the mood to discuss much of anything right now, let alone endure another lecture on the perils of an overdeveloped sense of responsibility. Interestingly—considering the critical circumstances—Rogan felt good and his mind was full of the delightful interlude with Lily. The little flower, as Andrew called her.

A sleepy page intercepted him and said he would show Rogan to his quarters. Following the boy, he climbed the great stone staircase that wound around the inside wall of the keep, then into a vaulted corridor lit with an abundance of torches. The lad led him to a chamber that was rather small, though nicely appointed. It held a good-sized bed, a stool and a shuttered window. The fire had been lit and there was a steaming tub by it. He was surprised by this hospitality, then thought that these amenities perhaps reflected the Marshands' goodwill. His mood improved even more at this observance.

The servant left him and Rogan was about to undress when his door opened. Surprised, he turned. Catherine Marshand came into the room.

"Good eve to you," she said as she moved toward him. "I have come to help you with your bath."

It was common custom that visitors be offered such service, but it was usually the married women who performed the honor of undressing and washing their guests. In the absence of such a person, it was conceivable that the eldest daughter would offer. However, Rogan's instincts were instantly alerted.

He did not stop her when she placed her hands on the thick band of leather at his waist. He experienced a distinct revulsion at her touch, but he was wary. He had dealt this proud woman a crushing blow today, and he did not want to lose what ground he had gained toward keeping peace.

Her slim hands did their work and his belt came undone. She laid it carefully on the back of a chair by the tub. When she turned back to him, he saw the burning in her dark eyes and a tight smile played on her face.

Rogan groaned inwardly. There was no way for him to stop this without appearing rude. It was ironic that an able-bodied man such as himself would feel these trepidations with a mere woman, but there was something about this one that made his flesh crawl.

"I am relieved you and your family have chosen not to take exception to my brother's brutish behavior."

"What's done is done." Catherine pulled off his tunic and untied his undershirt. She was close to him and he could smell her cloying scent. It was making him mildly ill.

Her hands went to the ties of his leggings.

"Do you not think it would be best to remove my boots first?" he asked. Verily, was this woman so anxious to get into his braes she would leave him standing with them caught up around his knees?

She knelt to perform the duty, then stood to address the leggings once again. He was not a modest man, but he found he had an aversion to being viewed intimately by Catherine's devouring eyes. When he was naked, he quickly stepped into the tub and picked up the soap.

"Nay, I shall do that for you, Lord Rogan."

With a shrug, he handed it to her and she lathered up her hands and began to rub his chest.

Rogan pretended to relax, leaning his head back and closing his eyes. "What can you tell me of your sister, Lily?"

The stroking stopped for a moment, then resumed. "Why do you ask about Lily?"

"I was curious. Has your family chosen someone for her to wed?"

"Lily is a pleasant girl. But she is young, and still unrefined. I have done my best with her, but she can be headstrong. As to her marriage prospects, I am sure my father shall have no difficulty finding someone suitable. When the time comes. It is traditional for the eldest to marry first. And it may be difficult to find someone after this scandal."

"Rich enough."

"Pardon me?"

"I said, rich enough. Certainly with a prize such as yourself, you would want to make the best possible liaison, am I correct? Another duke, perhaps?"

Catherine shrugged mildly. "I do not know. Certainly someone of good family. But I only received the news today of my betrothed…that the duke married another. But these are matters for my father."

Her hands trailed down his chest. She rubbed his legs, stroking the washing rag over them each in turn.

"I tell you, I am most impressed with her," he continued, pretending to be unperturbed by her ministrations.

Her voice betrayed her tension. "Let us not talk of her. Surely we can find something else more amusing for our conversation?" She was not going to be dissuaded by his lofty praise of her sister. "May I speak plainly, Lord Rogan?" she asked.

He was never to know what plain conversation she had planned, for it was then his chamber door opened. Andrew stood at the threshold.

"Ro—" he started, then stopped just inside the doorway, visibly taken aback by the scene before him.

Rogan called out to him pleasantly. "Come, Andrew, for I was just speaking to the Lady Catherine on her future prospects of marriage. Did you get a chance to discuss our family's concerns with her when she attended you at your bath?"

There was a short silence, then Andrew said, "Ah, the Lady Catherine did not attend me in my bath— eh, that is to say, I had no bath."

Catherine stood, finally flustered. "Well, there is

only one tub, and you must understand that Lord Rogan, being the elder, was chosen to—''

"Nonsense, think nothing of it," Andrew said, waving his hand nonchalantly. "I rarely bathe anyway."

Catherine hurriedly brought forth the drying linen when she saw Andrew settle into a chair, apparently determined to stay.

"If you will not be needing me any further this eve, I will see you on the morrow," she said stiffly, and exited the room before Rogan could reply.

When the door had shut behind her, Rogan grunted, "That was close."

"Afraid the lady would compromise your reputation, were you?" Andrew teased. "I must say that I am more than passing insulted. I would have very much liked a bath and a brisk *rub!*"

"It is cruel to tease me," Rogan said dangerously. "I could barely stand the feel of those bony hands on my flesh with that feral gleam in her eye."

"I will be glad to be away from this place. Enguerrand seems to have recovered well. But that woman. Do you think you can escape the attentions of Lady Catherine?"

Rogan didn't answer. He climbed in bed and pulled the furs up over him. "I shall be safe. Douse the candle on your way out, will you? And relax, brother. If all else fails, I do have my sword."

"My good fellow, it is something of a sword the woman is after!"

After breaking their fast the next morning, Rogan and Andrew were invited to accompany their host to the practice field where, he boasted, he would show them a fine display of fighting prowess.

Rogan stood quietly as he watched Enguerrand's men go through their drills, working with swords and maces. Andrew, who was off a little ways behind Marshand, amused himself by rolling his eyes at the stumbling maneuverings of the soldiers, then offering facetious compliments. Rogan scowled in mute warning for him to stop, but Andrew merely smirked.

His mind wandered to Catherine. Andrew had been right when he had said that her obvious interest in him could be a problem. And there was Lily. Thoughts of their meeting last evening in the garden still made him smile. She was a strange girl. She was beautiful and proud and yet unassuming, so unlike her elder sister.

"What say you, Rogan?" Enguerrand said, and Rogan snapped back into awareness. He glanced over at Andrew who was wearing his usual expression of ill-concealed mockery, brows raised in expectation.

"What was that? I am afraid I was distracted for a moment."

"Thinking twice, eh, St. Cyr?" Enguerrand hooted.

Andrew leaned forward. "He wants to know if you want to take a chance with one of his men." He rolled his eyes. "Damn daunting challenge."

Rogan ignored Andrew's jest and considered the invitation. With all of this pent-up tension, swinging a sword would feel wonderful right now.

"Very good," he said, and Enguerrand announced the match.

Rogan doffed his jerkin and shirt, surprising his host when he strolled onto the field bare chested.

"No chain mail?" Enguerrand asked Andrew.

Andrew shrugged. "Too hot. Rogan despises the heat."

"But without the protection..."

Andrew smiled. "Not to worry. He'll not receive a mark."

Enguerrand frowned, a bit insulted.

Behind a large piling of crates and barrels at the edge of the practice field, Lily hunkered down out of sight. She peered around the corner of her hiding place, trying to keep herself concealed and at the same time get a clear view of the goings-on.

She must be mad, she told herself. If her father saw her he would be furious. Worse, if Rogan spied her scampering about like an urchin, she knew she would never survive the humiliation.

But she had to see him again.

She had not been able to stop thinking of him all last night. She had been sorely disappointed this morn when she had found her father had taken him off so early. When she learned he was to fight one of her father's men, she could not have stayed away for all the riches of the Holy See.

As Rogan walked onto the field, stripped to the waist as he was, Lily dove deeper under cover. Her heart thundered in her chest as panic arose. He was half-naked!

Oh, she should run back while she still had the chance, steal into the solar where she was supposed to be, quietly sewing and gossiping with the other women. Aye, most certainly she had been foolish to give in to her impulses. She stood, firmly resolved.

But somehow, instead of going back to the keep, she crept closer, slipping behind a cart nearer to the perimeter of the field.

From here she could view everything much better. She was close enough to see the movement of muscle as Rogan swung the broadsword over his head to limber up. Fascinated, she noted the slight beading of perspiration glisten on bare flesh. She felt faint, closing her eyes to steady herself.

He was magnificent, more physically glorious than any hero of a bard's tale. His arms were thick with sinewed definition, sculpted as perfectly as the god Hermes in the garden, and his chest was broad with a light furring of auburn to match his wild mane of hair. It spread across his skin, tapering to a trail over the flat stomach. He turned, his back flexing with each of his powerful movements. Bracing himself, legs apart, he nodded to his opponent that he was ready.

Lily almost gave away her hiding place when she saw who it was her father had chosen to face Rogan. Latvar the Dane—a huge, ugly monster of a man. He was by far her father's most accomplished warrior, held in awe among the men for both his skill and merciless strength. As he approached, swinging his spiked mace, Rogan only waited with deadly calm.

They circled each other. Rogan's movements were smooth, like some wild animal of prey stalking with deliberate care. Finally, Latvar swung, the whooshing sound of the mace slicing through the still air. Rogan ducked, avoiding the mace easily. Latvar swung again, but his blow was once more evaded.

Latvar's war cry resounded and he lunged. Rogan maneuvered himself away from the brutal onslaught without a scratch. They circled again, wary, taking measure.

In a rage, Latvar hurled the mace aside and drew his own sword. To this invitation, Rogan raised his own weapon, swinging it over his head in an arc and bringing it down against the Dane's. The deafening sound of steel against steel sounded out, making Lily start.

Latvar was larger, but Rogan was unbelievably quick. The Dane could not bring the sword back up fast enough to see each of Rogan's swings. Lily saw Rogan unleash a barrage of blows that left his opponent backwheeling, panting and exhausted. When Latvar dropped to one knee, Rogan placed a booted foot on his chest, laying his blade gently against the thick neck.

Lily waited in tense anticipation as the two remained in perfect stillness before Latvar nodded, admitting defeat. Lily craned her neck to see her father's reaction. Enguerrand's face was red, his lips tight, but he only stared stonily at the Dane. Behind him, Andrew bounced on his heels, gloating.

What would her father do now? Lily wondered. Rogan inclined his head to Latvar and offered him a hand. Poor Latvar looked guiltily at his master. Enguerrand said something to the men and Andrew laughed and gave her father a good-natured slam on the back. He shrugged and turned away, stalking off toward the stables with Andrew sauntering behind.

The crowd that had gathered broke up. Rogan came over to the water barrel, which was perilously close to where Lily lay hidden. She shrank back, angry with herself for not stealing away. She should have left while she had the chance! She was very still, very quiet. Her pulse thumped wildly in her throat.

Taking up the dipper, he poured water over his shoulders and back. He tilted his head up, splashing his face and running wet hands through his hair.

"Well, are you not going to come out and congratulate me?" he asked casually, "or are you still angry with me for last night?"

Chapter Five

Closing her eyes, Lily wished fervently that her ears had deceived her, that Rogan had not discovered her in this humiliating position. After a minute, she rose and stood before him like a penitent child.

"Well?" he prodded. "*Are* you still angry?"

"N-no," she stammered.

"I should not have been so boorish. It was rude of me to ask such an unseemly question. However, I could not resist, and sometimes when men and women are alone, strange things are said. Even stranger done. I suppose that is why fathers are so determined to keep their daughters locked away." His eyes held a curious blend of sincerity and laughter. "Your father should take better care to keep you locked away, you know. Your freedoms, meager though they are, do tempt me."

"Oh," Lily said, surprised by this contrite statement. She had been afraid he would tease her.

"So, do you forgive me?"

"I do," she agreed. Digging the toe of her slipper

in the dirt, she added, "I suppose I overreacted a bit. But you took me by surprise."

"What a shame, and when I was enjoying our conversation so much. I was sorry when you left."

She eyed him speculatively. "Sometimes I think you mock me."

"What?" he said, brows shooting up in surprise. "I, mock you? Why Lily, it is you who mock me to accuse me of being insincere. I speak my mind, though it might seem dense to you. But, I am only a soldier. I can only make the excuse that I am crude and unused to the company of ladies such as yourself."

"Oh, you are far from crude. If you never thought yourself charming, then you do not know yourself as well as you think. And I believe you are adequately acquainted with the company of ladies."

"But none such as yourself," he qualified. "And I do admit I tease you. I confess I rather enjoy your reaction. There is so much pretense and posturing between men and women, and I have little tolerance for it. I like the way you are so honest in your responses."

Feeling as though her breath had been stolen away by the unexpected compliment, Lily blushed. "I suppose I am to blame as well for our *misunderstanding*." She shot him a mischievous look from beneath her lashes. "I have been warned to beware of gardens in the evening and serpent-tongued rogues."

"So you think me a rogue, do you?" He laughed, as if that were the most ridiculous thing he ever heard.

The glow from last night was stealing over her

again. She felt her earlier caution desert her. Tilting her head to one side, she gave him an assessing look.

"Once," she said slowly, "when I was a child, some traveling troubadours and jugglers came to the castle. My mother was alive then, and she adored such entertainments. We had a celebration, a fair with exotic acts and sights. One of the attractions was a man from the East who wore no shirt and had a great linen wrapped around his head with a gigantic ruby in it. Catherine insisted it was merely glass, but I always liked to think that it was real. His skin was darker than the field workers. He would play his flute a certain way to make a snake rise up out of the basket he had with him. The snake was so enraptured by the song that it was rendered harmless. It did his bidding, and he played his flute to command the snake to rise and fall."

Rogan looked at her. He was standing so close. He still had not replaced his shirt and his hair was still tousled and damp. He was so appealing. She was acutely aware of every aspect of his body. Something inside her ached, making the little distance between them almost painfully undesirable. Lily knew if he made a move to close the gap, she would not be able to recapture her indignation from last night. There was something pulling her toward him, and she was losing both her ability and her desire to deny it.

"Why do you tell me this tale?" he murmured.

"Because I sometimes feel with you that I am that snake and you are that man with the flute and..." She could not finish.

Rogan pulled his shirt over his head. When that

was done, he explained, "I thought I had better minimize my similarity to the bare-chested Saracen." His eyes were warm, those eyes that looked like a wolf's. It made her shiver.

"You say the most astonishing things," he murmured. "Do you not know the coquette's teasing ways, the power of the great eyelash-flutter maneuver, how to purse your lips in a flattering pout?" At first, Lily thought he was admonishing her for her forwardness, but the gentle smile that played on his lips reassured her. "You do none of these things. And yet, you achieve their goal with greater acuity than the most accomplished flirt. For you, it is natural, and that makes it all the more alluring."

His hand came up to touch her cheek with the lightest whisper of touch. Her mind was muddled; she could not think of what she should do in the face of such boldness.

"You have called me a rogue, and I have to admit I have given you cause to suspect as much. But I am no romancer." He added with a laugh, "And I am no snake charmer."

"I should not have said that. Catherine is forever chiding me for being too bold."

"And yet," he said, "I find it a most endearing quality." He paused, as if searching for the exact words. "I do not play fast and loose with the ladies, and I am not trying to seduce you, Lily."

"That is a relief," Lily said, vaguely disappointed.

"Since you have always been so honest with me, I will return the favor."

His hand was moving ever so slightly over her

cheek and imperceptibly his face seemed to be coming nearer. She fastened her eyes on his mouth.

"I cannot say that I have ever found another to interest me as you do," he said quietly.

"You say that you are no charmer, but you use flattery well."

"Is it flattery? I was merely being honest. Honesty can flatter, when it is complimentary. I say neither any falsehood nor do I try to persuade you with my words. I simply want you to know."

"Then you do not mean for this honesty of yours to draw me to you?" she asked.

"Does it?"

She paused. "You know it does."

His head lowered, and he said softly, "I am glad," just before his lips touched hers.

She had never been kissed before. Besides her fantasy heroes, there had never been anyone who would have inspired maidenly dreams of sweet, sweeping love. Therefore, she was sadly unprepared for the deep flare of sensation as Rogan St. Cyr's lips touched hers.

She couldn't know how much he held back. He really only brushed his mouth against hers, sensing her inexperience. But for Lily it was an instantaneous leaping of sensation within her, a trembling excitement that sprang up somewhere low in her belly and flowed like molten fire through her limbs. When he made to draw away, she let out a small sound of protest and leaned forward in a motion that told him that he should not retreat, not yet. He obliged, his pleasant chuckle rumbling in his chest as he drew her closer into the tight circle of his arms.

There was no telling what would have followed if not for the shrill sound of Catherine's voice calling for Lily. It was like a dousing of ice, that voice, and it made Lily start and pull away. She stumbled back, staring wide-eyed at Rogan as if suddenly shocked at what they had done. Her hand came up to her mouth, touching scalded lips in wonder.

She watched as his brows drew down, his expression changed to one of annoyance.

"Lily!" The call came again.

"She cannot find me here with you!" Lily whispered.

"Lily, calm down. You've done nothing wrong," Rogan urged.

"There you are!" Catherine called. Lily whirled around to find her sister standing only a few feet away. In an instant, Catherine's eyes flickered over her, then darted to Rogan.

As if smelling Lily's fear, her nostrils flared and her eyes narrowed. "What are you doing out here? You are supposed to be in the solar. Get back at once."

Flushed and confused, Lily looked from one to the other. She pressed her hands to her face, backwheeling before turning to run into the keep.

Rogan watched Catherine glare after her younger sister, witnessing the unveiled moment of pure malice before she composed her face and turned back to him.

"Has my sister been bothering you, Lord Rogan?" she said smoothly. "I swear, I despair of her sometimes. She is such a child, and a bit unruly. I must speak to Father about her. We cannot have her pestering our guests in this manner."

Rogan shrugged. "Lily was not bothering me. Do not trouble yourself." As he made to brush past her, he said, "If you will excuse me—"

"Lord Rogan!" Catherine interrupted. "There is something I wish to discuss with you. I have been thinking on your family's debt to me."

Rogan stopped and turned slowly. "Debt? I am not aware we owed you any debt. No money had exchanged hands."

"I was thinking more of a debt of decency," she explained. "On account of my having been so mistreated by your brother."

"I thought that issue was settled," Rogan said tightly.

"My father and I were counting on the marriage to the duke. You cannot know what humiliation this has caused me. We had told our friends. When they learn of what has happened, there will be great scandal. I feel it is very unfair for my reputation to be stained so, especially when I have done nothing to deserve it."

Rogan watched her carefully. Instincts told him that under the carefully groomed exterior, Catherine was as crafty as a fox. There was a vague threat here, one that did not escape his notice.

"I would think that your family would wish to make amends," she said.

"That is why I am here. My brother's choice of

wife is as unfortunate for us as it is for you. I have no more love of scandal than you, Lady Catherine."

She lowered her lashes. A calculated gesture, he was sure. An airy sigh issued from her ruby-red lips. "I know this has been difficult for you. I can see how much you desire to avoid ill feelings between your family and ours. My father sees it, as well. Yet, the matter still remains the same."

Although he was irritated, Rogan forced himself to be calm. "Yes, it is true. You have been wronged, lady, and nothing I can do will change that."

Her eyes sparkled at his kind words. Her posture changed, losing its rigidity and a beguiling smile appeared. "I am pleased you accepted my father's invitation to stay," she said.

Rogan nodded. "Yes, for a while."

The smile deepened, but her eyes remained cold. "That is most gratifying. I think you shall enjoy our hospitality."

"You have already been most gracious." The compliment almost stuck in his throat. Remembering Andrew's tactics the previous day, he added, "You have much cause for insult, no one would argue with that, but you have responded quite generously. I hope my family will be able to remain in your charitable esteem."

She inclined her head at the praise. Rogan fought his irritation at this regal gesture.

"We shall see you at supper, then," she said. "Father has planned some diverting entertainments. Good day, Lord Rogan."

When she was gone, Rogan raked his hand viciously through his hair. What was she about? She had reminded him of the injustice done her, a way to hold sway over him because of it. She wanted something, but he could not yet see what it was. Puzzled, Rogan mulled it over.

Damnation! he swore silently. The delicacy of this situation strained his meager skills at subtlety and intrigue, and rankled his pride. Andrew was right—Alexander should be here to prostrate himself for Marshand's pardon. The mental image of his arrogant elder brother in such a state made him smile, then he shrugged off his resentment.

It was done. And after all, it had occasioned him to meet the Lady Lily. He could never be sorry about that.

Catherine was aware of Rogan's growing fondness for her sister, and it did not please her.

Very soon after Rogan's arrival, Catherine's cunning mind had begun to formulate a plan. At first, it was merely for retribution, but as it took shape and grew in proportion, Catherine knew she must have Rogan for her own.

Oh, he was marvelous. He was like no other male she had ever encountered, and she wanted him with a desire she had never before known. But she was not about to settle just for a second son, no matter how magnificent the man. And she knew of a way she would not have to settle at all. She could get everything that she wanted. Everything she had a right to. A rich, handsome husband. *And* the duchy.

After all, accidents happened all the time, didn't

they? Even to the Duke of Windemere. Misfortune could easily befall Alexander, leaving Rogan to inherit the title.

It would be relatively simple to arrange. As for the wife, the cherished little merchant's daughter, she would be no obstacle. And if she were with child already, so much the better. Countless women and their infants were lost during a difficult birthing.

Oh, it was a lovely plan. And it *would* work.

Pausing by the looking glass in her chamber, she stared at her reflection. What in the world could the man see in stupid little Lily? Was she, Catherine, not the greater beauty? It was she, not Lily, who deserved Rogan. She had always known she was destined for greatness. Even as a child. Her mother had tried to dissuade her of her superiority, but she had only made Catherine hate and pity the foolish woman's lack of insight. When she had died, it was a relief. Without a moment of grief, Catherine had easily assumed her mother's position in the family and went to work, preying on her father to secure her a future worthy of her.

She would not allow herself to be cheated of it now.

Her door opened and a dark-haired man slipped into her chamber. Catherine did not turn around. He came up behind her, slipping her arms about her waist and pulling her stiff body up against his.

"Ah, you are so tense, *ma chérie,*" he whispered into her ear. Annoyed, Catherine turned away, but he pulled her back roughly. He chuckled. "You are in a mood. Does Phillippe not know how to soothe you when you are like this?''

Despite his smooth words, his hand crudely slipped between her legs. Catherine stiffened but did not push him away.

"You called for me," Phillippe purred. "You need me tonight."

His hand began to move in a rhythmic motion, and gradually Catherine relaxed against him. "Ah, that is good to relieve what is on your mind."

"Shut up and take off your clothes," Catherine snapped. She tugged off her own dress, carelessly casting aside the expensive garment and her costly jewels. She stood by the fire and watched Phillippe come to her. When he took her in his arms, she closed her eyes. Instead of his swarthy complexion, she envisioned a more bronze tone. Broader shoulders, thicker arms, hair a rich russet and eyes the haunting gray of the wolf. Tonight she would let Phillippe bring her body relief, but in her mind it would be Rogan making love to her.

Enguerrand Marshand was not a stupid man. He had many faults, and to his credit he was even aware of most of them, but lack of mental acuity was not one. Thus, he was well aware of his eldest daughter's calculating nature. In fact, he quite approved of it most of the time. She took after him in many regards, and he liked to think that her shrewdness was one of them.

He was also aware of her cruelty, but he preferred to think of it as more a lack of sensitivity. That quality he did not lay claim to. He did not approve of it, but he accepted it as part of Catherine. No one was perfect, after all.

Pride was taken in the sweet blessing of Elspeth. Another man might resent the third of a trio of daughters most of all; the last chance at a son and heir gone. But Enguerrand doted on his youngest. She was an extraordinary child, had been since birth. Serene, with a wisdom beyond her years yet ever innocent, he cherished her. As much as he loved her, he could not bear to grant her only wish. To send Elspeth to the convent would be to lose the only joy in his life.

As for Lily, he gave his middle daughter little thought. She had always been stubbornly independent, not anything like his beloved Elspeth. Nor was she cunning like himself, like Catherine. She was more like his wife, whom he had married in accordance with his parents' wishes and never understood. So, he had mostly left Lily alone, trusting Catherine to see to her rearing, and never really giving her much thought.

Which was why he was so surprised when Rogan asked to marry her.

Catherine wanted him. She had come to him and said she would take Rogan as husband. Knowing well the machinations of his daughter's nimble mind, he sensed that she had strong reasons for wanting the match, and so he had agreed.

What he had never considered was that Rogan would not want Catherine. When Enguerrand broached the subject, Rogan simply said, "I must decline."

Enguerrand pressed him for an explanation, but the man only shrugged, offering only that Catherine was not to his liking.

Enguerrand grew irate. "You insult me, St. Cyr. Your brother deals dirty with me, now you refuse to make the matter right. Good God, you had the gall to best the Dane. Do you not even have the decency to lose to your host's champion?"

"I never lose, not even on purpose," Rogan answered calmly.

"The only person who has shown me respect has been young Andrew. Yes, Andrew. You may not think much of him, judging by that look on your face, but the young priest is the only one who has gone out of his way to treat me with deference."

Rogan maintained a stony silence.

"You have done nothing to mend the breach between our families. For all of your talk of wanting to preserve the goodwill of the Marshands, you are doing nothing to secure it."

It was a heavy threat. Again, Enguerrand was not stupid. He knew this man wanted peace. Desperately. Enguerrand pressed his advantage. "I have shown great restraint, giving you the chance to redeem yourself, and you flaunt this chance and insult Catherine. That is two rejections from you St. Cyrs. That hardly bodes well for reconciliation. Tell me, Lord Rogan, what do you find objectionable about my daughter?"

After a pause, Rogan answered carefully, "Nothing objectionable, I assure you." He seemed to wrestle within himself for a long moment. "It is just that I would ask you to extend your generosity once more," he said at last, "and give to me Lily's hand instead."

Enguerrand was astonished. "Lily? Why do you want her?"

"I had been thinking of it in any case, but your proposition forces me to act more quickly than I would have liked."

"You want Lily?"

"She has impressed me favorably, and she seems more of a wife to suit my particular temperament. Catherine is lovely, well-bred and exemplary in every way. But she is too fine and would require attention I cannot give her. I am not a duke, but merely a soldier."

"A damn fine warrior, I would say," Enguerrand said, despite himself. "Lily, eh?"

Rogan nodded. "Yes. Surely you cannot deny she is beautiful, but more importantly, I must say I find her enchanting. On the few occasions I have spoken to her, I have been greatly impressed with her spirit and interesting mind." A slow smile tugged at the corners of his mouth. "I shall certainly find it no hardship to take her to wife."

Enguerrand shook his head and muttered something unintelligible.

Rogan continued, "I believe she would be favorably disposed to my offer."

That aspect of the bargain had not occurred to Enguerrand, nor did he much care. He rubbed his bristled chin. This Rogan St. Cyr's choice of Lily he certainly could not understand. And Catherine would be furious. Still there was no reason to refuse. He gained his ends just as well with the second daughter as the first. And with Lily married off, he still had Catherine to bargain with in a future alliance. Perhaps another powerful family could be approached.

"All right then, let us discuss the bride-price."

Rogan held up a hand. "In the interest of healing the wounds of our families, I will waive the dowry. And as my new father-in-law, I shall make, shall we say, a small gift to you in appreciation for your sacrifice of your daughter who is to become my wife."

"But that is—"

"Unconventional, I know. But I insist."

Enguerrand paused. The man was obviously trying to buy him, but it was unnecessary. Enguerrand had already agreed. What a fool!

"Very well," Enguerrand said. "I shall announce it at once."

"I wish to have the ceremony as soon as possible. Three weeks should be sufficient to have the banns read and make the necessary preparations. I have urgent business in the northern shires and must leave as soon as we can accomplish this."

"Very good." Enguerrand nodded. He rubbed his hands together, planning. He hardly noticed when Rogan took his leave.

This was unbelievable! To get a daughter married without a dowry was incredible enough, but to actually profit from the deal—marvelous!

Immediately, his spirits plummeted when he remembered Catherine. He dreaded telling her Rogan wished to marry her sister.

Suddenly Rogan's bribe seemed not so foolish after all.

Chapter Six

Enguerrand made the announcement that night at dinner, standing without preamble and roaring for the entire hall to hush and attend him.

Rogan was surprised to note the thrill of excitement go through him. He had not had a chance to speak to Lily today. They had only exchanged glances, hers shy but unable to hide her pleasure. He was, surprisingly, anxious to speak with her and impatient to know her reaction to their impending marriage.

Enguerrand called out, "Listen up, all and everyone! I have an important announcement." The noise dimmed. Rogan caught Catherine's eye and was surprised to see the glimmer of triumph there. His stomach clenched as he realized she thought the announcement would be of *her* marriage to Rogan.

Damn Enguerrand, the old fool!

And if Catherine had not been apprised of the change in her plan, then it stood to reason that Lily was likewise uninformed. He whipped his head around to watch her as Enguerrand said, "Rogan St. Cyr has requested the hand of my daughter, Lily..."

His voice faded, and Catherine was forgotten, for as the words descended, Rogan could only stare at his wife-to-be.

The naked emotion on her face attested to her ignorance of the arrangements that had been made that day for her future. Her features registered shock, quickly replaced by a look of purest joy as she swung toward him in disbelief. Her clear eyes, such a singular shade of blue-green, opened round and wide and looked like brilliant bits of aquamarine.

Rogan felt something inside of him twist in an oddly pleasant way. Good God, if he had ever had a moment's doubt about the matter, it was put to rest as he smiled at Lily. He had never seen her look so exquisite. And he had never felt so sure of anything, he reflected. He rose and held out his hand. She fairly beamed as she stood and allowed her father to place her slim hand in his palm.

They turned together with stiff formality to receive the congratulations of the others. Bracing himself, Rogan saw Catherine was to be the first. But she merely stood rigid, lips pulled taut and eyes smoldering with tightly checked rage. "Congratulations, Lily. Rogan," she said before turning away. Elspeth rushed forward and flung herself in Lily's arms, distracting her, and Rogan turned to face the smirking face of his brother.

"That went well enough," Andrew said. "And so, I congratulate you. May happiness be yours. And may the dour face of misfortune—" this with a surreptitious glance at Catherine "—be stayed."

The minstrels stuck up a gay tune and the wine

flowed freely. Rogan wished he could steal Lily away, speak to her alone, but the castle women surrounded her now, chattering wildly in excitement. She kept peering at him with the pleasure she was too ingenuous to hide. There would be time enough to talk privately. He would see to it.

As for Catherine, he saw no more of her that night. But though it was a relief for the moment, an uneasy feeling would not leave him alone. She was not done with him yet. He felt it.

Lily sped down the perilous path along the cliff face to the tiny stretch of beach below. Beyond was the quay, with its neat rows of fishing boats bobbing on the sun-splashed sea. She was late.

Across the strand she ran, her skirts hiked up, kicking sprays of sand out behind her. The docks were busy with men unloading the day's catch onto long carts while women picked over the piles of fish to make their selections before the crop was brought to market. Children weaved daringly among them, finding games to amuse themselves while their parents attended their chores.

Pushing through the throng, Lily hurried to the wharf. She spied Rogan in one of the small boats. He looked unperturbed enough at her tardiness, reclining on the edge of the hull, one knee drawn up upon which he rested an arm.

She realized after a moment that she had been holding her breath. He looked casual, so at ease lounging thusly in the sun-kissed afternoon, that she had simply forgotten to breathe.

"Hello," she called, "I am sorry to be late."

"No bother." He raised a challenging brow. "I was thinking you might be having second thoughts."

The effect was utterly charming, a slight mockery adding a sparkle to her eyes. She was feeling a bit giddy at the glow of pleasure that stole through her body.

Cocking a hand on her hip, she said, "You think me a coward, do you?"

"Not at all, but," he said, sweeping his hand toward the vast horizon where pale azure met deep aquamarine, "the sea can be intimidating."

She hesitated. It was true, she *was* more than a bit daunted at the prospect of sailing for the first time, but any trepidations she had were completely overridden by the excitement of being with Rogan, alone.

"Come on board, then," he dared. Gingerly she stepped over the bulkhead, wavering a moment at the sway of the deck. Rogan was on his feet in an instant, moving forward with uncanny balance. He reached out strong arms to hold her steady. When he did not release her right away, she gave him a sheepish look. He was grinning down at her, so close she could see that in the sunlight, his eyes appeared dark, slate blue with flecks of gray.

"It will take a while to get your sea legs," he murmured. It was a perfectly neutral statement, yet he made it sound like an endearment.

"I think you should know I cannot swim."

Rogan chuckled. "I am an experienced seaman. And have I not already proved my competence to save you from the perils of water? Now, sit here and I will lead us out."

Doing as he instructed, Lily perched on the crude plank bench, gripping the railing until her hands ached. Rogan smiled at her over his shoulder as he took up the oars and maneuvered the small craft out of its mooring and into the open sea.

"There," he said pleasantly, coming to sit beside her once they had cleared the maze of rocks in the shallows. "You can let go now."

Lily did not think she could. The water slapped rudely against the sides, rocking the boat as the currents took over. She forced herself to unfurl her grip, not wanting to appear childish.

He slipped a protective arm about her, pulling her against the hard mass of his chest. "Hold on to me, or rather I shall hold on to you and make sure you do not spill overboard."

"I know I am being silly," Lily murmured. Her fear of the ocean was being replaced by the overwhelming awareness of his male body. The scent of him, mild and masculine and unbearably stirring, was having a dangerous yet familiar effect on her senses.

"See, look," he said, pointing back to the coast. Lily peered over his broad shoulder. The beach was already reduced to a pale ribbon between the water and the stark gray of the cliff. The docks, so alive a moment ago with the daily activities of fishmongering, looked merely like a placid spray of color. She could not even distinguish people.

Uncoiling from him, she sat upright, forgetting for a moment the tiny boat surrounded by sea. "It's beautiful!'' she breathed. The cliffs were monstrous, dominating the horizon. She had never seen anything so majestic, so seemingly impenetrable. And Charolais, resting on top like a crown, its towers stretching to the sky like a fairy castle amidst the clouds. The sandstone walls were bleached by the sun, making them glimmer like some enchanted place.

"It is a breathtaking sight," said Lily. "One can almost imagine the Vikings sailing up in their longboats, greedy for the tin to be pilfered in the moors beyond the cliffs. Or think of the generations of English sailors, weary and homesick, laying sight of this land, knowing their journey was almost at an end."

"How many thought themselves safe when they spied land, heading toward the guiding lights only to find the wreckers were about their evil business?"

Startled at this dark observation, she looked at him. "Those are just stories," she said. "No one would do such a thing."

His eyes darkened. "Darling, you are an innocent. Men—and women—have indeed done such things. And worse."

She turned away, troubled.

"Will you regret leaving?" he asked.

She blinked in surprise. "No. When Mother was alive, Charolais was a happy place. But there has not been any joy within those walls in a long time. I will be glad to leave it behind."

"What a sad tale," he commented.

"Oh, not so much," she said, and laughed. Her eyes sparkled as they met his. "It does have a happy ending."

"Ah—" he nodded "—as it should."

"What of you?" she asked. "Were your childhood days happy ones?"

"Fairly typical." A slight smile curled the edges of his mouth.

Lord, he was handsome, she reflected, studying the chiseled jaw and hard planes of his face, softened now by fond remembrance.

"I was always fetching Alexander out of trouble. He was a bully even as a boy, and it tended to annoy people." His wry look marked this as an understatement. "But I was not fostered away from home, which was lucky. My father could see no merit in it since he said he had the best training in the shire. Besides, I like to think he was rather proud of me. He liked to watch me practice. My mother, on the other hand, busied herself with my sister. The boys, she would say, were my father's job." He paused. "They both died of fever when I was away on Crusade, along with my sister."

"I am sorry," she said. "I noticed you and Andrew are close."

"Yes, he came to live with me at Kensmouth when I returned home."

"And Alexander?" she asked.

"He sees himself as the patriarch, which is reasonable given he's the eldest. Though he is not in favor with me at the moment, I must admit, however grudgingly, he is fond of his family and a good brother." He winced, then grinned. "That was almost painful to say."

Lily laughed. Her spirits felt as if they were soaring. Everything was so easy when she was with Rogan, all of the darkness and confusion of life at Charolais faded and was replaced with brilliant, serene simplicity.

Rogan interrupted her musings. "Part of the reason I brought you out here was to speak to you about our marriage. I do not know what your father has told you, if indeed he has said anything. You should know it was he who proposed it, to align our families as was originally intended. It is a good idea, fortuitous for both houses."

"Yes, it keeps the peace," she said quickly, hoping to hide the crushing impact of his words. She had suspected this was his reason of course, at times convinced it was the *only* reason a man like Rogan St. Cyr would bother with her.

"You have a quick mind," he said approvingly, "and it does serve that purpose well. But when your father approached me, it was Catherine he wished to be wed. I asked for you instead." At her shocked expression, he laughed. "I will not speak ill of her, for she is your sister, but suffice to say that I did not feel Catherine and I would suit."

He grew serious. "But I want you to know I feel very differently about you. I was not at all displeased with the alliance. So, though it was prompted by your father, never think that I was unwilling to take you as my wife. And despite the advantages for both our families, my motivations were not simply duty. I can even admit that the thought had crossed my mind before Enguerrand and I spoke. It simply happened faster than I had anticipated."

She gaped at him for a moment before she remembered herself and snapped her mouth shut. His eyes creased in amusement and, despite herself, Lily laughed. As quickly as her sadness had descended, it was gone. She grew daring. Gazing at him through her eyelashes, she asked, "Do you remember that first night, when you surprised me in the garden?"

The corners of his mouth quirked. "Yes, I recall the night."

She gave him a look that was both playful and reproachful. "I often go to that place. I have done so since I was a child. In the center of the pool is a statue. Did you notice it? It is Hermes, with his winged cap and feet. I always loved tales of the Greek gods, though I had to practically beg old Absalom to tell me them in secret. My father frowned on such tales."

"Sometimes, Lily, it nearly breaks my heart to think of you under such stifling influence."

"Oh," she mused, a devilish light in her eye, "I became rather adept at working around it. Anyway, I always loved the tales of Hermes. He was heroic, but he was best known as a messenger of the gods."

"Yes, I recall."

"Well, I was thinking that night of you being a messenger of sorts. Like Hermes."

"Ah, so therein lies my similarity with your hero. It is a decided improvement over a snake-charming Saracen."

She blushed, regretting her impulsive confession. "It just seems coincidental," she muttered lamely.

As ever, Rogan was gracious. "I remember an old

priest I knew as a lad. He used to say coincidence is when God is quietly at work." His eyes slanted toward the sun, swollen and dipping low. The sky was transformed into a vista of flame, its brilliant color reflected in the molten sea. "It grows late. We should head to shore."

She followed his glance and sighed. When she turned back to him, she found him watching her with a softness in his eye that sent a tremulous shiver throughout her limbs.

He was going to kiss her again. She could tell by the way he was staring at her mouth, studying it with his brows slightly drawn and his eyes smoky and intense, like a starving man before a banquet. Her body moved forward, shamelessly eager.

His head inclined, closing the space between them and then he stopped, hovering for a moment before pulling away.

"You will be mine soon enough," he said hoarsely. "We have little more than a fortnight wait." He hiked one corner of his mouth up. "Though it is not easy to behave."

She opened her mouth to tell him that she did not wish to behave, that it was perfectly agreeable to her for him to take her in his arms, but her courage failed her.

Without another glance, he took up the oars. Sighing, she bit her lips together and fussed over the drape of her skirts. It took her a moment to realize he had paused to watch her. He put down the paddle and leaned forward, catching her hand in his and pressing her fingers to his lips.

"We shall do quite well," he said.

Lily swallowed, determined that she should not transgress the bounds of decorum any further, for a swell of emotion surged in her breast and she felt the prickly sensation of tears being born. Quite calmly, she answered, "I should think so."

Chapter Seven

Catherine entered the deserted chapel. Genuflecting in front of the tabernacle, she went to the small side alter and knelt before the Madonna.

He came in just after her, his footfalls heralding his approach. She bowed her head as if deep in prayer.

"My lady?"

She raised her head and turned. "My lord."

Rogan stood in the doorway. His face was blank, guarded.

Catherine rose. "Thank you for seeing me." She sighed petulantly. "Though it is the least you can do, after all you have put me through."

His forehead creased slightly. "What exactly have I done, lady?"

She bestowed upon him her most practiced pout. "You have been trying to make me jealous."

"Pardon me?"

Her laughter tinkled in the hollow space like shards of glass falling on stone. "Why else would you play this game? Marry Lily, indeed."

He drew in a slow breath. "When your father suggested we wed, I explained to him I was honored, but Lily was more suited to my temperament. I have no wish to offend you, however—''

"But you see, that is exactly it," she snapped. "I *am* offended. You do not understand at all. It was I who convinced Father a marriage between our families would be best."

"And so it shall be," Rogan replied.

"But 'twas to be with *me!* Lord Rogan, Lily is a simple child. You cannot be serious in your choice of her over me. What game are you about?"

His face grew cold. "No game, my lady. I simply prefer your sister."

"That," she spat, "is impossible. That simpering idiot?"

"You insult my betrothed," Rogan said gravely.

Catherine's laugh was harsh. "Tell Father you wish to have me after all, or I shall do worse than that."

"Do not threaten me," he warned.

She narrowed her eyes, her hands curling into claws at her side. "You forget your place, St. Cyr. Did you not come here for peace? You should be thinking about how to appease me, not whetting my displeasure."

"It is true, I abhor war. As I have discovered, so does your father. Oh, he talks a bold game, but he has no stomach for the fight."

Seething with frustration, Catherine prowled a tight circle around him. "Then you will deal with me, and you shall see *I* have the stomach for the fight."

"You can make no trouble for me," he scoffed.

"Can I not?"

He hesitated. "If you do, you shall pay a hundredfold. I have known persons like you before, Catherine. You covet, and what you cannot possess, you seek to destroy. Your foolishness does not frighten me. It disgusts me. I would not have you for my wife should the whole of England depend on it."

He spun on his heel and headed toward the nave. Catherine shouted, "Do not dare leave!" He didn't hesitate. The closing of the studded oak door resounded with a defining thud.

Catherine stood frozen in place, her mind full of vengeful thoughts. She would make him pay for his vicious rejection!

On the heels of rage came something else. How exciting he understood her so well! "Either possess or destroy" was what he had said. He knew her. Yes, oh, yes, she would have him yet, else she would crush him like an ant under her heel.

Lily sat at the small table in her chamber on the morning of her wedding, staring at the small looking glass and turning her head this way and that in order to inspect the intricate braid that bound her hair. It was piled high on her head and woven with sprigs of flowers and ribbon. "Yes, thank you, Ingred, that will be all."

The servant smiled proudly at her handiwork. Ingred was Catherine's maid, sent by her sister as Lily had no one of her own to help her dress. Lily had always worn her hair simply, but Catherine had insisted, in an unexpectedly generous gesture, on the loan of her handmaid to create "something spectacular for this special day."

At Lily's dismissal, the servant's face fell in disappointment. Too well trained to protest, she left quietly.

Immediately Lily's hands flew to the elaborate coif and began pulling it out.

"Elspeth, quickly, help me get this stuff out of my hair. I have less than two hours to come up with something less...less...less like Catherine."

Her younger sister stood off near the window, staring with unseeing eyes out onto the courtyard. Her youthful looks were creased with worry.

"Elspeth, come, I am in a frightful hurry."

The girl started. "What?"

"My hair, please help me," Lily prompted. Elspeth murmured, "Yes, of course."

"My goodness, this is really impossible. If I did not know better, I would think Catherine instructed Ingred to make me look ridiculous apurpose. Oh, I am nervous, please work faster."

When she was at last brushing out her unbound hair, Lily noticed that Elspeth had withdrawn again. Laying her brush down, she rose and went to her sister, placing her arms gently around the frail shoulders.

"My goodness, you seem lost." Lily laughed, hugging her closer. "You are much preoccupied, and I think I know why."

It was startling to see the look that came over Elspeth's face. "You do?" she gasped.

"There is no shame in what you are feeling. I too shall miss you. You may be the only part of Charolais it hurts to leave. Oh, there is Father, but he is always much too busy with his knights and the other lords to ever pay much attention to us. And I know that it will distress you to hear it, but I shall not miss Catherine.''

Seeing that Elspeth's pallor had increased, Lily questioned, "Elspeth, please tell me, what is it? Is there something else that troubles you?''

"N-no," Elspeth stammered, her eyes round with panic. "'Tis what you said. I shall miss you so.''

Lily considered her for a moment, comprehension dawning, "Poor Elspeth. Are you afraid to be left alone with Catherine?'' Lily had always served as a buffer between her overbearing older sister and her sensitive younger one. "Elspeth, Father has promised to send you to convent, as you have wanted. You will be where you long to be, as will I. You will not be left behind for long.'' Seeing that this was not making any difference, Lily said firmly, "I shall speak to Father before Rogan and I leave for Kensmouth. Will that ease your mind?''

Elspeth tried a smile and turned back to look out the window. Lily sighed. Her younger sister was always a mystery. Catherine caustically referred to her as "our little saint," and that was not very far from the truth.

Reluctantly Lily released her, not knowing what else to say. With a heavy heart, she watched her sister's mournful face.

"Be happy for me, Elspeth. I am marrying a man who surpasses any other I have known. I have never been happier, could never *be* happier. Today begins a new life for me. A life with Rogan, filled with such wondrous excitement I never dreamed possible. I know 'tis difficult to say goodbye, but can we just for today think of things that will gladden our hearts?''

Elspeth looked more pained at Lily's statement. Unexpectantly she leaped to her feet and fled the room.

Lily sighed, aggrieved at seeing her beloved sister so distressed. But the ceremony was only one hour away, and she was despairingly behind in her preparations. With a steadying breath, she sat back down at the dressing table and set to work on her hair.

There were several indelible images Lily would always recall about her wedding day: her father's puffed-up pride, Catherine's pinched face, Elspeth's wan expression and Andrew looking serious for the first time since she had met him. The rest was a blur of happiness, because after all of it, there was only Rogan, standing tall and handsome, outfitted in tight-fitting hose tucked into boots and a dark tunic adorned only by a thick golden medallion bearing his family's crest. Beside her at the altar, he repeated his vows in a deep voice that seemed to resound in every bone of her body. His large hands engulfed hers and his eyes seemed to pierce her in that way he had whenever he looked at her, as if he were seeing things within her she herself had yet to discover. How could it be a mere look could bring her to such breathless excitement as his did?

Her own promises she spoke in a voice that surprised her in its strength and assurance. She felt none of this confidence. Inside she was quaking, though she was not quite sure why. It was not exactly fear, and yet it was, but somehow pleasant and titillating.

At the celebration immediately following, Lily moved through the crowd gathered in the hall, feeling at once giddy and numb. People pressed in, smiling and hugging her, raising their cups in toast after toast. Disembodied voices chattered gaily, pouring out congratulations and well wishes of happiness, prosperity and long life. To these, she responded reflexively, hardly aware of what pleasantries tripped from her lips. And Rogan stayed beside her through all of it. The warmth of his fingers lightly grasping her elbow was the only thing that seemed real.

"Are you chilled?" Rogan asked, noticing her shiver.

"I suppose I am, a bit. Perhaps I should send Dynna to fetch my shawl."

"It is almost time to retire anyway. Why do you not go on ahead?" He smiled at her, his gaze lingering on her mouth. "I will join you before long. Go, I will make your excuses for you."

"Do you not think we should tell Father? The toasts—"

He waved her objections away. "I will have none of the usual foolishness that torment couples newly married. When I arrive, I guarantee I will be alone."

She nodded, feeling not a bit guilty at cheating her guests of their ribald cheer. It was customary for the woman to be taken to the bridal chamber by her ladies and subjected to a lengthy toilette while the groom was carried upstairs, stripped naked and thrown in bed with his new wife, all the while taunted by raucous "instruction" as to his duties. But no one would dare such crass humor with Rogan.

The fire in her chamber had already been lit, and a bath set out. But even the steaming water could not calm her mind. Rogan would be here shortly, and tonight she would lie with him, become his wife in every way. And although the idea thrilled her, causing a strange tightening in the pit of her belly, she was terrified as well. How was she to know what to do? What if she did not please him? Lord, she hadn't the slightest idea what it was he would expect from her.

This was no time to turn cowardly she chastised. Today she had wed before God, promised and forsworn to love and obey, and tomorrow she would leave with Rogan to begin their life together.

But before tomorrow's journey there was tonight.

Rogan found the way to Lily's chamber easily enough. From below, the sounds of the revelers echoed through the stone corridors. They would drink late into the night, the wedding a fine excuse to abuse Enguerrand Marshand's butlery stores.

But he had a warm bed waiting for him, and an even warmer maid. His wife, who would be a maid no longer after tonight. His pulse quickened at the thought.

Opening the door, he stepped inside the comfortable room aglow with firelight and nicely appointed with comfortable furnishings, an abundance of cushions and even a thick rug on the floor—a rare indulgence. His eyes sought Lily. She was standing to one side, looking something like a cornered doe.

Rogan closed the door softly. With no mother to guide her, he doubted that anyone had counseled her as to what the sexual act entailed. Somehow, he could hardly imagine Catherine doing it. Such acts of kindness were likely foreign to her. Exhaling, he approached Lily.

"Do you wish something, my lord?" she asked, nervous.

He looked at her stiff posture, her anxious expression. Where was the spirited nymph who had lifted her skirts like a peasant and dangled her bare legs into the garden pool? He was determined to have her back.

"Nothing, wife," he answered and watched for her reaction to the title. It came in a gentle suffusion of color. Yes, there was Lily, raw emotion clearly written on her face, without pretense, without guile. He chuckled as he moved closer. "How does the sound of that seem to you?"

"It pleases me well," she replied. It was a dutiful answer, but the light in her eye spoke of how much those words were true.

She was so very beautiful. He studied the warm glow of her skin in the firelight, the gentle curve of her high cheekbones, that noble arch of her nose. And mostly, the full, pouting lips that could part unexpectedly to a brilliant smile. They were lips full of sensuality, and suddenly the longing to taste their promise was nearly unbearable.

He drew closer, approaching carefully. He was oddly touched by the demure casting-down of her eyes. "Why are you so quiet?"

Her gaze lifted to his. "I do not know what to say. What does one say to one's husband?"

"Lily, I am your husband, but I have not ceased being Rogan. You have never been lacking in conversation with me before."

He could see the tension in her spine relax slightly. "This is all so sudden and strange," she said in way of explanation.

He paused. "Do you regret it?"

"Oh, no!" she exclaimed. "You must not think that. It is just that we are married." She said it with so much awe that he suddenly felt contrite at his lack of understanding.

"I suppose it has all happened fast. Perhaps too fast."

"I didn't mind. It didn't seem fast enough. It felt as though it took forever for today to arrive. But now that it is here, I admit I am…"

"A bit overwhelmed?"

She responded to his kindness with a conspiratorial smile. "Yes, perhaps that. It is such a large thing, marriage. It is done, and now we are bound together. Forever."

"You make it sound like a sentence of doom!" Rogan laughed, though he, too, could confess to a certain degree of shock over such an unlikely event as his marriage.

"I didn't—"

"Lily, I was only teasing you and do not apologize again!" He was exasperated, but also more than a little amused. She looked at him, confused, and he held his hand out to her. "Come here."

She stepped forward, slipping her hand into his. He pulled her to him with a playful jerk, hoping to tease her out of this recalcitrant mood.

"It is all right for you to be nervous. I understand it is a common condition among new brides." He studied her face, as open to him as a rose in full blossom. She really was just a child in so many ways. Yet at the same time, he was acutely aware of her slender body, only inches from his own and that it was the form of a woman full-grown. She had the power to stir his blood and his tenderness, and no woman had ever been able to do that before. "Do you remember the day by the practice field, when I fought the Dane and found you hiding? Do you recall that we kissed?"

Lily bit her bottom lip as she nodded. Rogan drew her closer so that their bodies brushed lightly against each other. Not too close, yet every inch of his flesh tingled in awareness of her proximity. "I got the distinct impression that you did not find that unpleasant."

"No," she said. A tender smile curved her lips as she relaxed against him. His own tension mounted.

"Tonight," he murmured as he bent his head toward her, "we will start there."

He saw the thick lashes flutter down as he touched his lips to hers. She did not stiffen, nor did she hesitate, but leaned hungrily into the kiss. He almost laughed. He should have known to expect an unaffected response from Lily.

Her fears seemed to be dispelled. The little flower was not as fragile as she looked. Giving in to the pressing need gathering in his loins, he pulled her tightly into his arms, bringing her full length against his body. The feel of her supple form yielding to him sent a wild pulse slamming through his veins and thundering in his ears.

The madness of unleashed passion was claiming his control. He plumbed the depths of her mouth, honey sweet and as intoxicating as spiced mead. She made a small sound, reaching up to entwine her arms around his neck, touching her own tongue hesitantly to his. The contact shot a bolt of pleasure through his trembling core, leaving him ravenous.

He dipped his head, pressing his mouth along the ridge of her collarbone, tasting her in small nibbles as his teeth teased her heated flesh. Her hands threaded into his hair, then fell to his shoulders, cling-ing to him tightly as he moved up the column of her throat to press soft, faint kisses into the hollow at the base. When he claimed her mouth again, her ardor matched his own with a raw sensuality sparked to life.

"Come to the bed, love," he whispered hoarsely. She nodded, dazed, breathless, with lips swollen and eyes heavy lidded with passion. He led her to the pallet piled high with plush furs, kissing and nuzzling her on the way. He felt for the bed with his knee, then gently he eased her back, leaning over her so that his mouth never left hers.

When she was fully reclined, he pulled back, study-ing the alluring vision before him. Her golden hair fanned out like a shimmering cloud. Her eyes gazed up at him, those brilliant blue-green orbs that took him to places lost in memory, as she watched him grab his shirt by the back collar and pull it over his head. She flicked her tongue over her parched lips, and the simple, unconscious gesture sent his pulse into a frenzy, making him grind his teeth together in determination. *Slowly,* he cautioned, reminding himself of her inexperience.

"Do not be frightened," he said softly. "I will move slowly, gently." He rose and shucked the rest of his clothes, then doused the candles, casting the room in the rosy glow of the dying fire.

He lay down beside her. Her eyelids drifted down as he drew her into his arms again. The gesture was vulnerable and demanding at the same time. When had he ever had a lover like this—so open, so giving? She was like a flower, indeed, this Lily, delicate and beautiful and intoxicating, begging to be touched.

The ribbon holding her gown in place at her neck unraveled with only a small tug and the soft, prim lace fell open, revealing the smooth skin that seemed to glow, bathed in the flickering light of the fire. He ached to savor the silken flesh, test the texture, the taste of it against his lips.

She was his, he thought, and something lurched in his chest. Rogan bent to indulge the desire, kissing her neck, her shoulder, her throat, nibbling gently as he moved down farther to the soft swell of her breasts. She gasped a quick inhalation of delight when he gathered the supple flesh into his hands and took each taut peak into his mouth and sucked. His tongue he swirled enticingly, teasing the sensitive nub until she arched, making tiny sounds of pleasure that fanned the flames of his lust until it was an inferno raging out of control.

He was mad for her. Each cry, each moan, each sensual writhing inflamed his blood to an unbearable pitch. Slashing his mouth over hers, he slipped his hands over her buttocks, ridding them of the thin barrier of the delicate linen nightdress.

Impatient to feel her flesh against his own, he pulled her in tight and lifted her hips up to brush against his arousal. Groaning, he pressed her down into the furs. He would have waited, preparing her for the intimacy, but he could manage restraint no longer. Murmuring tender, breathless words of reassurance, he rolled over her eager body. Easing her legs apart with his knee, he paused a moment before slipping into the moist heat. The feel of her inner flesh around him, a tight sheath of sensation, was an explosion of pleasure that tore away the shattered remnants of his reserve. He pushed on and felt the barrier of her maidenhead just before it yielded to his thrust.

She recoiled, letting out a small cry only once. He tried to wait for her to recover, but she moved against him. He did not hesitate to oblige, marveling at her abandon. Over and over again he drove himself inside her. She clung to him, moving to match his rhythm. He could feel her tensing in his arms.

"Let go, Lily," he rasped, joyous that she would find such pleasure this, her first time. Controlling his strokes, he pushed deeper. A soft moan escaped her and he covered her mouth with his, his body continuing to coax her to the brink of fulfilment. At last, he felt her stiffen, gasp and her eyes flew wide for a moment before she buried her face in his neck. He held her tight, able to feel the tremors shudder through her slight form just before the waves of pleasure lifted him up and bore him aloft for an endless moment.

He drifted back to his body slowly. Rolling to his side, he gathered Lily tight into his arms, not wanting to let her go. God, she was a wonder. She snuggled against his chest like a cat nestling in a comfortable bed. He smiled at the artless movement, so innocent and sensual at the same time.

"I had no idea it was like this," she said. Her breath fanned across his chest. "Now I see, I understand. If this is the way it is between a man and a woman, I know what all the fuss is about. 'Tis wonderful. But why does everyone refuse to speak of it?"

He smiled against her hair. "This is the best of what lies between a man and woman. We are lucky, love."

Her voice was full of amazement. "I never even knew that such feelings existed."

Nor I, Rogan thought, but he did not say it. Instead, he tilted her face up to his and kissed her again.

"If this is what the marriage bed is about, it is a wonder anything else gets done," she said after a while.

"'Tis a problem for some." Rogan chuckled. "Much of this world's problems are the worse for desire and passion."

She curled tighter against him. He gritted his teeth, wanting her already yet knowing that it would be awhile before she would be ready for him again.

"We should sleep," he said unenthusiastically, "for we have a long journey ahead of us tomorrow."

"Yes, we should sleep," she agreed. "Good night, Rogan."

"Good night, wife." Rogan closed his eyes, but it was a long time before he found sleep.

"I shall go mad, Phillippe, I swear it."

The swarthy Frenchman took a long sip of wine. "The little one will not do it?"

"She refuses. Damn her! She was my only hope of stopping the wedding, and now it is too late for that. But I am not through, Phillippe. I *will* not be thwarted."

Catherine sat stiffly on the edge of a tufted chair. From his position lounging on the bed, Phillippe thought she never looked more desirable. Or exciting. The look in her eyes sent a thrill through his slender frame. He loved her like this, brittle and dangerous and capable of anything.

He rose from the bed in a fluid movement and went to refill his cup. Gazing down at Catherine as he drank, he felt a surge of power. He savored it, smiling into his cup. He could give her Rogan.

"I know your obsession," he stated. "Another man might be jealous, but not I. See how well I know you? I would even find a way to deliver him to you." Placing the chalice on a nearby table, he went to kneel before her. "And I can."

Ah, the flicker of rabid interest in her eyes was like an aphrodisiac, sending his body into thrilling stimulation. She reached out two hands to grasp his tunic. "How?" she whispered.

"We shall go visit your sister, together this time. Perhaps there is something I can say that will persuade her, eh? She loves Lily. She would never harm her, nor would she wish to see her harmed. That is why she will lie for us."

Laughing, he rose and grasped her hands, pulling her upright. "Let us be off. We go to her tonight— now—and inform her that if she does not do as we wish…"

He paused, relishing the way the gleam of anticipation lit his beloved's face. "Then, I shall be forced to take Lily's life."

"Kill Lily?" A slow, brilliant smile spread on Catherine's face. "Oh, yes, Phillippe. Let us go!"

Chapter Eight

Lily awoke the following morning to a sudden awareness of the warm press of Rogan's body full against her side. In the silence of the room, his soft breathing seemed loud. She turned to gaze at him and to study his handsome face in repose. Still heart-stoppingly handsome, he looked different. Somehow boyish. His hair was tousled, that errant lock falling near one closed eye. If she dared, she would have smoothed it away, but she didn't want to wake him.

How lucky she was to have married for love. Oh, she had known for quite some time that she was in love with Rogan. Under the tender nurturing of his kindness, her attraction blossomed into that deeper emotion almost immediately. And surely his gentleness and admitted enjoyment of her was the same thing, though he had not exactly said so. Yet he was kind and passionate and always attentive. She concluded men just took longer to realize these things.

Since the death of her mother seven years ago, Lily had not really known happiness. The closest she had come was contentment, and that only in the moments she shared with Elspeth. Now she felt the sheer euphoria of it welling inside her, obliterating the years of struggle under Catherine's harsh yoke. She felt free. She felt reborn. She felt distinctly, unmistakably and incredibly...happy. Just then, Rogan's eyes opened.

"Good morn, husband," she said warmly.

"Yes, it is, isn't it?" Rogan answered, stretching. "Do you know the hour?"

"No, but I believe it is early yet."

"We should rise. If we are to leave by noon, there will be much to do."

"I cannot wait to see Kensmouth," she said.

Rogan smiled and reached out to touch her face. "It is not nearly so grand a place as this. It is a much smaller household." His lips moved closer to hers. "You may find it boring."

"I do not imagine anything in my life with you will be boring."

He gave her a look that made her belly flutter. "You always say the most startling things."

It was a compliment, she could tell by the lovely way his eyes caressed her and by the appreciative tone of his voice. That he liked all the things about her she had been taught to suppress amazed her. She giggled, leaning forward impulsively to kiss him.

He looked taken aback at first, then immediately his hand slipped behind her neck and brought her down to kiss her again. Lily felt the spark of hunger flare to life as his hand closed over a breast. "They are waiting below," she gasped.

"Let them," Rogan answered roughly, rolling

them both over. Lily laughed. It was starting again, every delicious sensation he had brought upon her last night. Liquid fire poured through her veins and her mind clouded as his mouth descended once again to hers.

When the pounding sounded, Lily thought it was merely the blood pulsing in her head. It was not until the voices started calling that she realized someone was pummeling their door.

"What the devil?" Rogan muttered, rising quickly and pulling on his leggings. They had bolted the door against any addlepated pranksters who would get it in their heads to harass the newly married couple on their wedding night.

Rogan looked over his shoulder as he headed for the door, waiting as Lily pulled on her dressing gown. She gave him a brief nod to indicate she was ready and he threw back the bolt.

"What is going on here?" he demanded roughly. Lily skittered behind him to peer at the intruders. She had a brief glimpse of several soldiers, four or five, all in chain mail and armed with swords. Two of the men lunged forward and grabbed hold of her husband.

Rogan looked at them contemptuously and snarled in a low voice, "Kindly tell me what this is all about before I set the lot of you on your arses."

The men froze, looking at one another for mutual support. Most certainly, they had seen Rogan's prowess on the practice field and they were intimidated by the threat.

One, apparently a leader, said, "We are to bring you to Lord Enguerrand immediately."

"Why?"

The soldier stood solid. "Those are my orders."

Rogan paused. He looked to Lily. "Stay here. I will return when this has been sorted out." Turning to the men, he said, "No need to maul me, I am going willingly."

The soldier who had spoken shifted uncomfortably. "Still, my lord, we have to do our duty." He paused, obviously daunted by the gaze of steely gray that held him. Reconsidering, he said, "Lionel, William, Kenneth, let him go. Keep your weapons trained. Lord Rogan, I suggest that you keep your word. My men will not hesitate to act should you try to break away."

Lily would have thought Rogan would laugh at the threat, but he nodded his head solemnly. He left with them, not giving her another look.

It took only a few moments to find a suitable gown and throw it on. She did not fuss with accessories, pausing only to put on a pair of slippers and run a brush hurriedly through her hair before she was out of the chamber and down the stairs. She had no intention of sitting calmly in the room, even if her lord and husband did command it.

The hall was all but deserted. A chorus of voices led her into the bailey. Darting outside, Lily saw a large crowd gathered. Shoving aside those who blocked her path, she reached the center to find her father and Rogan facing each other. Her husband was still held at sword point by the soldiers. Without hesitation, she stepped forward to stand at his side.

"You deny it?" Enguerrand boomed. His face was florid crimson. She had seen her father in fits of temper to shake Charolais's foundations, but never had she seen him like this.

"Of course I do, Enguerrand," Rogan snapped back, not as cool as he was before.

"My daughter does not lie."

"And yet she has done so."

Lily interrupted. "Father, what is going on?"

Rogan whipped around. Seeing her, his eyes narrowed. The sight of his anger made her step back. "Lily, I told you to stay in the room!"

She had never suspected his displeasure could be so awesome. She swallowed her fear and stuck out her chin. "No, I will not stay in my room, Rogan, even if it is your order. Please, someone tell me what is happening."

Enguerrand sputtered, "Listen to your husband, child, get to your chamber."

Courage borne of fear made her obstinate. "I will not. Explain this to me!"

Catherine floated forward, seeming to be propelled upon a cloud. Her face was transformed from its usual stern composure to an expression of near rapture. "There has been a terrible tragedy, Lily dear."

"Catherine, not now," Enguerrand warned.

"She needs to know, Father. It is not as if this thing could be kept from her. Do you not think she should be told what manner of man she has married?"

"I think, rather, your father should know what manner of woman he has sired," Rogan shot. "This is your doing, Catherine. Your hand is behind this preposterous accusation."

"You lie to save yourself!" Catherine cried.

Lily's panic was rising. "My lord, please, if you have any regard for me at all, tell me what is happening."

Rogan made to move toward her, but the point of a sword came up to stop him. He leveled a glare at its owner. The poor man took an involuntary step backward and Rogan passed.

"Listen to me," he said to her gently, laying his hands on her shoulders. "You must be very strong. This will be straightened out presently. 'Tis some kind of terrible mistake." He paused, drawing a breath. "Your sister has claimed I raped her."

Lily felt an instant flood of relief. "Catherine is lying, of course. You know she is jealous. She is saying this to—"

"Not Catherine, Lily. 'Tis Elspeth who has said it."

A dizzying moment of shock drained the strength from her body. Reflexively Lily whispered, "She is lying," but the words were not convincing. Elspeth did not lie. Elspeth was the purest person on this earth, devoted to God and completely without malice. "Perhaps it is some mistake."

"Yes, it is," he answered, but he had heard the doubt in her voice. "Lily?"

She wanted to believe him. *If it were anyone but Elspeth...*

Andrew's voice sounded just at that moment. "What is this? Rogan? Enguerrand? I demand an explanation."

Rogan reached out a hand and restrained him. "Hold, brother, 'tis nothing but a misunderstanding."

"What kind of misunderstanding?"

Rogan paused. "The little girl says that I raped her."

"What?" Andrew exploded. He spun to confront Enguerrand. "What purpose do you have with this hideous lie?" He turned his head, glaring at Lily in suspicious assessment. "Did you know about this?"

"I just heard of it," Lily said defensively, then wondered why she felt accused. She looked at Rogan. He was studying her.

"This is ridiculous!" Lily announced, glaring at all of them. "I will speak to Elspeth myself."

"Elspeth can see no one!" Catherine interrupted.

Lily gave her a withering glare. "Surely she can see me, Catherine, as I am the closest to her of anyone."

"She is too distressed."

"Then I will comfort her." Lily brushed past her, hurrying back into the keep. She was surprised when Catherine came fast upon her heels.

"Elspeth cannot face you. She thinks that you care for him more than her, that is why she did not come to you. She was afraid that your love for Rogan would turn you against her."

Lily whirled. "That is absurd. Elspeth knows I would never forsake her, and if she tells the truth, then I will know it and believe her. As for you Catherine, it is your involvement in this that causes me to doubt the most. I find it unlikely that she would confide in you. She is terrified of you!"

"I know I have been—at times—less than understanding, perhaps," Catherine purred, "but in urgent

situations such as these, trivial misunderstandings are
unimportant. Elspeth came to me and it is right that
she did. I am her sister every bit as much as you are!''

Lily hurried faster through the dim corridors of the
castle, hoping to escape Catherine and the disturbing
things she was saying. Her explanation had a ring of
plausibility.

And there was the matter of Elspeth's behavior of
late, so obviously distressed and piteously withdrawn.
If she knew her beloved sister was marrying the man
who had raped her, would she not be this way?

And after all, how well did she really know Rogan
St. Cyr?

They came to the portal to Elspeth's chamber, and
Lily whirled on Catherine. ''Alone,'' she announced.

Catherine hesitated, wetting her lips. ''Of course,''
she conceded after a moment, stepping back.

Elspeth lay in her bed, her eyes huge and red, staring at nothing. Lily's feet whispered on the rushes as
she went to her side. ''Elspeth, 'tis I, Lily.''

Elspeth did not respond. ''Can you speak to me?''
Lily asked softly.

''She told you,'' Elspeth said, turning to meet
Lily's gaze. ''She told you and now you hate me!''

''No, no, sweet, I do not hate you. I did not come
here to berate you, I promise. I only want to know
the truth.''

''She said I would not have to speak to anyone,
that I could remain quiet and she would take care of
everything.''

Lily took Elspeth's hand in hers, feeling how cold

the slim fingers felt. "I am afraid I insisted. I have to hear it from you. I know you would never lie to me."

Elspeth paled, appearing wraithlike. "Ask Catherine. Go away, please!"

"Darling," Lily urged, "I just need to know from you if it is true what Catherine has told us. Did Rogan…did Rogan hurt you?"

"Speak to Catherine," Elspeth cried again.

Lily paused, not knowing if she dared press further. Elspeth was in a fragile state. Still she had to know. There was too much at risk. "Tell me just once, yes or no. Did my husband force himself on you? Tell me, Elspeth, and we will never speak of it again."

Elspeth thrashed, "No. No!"

Hope leaped violently in Lily's heart. "No, he did not?"

"No, no, no. I will not say it."

"Then he did do it?" Lily rushed, desperate. "I beg you to tell me. For me, Elspeth, please. If you love me, then answer. My entire life is at stake. Did he hurt you?"

Elspeth calmed suddenly, and her glazed, wild eyes stared at Lily as her mouth worked mutely. At last, she cried, "Yes!"

Lily forced herself to remain calm. "Are you certain it was he? Could there be a mistake?"

Elspeth shook her head. "No. It was Rogan. No more!"

Lily closed her eyes and withdrew, pulling herself upright. She looked down at her sister, lying rigid and silent now. There were so many other questions, but she did not dare ask.

Elspeth's face was a mask of grief. "I am sorry, Lily."

Distracted, Lily murmured, "It is not your fault, sweetling. Never, never be sorry, for the one who did this to you bears the burden of guilt." Lily wished she had it in her to comfort her sister, but her own heart was ripping apart and a shocked numbness had come over her. "He will be punished."

"No," Elspeth cried, "just send him away. Never go near him again. Just send him away and the bishops will annul!"

Now it was Lily who could not speak. Nor could she bear to look at her sister. She managed to say, "Rest now. I will take care of it." And then she left.

Chapter Nine

Rogan stood in the courtyard, impatient for Lily and Catherine to return. Pacing like a caged leopard, Andrew was silent. He kept glancing to Rogan, waiting for instruction as to what to do. Rogan sent a silent message with a stony look: *wait*.

Taking a deep breath, he turned to Lily's father. "Let me speak with the child. I am certain if I can only confront her, we will learn the truth."

"I am convinced we know the truth," Enguerrand growled. "Here come my daughters."

Rogan turned to observe his wife as she approached, Catherine with her. "Where is the child? I want to speak to her myself," he said.

"Elspeth cannot speak to you or anyone," Lily said quietly.

She did not look at him. Her expression was cold, and he realized with a shock she was regarding him as if... "Lily, tell me what happened with Elspeth!"

She stood by her father, stiff and rigid. "I spoke with my sister," she said, her voice hardly more than a whisper, "and I am convinced she is telling the truth. She told me what you did to her.'' She turned away from him then, addressing her father. "She told me that my husband did indeed rape her.''

"This is ridiculous!'' Andrew thundered. "When? How?''

Catherine stepped up. "It was the night before last. He stole into her room while she slept and violated her in her own bed!''

Andrew was almost triumphant. "Rogan was with me until late, and I saw him retire before I adjourned to my own chamber.''

"You will forgive us for not having confidence in your testimony,'' Catherine sneered. Her eyes glowed like a venomous cat who had finally captured her prey. "You are hardly reliable, being his kin.''

"Shut up, Catherine!'' Rogan turned to his wife. "Lily!'' He saw her flinch at his call, but still she refused to meet his gaze. He grew angry. "Yesterday, you swore before God to obey me. Now, I want you to look at me and tell me that you believe these lies, that you condemn me. Say it to me.''

She took so long to oblige, he thought she might disregard his order. But she swung on him all at once, her eyes clear with bitterness, her jaw set. That lovely, strong nose he had always admired flared now with a rage barely contained. "Then I will say it clearly for you. I do believe Elspeth. I had it straight from her.'' Weakly she added, "I have no choice.''

"My God!'' Andrew exploded. "Lily, you know him. How can you believe this!''

Pain clouded those sea-green eyes. "Elspeth would never lie.'' When her gaze slid to Rogan, her lips trembled. "You are a demon who preys on the purest of innocents. I revile the fact you are my husband, and as of now I denounce you. And I join my family and condemn you for the disgusting monster you are."

"There is no mercy for his kind," Catherine said, unable to hide her glee. "He is to be executed."

"You cannot do that!" Andrew protested. "You have no authority to kill another noble. You need the sanction of the king's law for that."

"He raped our sister!" Catherine shouted back.

Rogan stared at Lily, who stood under the scathing glare with a fine rage of her own. Around him, voices argued, but nothing penetrated the red haze filling his brain. Lily had just condemned him, and the shock of that left him suddenly drained.

Andrew was saying, "You will have much to answer for if you do not respect the king's authority here, both from the crown and from my family. Rest assured that there is little Alexander will not dare to avenge Rogan should you harm him."

Slowly Rogan turned away from Lily. The betrayer. His eyes lingered, pinning her over his shoulder until she at last looked away with a trembling gasp.

Enguerrand was half-mad with grief, but he was shrewd and too aware of his position to totally abandon convention, and the law. "No, Catherine, we cannot kill him. Though I would like to. My Elspeth!" He choked on the word and for a moment, Rogan thought he would weep openly.

Regaining his composure, he gave Rogan a look of

pure malice. "But I can hold you until a court of justice can be convened by a representative of the king's to hear the evidence."

"Father!" Catherine began, clearly disappointed. Enguerrand waved his hand sharply to silence her. Rogan was dully surprised it worked, and she snapped her venomous mouth shut.

"But he will not escape my wrath so easily," Enguerrand continued darkly. "He is a man who preys on helpless children, and so he shall receive just recompense. Perhaps if he is without the pains of conscience, then he needs another kind of pain to encourage remorse. Thus, I will give him pain aplenty to keep him company while he awaits judgment in my dungeons. Tiebold! Fetch the bullwhip. I shall have him flogged!"

Rogan realized these words should have made some impact on him. But as they dragged him away to lash him to the posts in the lower bailey, he could think only of Lily standing like an ivory statue, cold and rigid and unreachable. Nothing of the Lily he had married only yesterday, loved only just last night, remained in the stone-faced woman who now stood with her family against him.

He didn't bother to resist when they bound his hands to the posts and ripped off his shirt. He fixed his eyes upon *her,* silently daring her to relent, to speak even now in his support.

Andrew continued to protest loudly and vehemently. At Enguerrand's sharp order, he was held to prevent interference.

A sharp sound ripped through his brain, and he

knew the man behind him was warming up his arm, snapping the deadly coil of leather in the air. Rogan was surprised to feel a cold, numbing dread seep through his limbs, leaving him trembling. He was not a man who feared much, and he had borne pain before. But he had also seen what a bullwhip could do in the hands of an experienced man and, yes, he was afraid.

Eyes still fixed on his wife, he saw when Lily spoke urgently to her father, but he could not hear what it was she said. He saw Enguerrand's head shake in a definitive denial. Then the first blow fell.

An excruciating flare of fire burst across his back. The wound immediately pulsed and stung, alive with agonizing feeling. Again an explosion of pain came as another welt was opened.

On the fifteenth stroke, he let his head sag and the agony made him senseless. He thought he heard someone weeping. He wondered who it was who would cry out at his suffering here in the midst of his tormentors.

For himself, he did not make a sound.

He was taken into one of the tiny cells in the bowels of Charolais, a dark place that stank of human waste and damp. The amplified sound of dripping echoed around him. It drowned out the gruff commands of his unkind companions—two burly soldiers who bore him down the steps. He could not stand, let alone walk, so his feet dangled helplessly after him and his head lolled with the limpness of a well-worn doll. Not that Rogan was aware of any of this; he was not. He had forgotten where he was, who he was. He was only dimly aware of some delirium nightmare, of a pain that seemed blessedly remote at the moment. Only one thing was real to him: Lily's betrayal. That anguish burned savagely in his heart.

He was shoved into a small chamber. It was too dark to see anything, but he heard the final thud of the door slamming shut and the high-pitched squeal of an indignant rat put to flight.

He lay still, studying the darkness creeping in upon him. He was falling into a vortex, one he found strangely—dangerously—inviting. He fought against it for as long as he could, but it would not be denied. As it consumed him, he didn't know if he would ever wake, so he prayed for his soul in case he did not. He wondered if dying now, with so much hate in his heart, would damn him eternally.

Catherine stood over Rogan, Phillippe beside her holding the torch. St. Cyr was still unconscious, lying on the floor, unmoving. He was on his side, his mangled back away from her, so she could not see the damage. She had no wish to view it. The physician had just left, having reassured her that he did not think Rogan would live through the night. But Catherine was not satisfied with that. Rogan was a man of strength and endurance.

Possess or destroy. He himself had named her obsession.

"You should have come to me when you had the chance," she said in a deadly low voice. She stepped forward, placing the toe of her shoe against his ribs and giving him a shove. He fell onto his back and the pain of the ruined flesh hitting the stone floor brought him briefly awake in a stark flare of agony.

Catherine gave him a brittle smile as he struggled to focus on his tormentor before unconsciousness came again. When she turned away, she noticed that Phillippe's swarthy face held an unusual pallor.

"I want him dead as soon as possible. Tonight, or tomorrow night at the latest, set the dungeons afire. Have it discovered in time to save the rest of the castle, but I want these rooms destroyed completely."

She cast a lingering glance over her shoulder as Phillippe led the way out to the corridor. Rogan lay motionless. Even ravaged as he was, he was a magnificent specimen of man.

It was a waste, but leaving him alive was unthinkable.

The following day, there was not a moment that Lily did not think of him, despising him, yearning for him. She felt shattered, an excruciating sensation that made her stomach knot and her head pound with a constant, dull ache. He was a beast. The man she had loved was a ruthless animal, and all her dreams of happiness were dead.

She wanted answers. She wanted to scream at him, tell him how much she hated him for what he had done.

God help her, she wanted to kill him herself at times.

Her hatred, she could understand. What she could not fathom was her pity.

She had protested the lashing. Eventually, as Rogan's body had hung limp between his bindings, she had begged her father to stop it. Finally she simply sobbed and ran away, not even able to make herself see the end. What was it in her that she could take no joy in his punishment? He had no right to her compassion. And she felt like a traitor sitting by Elspeth's bed as that one slumbered in drug-induced sleep, wondering if Rogan's wounds had been properly dressed, thinking about his agony and tormenting herself with thoughts of his need.

Perhaps it was pity that drove her. Perhaps it was simply the necessity to see him again, confront him. Whatever it was, she finally decided she would go to him.

She gathered some bandages and a salve and made her way to the dungeon. The guard opened the door and fitted a sconce into the bracket on the wall.

He was lying on his back in the middle of the small chamber. She thought he was dead for a moment, surprised at the terrible grief that welled up inside of her. Then she noticed the slight rise and fall of his chest and she knew he still lived. She remembered laying her head on that chest just two nights ago. As much as she reviled what he had done, a wrenching pain gripped her at the memory. And with it came a strange thought, a deep conviction that startled her in its clarity and strength: he could not have done it. Not Rogan.

It was the first of many doubts she was to have, doubts that flew in the face of all sense. Telling herself it was merely a selfish wish borne of her own grief, she pushed it away. Kneeling, she gently rolled him over.

When she saw what her father's men had done to him, saw the blackened flesh of his back from the already festering welts, she had to look away. It took a few moments of deep, steady breathing to calm her stomach and keep herself from giving way to the wave of nausea. Steeling herself, she called to the guard to bring her hot water and set to work cleaning the wounds.

His body was ablaze with fever, and Lily felt inadequate. She knew little about medicines and healing. But there was no one else to do it since old Maida, the healer, had died, so she concentrated on getting the worst of the debris and dried blood out of his wounds.

He never stirred and Lily thanked God for that one blessing. If he had been conscious, the pain would have been unbearable. She finished the cleansing and smeared his whole back with a generous portion of salve, a mixture of healing herbs and goose fat, before wrapping clean linens lightly over his entire torso to protect the injured flesh and seal in the medicine. She said a quick prayer it would be enough, then thought of the fruitlessness of her efforts. He would likely hang for his crime in due time.

Finished, Lily stood on trembling legs and called the guard. She ordered a pallet brought in and she and the guard struggled to pull Rogan onto it. She insisted he be fed strong broth twice a day, pressing a silver piece into the guard's hand to insure it would be done. Looking at Rogan now, she found it difficult to muster her hate. He was so vulnerable, so helpless, so very unlike the man she had known. It was her second moment of doubt.

Once seated again by Elspeth's bedside, she was still thinking of him. She could not stem the flow of uncertainty that now bubbled up to cloud the safe, hollow hate that had sheltered her before. It was impossible he could be innocent. She knew that. And yet, fool that she was, she was unsure...

Her thoughts were suddenly interrupted by Elspeth. "I am a sinner!" she cried out, thrashing about in her sleep.

Lily leaped out of her chair and rushed to her side, holding her down and trying to calm her. The physicians had warned them not to wake her when she was in the grips of one of these sleep trances, cautioning that it could be damaging to her already fragile mind.

"Hush, Elspeth. Sleep now, my love."

"I am dirty! I am unclean."

This was her usual cry, and Lily felt a renewed surge of disgust for Rogan whom she had been so foolish as to feel pity for only moments before. "Shh, my little love, it is all right. You are but a sweet innocent." She rocked her in her arms like a babe. "Please rest now."

The seizures usually lasted only a few moments, and this one was already subsiding. Lily felt the small body relaxing, and the tortured voice fell off until it was barely discernible. Her murmurings were so soft, in fact, that when Lily heard her say "I have lied," she was not at all sure she had heard correctly.

* * *

Down in the dungeons, the men did their work in silence. The fire was to look as much like an accident as possible, so they rigged a pile of straw near a torch to ignite as the flame burned low. It was relatively simple, and they were finished quickly.

A short time later, a second group of men moved in, equal in stealth but intent on a mission of a different nature.

"Where is the guard?" someone hissed.

Andrew shook his head. "He is nowhere about. I do not like this. It seems a trap."

"Do we retreat?"

"No," Andrew said quickly. "I count myself lucky if my brother is not already dead. I will not have another chance as this. If it comes to it, we grab Rogan and slash our way out of it. If Rogan dies…" He paused, and his men looked away respectfully while he fought for control. "If Rogan dies, it is no comfort to me that I saved my own life." Andrew frowned into the dark maze of corridors. "I have no idea where he is, so we look in every cell. When you find him, give the whistle. I suggest we start."

"What is that smell?"

Andrew paused, sniffing the air. His eyes widened in alarm. "Fire!"

They all reacted in unison, racing down the corridors, flinging doors open as they went, shouting to one another as each cell turned up empty. They did not bother with stealth now; there was no time.

"I found him!" Garven, an older knight, called at last. Andrew was beside him in a flash and they went together into the moldy cell.

Garven knelt beside his master, feeling the timorous

pulse at Rogan's neck. "Just barely alive, sir. And maybe not for long."

"A fate we may all be sharing in if we cannot escape this Hades. John! Arwen! Lord Rogan is here!"

The men came and hoisted Rogan onto their shoulders. They had no time to be gentle, and Andrew winced as he thought of the pain for his brother. Blessedly, Rogan did not wake, though that fact worried Andrew all the more.

They raced against the encroaching flames as they threaded their way up through the labyrinth.

"Pray the alarm has not yet been raised," Andrew called. "If it has, we are likely to be met on the surface by half of the population of Charolais."

Garven grunted, bursting free of the choking flames and into the still night. "All clear!" he announced.

"Call for the alarm now," Andrew instructed, "and we will escape under cover of the confusion."

Andrew watched grimly as Rogan's limp body was slung on the back of a horse. His jaw worked as he thought what a shame it was that they could not simply let the flames take Charolais. A fitting end to such a hellish place.

Lily had spent the night by Elspeth's bedside, so it was not until morning that she heard the news of the dungeon fires.

Numb, Lily sat in silence before asking, "And my husband? Lord Rogan?"

"My lady, he is certainly dead."

Chapter Ten

Autumn came, staining the sparse greenery dead shades of brown and rust. It was followed quickly by winter with its bleak wastelands that so suited the Cornish coast. Through these changes, Charolais slept like an enchanted castle, its inhabitants still under the spell of the horror that had occurred that summer.

Everyone was changed, especially Lily. Life no longer held the slightest of joys, nor even the promise of such. She lived quietly, alone with her grief.

She had her chamber changed and the one that had been hers since childhood, the one she had shared only one night with Rogan, was closed up and left unused. She never went to the garden. She never walked by the sea.

Elspeth withdrew, causing her father so much worry that he at last granted her dearest wish: to be allowed to go to the convent. This news didn't cheer the child, and her delicate state was the preoccupation of Lily, who never dared ask again about the cryptic cry that fed so many of her tortured doubts.

Even Catherine was changed. And though she grew

meaner over the months, given to extreme moodiness and vicious outbursts, her sting was gone. Everyone was relieved when Enguerrand made quick arrangements for her marriage to an old earl. It was a suitable enough match, though disappointing after having had dreams of a duke. Catherine, surprisingly, seemed to be as anxious to be away as was her family to have her gone. She was wed and living with her new husband before Christ's Mass.

Nothing was heard from the St. Cyrs. Initially there had been some concern that Alexander might launch a retaliation for the death of his brother, but none came. The worry lessened over time and life at Charolais slipped into dull monotony.

When her father announced he had found her a husband, Lily reacted not at all.

It made no difference what happened to her now.

When Lily's wedding day arrived, it was the kind of day in late February that was deceptively mild, a kind of lull amidst the heart of the winter, and Lily was relieved to see that the chapel looked nothing like it had on the long-ago day when she had wed Rogan. Gone were the gay boughs of late-summer flowers. A few ribbons sufficed for decoration. Instead of the broad-shouldered warrior waiting for her at the altar, a thin, pale bridegroom stood. Leon de Aignier, a Norman relative. A pleasant enough fellow, smiling down the aisle at her, proud that he had made such a fine match.

She drew up to him, seeing him close for the first time. They had barely been introduced when her father informed her they were to wed. He was so young. Her heart ached for all she would not be able to give him.

The priest began the mass, droning the holy prayers in staccato Latin. Lily felt her bridegroom give her fingers a squeeze, as if to reassure her. *He thinks my pallor is due to nervousness,* she realized and a flush of shame passed through her. A good man, he deserved better, not a woman whose heart was dead.

The altar servers moved about, fetching the incense drum, bowing low in reverent acknowledgment before the Holy Sacrament. Ordinarily Lily would not have noticed them, but one happened to catch her eye. He was watching her, it seemed. The strangeness of that pierced her dysphoria. She looked closer.

He looked familiar, but she could not place him. She glanced toward the other server, but his head was bowed low so that she could not see him. But when he moved, there was something in his step that seemed to remind her of something…

Lily realized de Aignier was speaking his vows. She snapped out of her musings and forced herself to attend him. He was looking at her with such pleasure, enunciating each syllable enthusiastically.

When he was finished, the priest turned to her and began, ''I, Margaret Lily Elizabeth Louise.''

''I, Margaret Lily Elizabeth Louise,'' Lily repeated.

''Take thee, Leon Stephen Robert.''

''Take thee, Leon Stephen Robert.''

''As my husband.''

Another voice, rich and bold, and easily familiar cut through the silence of the chapel. ''I am afraid she cannot do that, Father, for she already has a husband.''

Immediately, sounds of dismay exploded. Lily's head shot up, and she was looking into the face of the altar server who had been bowed so low, concealing his face. It was Andrew! She whipped her head around toward the voice. That voice! It could only be...

Rogan stood directly in front of her, staring with a thunderous expression.

Rogan. Rogan was here. Alive. Impossibly, blessedly alive. Her legs gave way, and had it not been for the gallant de Aignier catching her, she would have collapsed onto the cold stones.

Staring at her with a terrible, evil-looking smile twisting his lips, his eyes gleamed silver by the dim flames of the candles. Trust him to appear in such a shocking manner, Lily thought distractedly, so smug and poised and magnificent.

''Block the doorways, do not let him escape!'' Lily recognized her father's voice. No one moved. Then, in unison, Rogan's men drew their swords and the slicing sound of unsheathed steel resounded in the chapel.

Alive. Alive, Lily was thinking stupidly, unable to will her limbs to move, wanting to cry, to shout— something. He was still watching her, looking incredibly at ease amidst all of the tension. And though his eyes held a fathomless intensity, she felt deliriously happy.

Her reaction was pure instinct. She dashed the small bouquet to the floor and ran straight into his arms. In a smooth motion, Rogan captured her around the waist. He did not embrace her, but swept her behind him. His hand he kept tight on her wrist, hurting her.

"You are alive!" she exclaimed. It was the only thought her brain could conjure.

"Obviously," Rogan muttered. "Disappointed?"

de Aignier leaped forward and demanded, "What the devil is going on?"

He had spoken to Enguerrand, but it was Rogan who answered. "Why, you have been had, my good man. The lady is already wed, you see. To me. And though I wonder at my own sanity for not counting myself well rid of her, I find I am curiously unable to see the woman who promised me to wife live a life of sin with another." He paused, letting de Aignier digest his news. "You were taken in, and that is regrettable. But it has happened to others before you. Me, for instance. So you see, I sympathize."

"St. Cyr, you are outrageous!" Enguerrand roared.

Suddenly Rogan dropped the sardonic mien. His whole body stiffened and his tone sharpened to match Enguerrand's. "No, 'tis you who are outrageous. Did you not do your best to destroy me? But I lived, Enguerrand, and I have returned. And today luck is with you, for I want no vengeance on you. I come only to claim my wife." He turned to Lily. Confused and suddenly wary of the dark light in his eye, she tried to step away but Rogan yanked her back to his side. His next words were for her alone. "The wife who handed me over like a female Judas."

Coldness crept over her, a mingling of shock and

fear, as the chapel exploded into action. Men rushed forward, but Rogan's soldiers, disguises now cast aside, had gathered into a small semicircle. Passing Lily to an older man who was waiting by the vestry door, Rogan turned back to the fray. Lily cried out his name, but she was already being dragged out through the sacristy. The last thing she saw was the wide, terrified eyes of Elspeth as Lily was taken down a narrow stair that led to an outer courtyard. Behind her, she could hear the furious clash of steel.

Too late she thought to struggle, but her captor was quick. He bound her hands together before lifting her atop a nervous stallion, and lashed them to the saddle. No sooner had she been secured than Rogan's men started racing out of the castle and mounting up. Lastly Rogan and Andrew came out at full run. Rogan shouted some orders and swung up onto the stallion.

The feel of him pressed fully against her back slammed into her like a blow, his hard chest like stone and his arm about her waist squeezing her like a vise. As he kicked the great beast into action, she was thrown against him, cushioned by the warm flesh that was cruelly inviting. She was grateful, however, for the benefit of stability his cold embrace afforded as they raced to the castle's main gate. There they were joined by several others, who had been set to insure a safe retreat.

As the troop of raiders passed under the gate tower, Rogan swept his sword expertly over the ropes that controlled the portcullis and it came crashing down just as they raced through the gate. Without pause, the raiders pounded over the moors at breakneck speed. By the time they reached the cover of the trees, they had not seen any sign of pursuit from the castle.

They rode at the jarring pace for hours. At times, the men would shout to one another in a brief interchange to clarify direction, but otherwise no one spoke.

Rogan continued to hold Lily tightly against him. She was acutely aware of his powerful thighs like granite behind her legs, his breath at her ear, warming it against the terrible wind. He did not speak, nor did Lily, though the need to do so burned in her throat. Or perhaps that was grief. In the silent tension of their mad escape, she could feel the heat of his anger burning into her back.

Darkness was beginning to fall when they finally stopped. Lily could make out a ramshackle hut in the dense twilight. She was filled with questions, but fear kept her mute as Rogan swung down from the horse and entered the small shack with Andrew. The man to whom Rogan had passed her in the chapel came up to her again and gently untied her hands, taking her down from the horse.

"I am hungry," Lily said meekly. Her legs were shaking and she feared she might faint, else she would not have complained.

"We will have something to eat on the boat," the man answered, not unkindly. At the mention of a boat, Lily realized she smelled the briny aroma of the sea.

"Where are you taking me?" she cried, instantly alarmed. She had heard tales of slavery inflicted on female captives—sexual and domestic servitude to lords in foreign countries. But no, Rogan would never do such a thing. He was angry at her, yes, but as much as he might despise her, he could not be that cruel—could he?

"Please!" she screamed, struggling against him. He was an older man, almost as old as her father, but he was strong and he held her easily. "Do not send me away, please. I don't want to go. I do not want to be a slave!"

"Silence," her captor urged. "Get on the boat. Lord Rogan will explain everything to you there."

His words were like an immediate balm. Rogan was coming with her. "Then I am not to be sold into slavery?"

The man chuckled. "Now, my lady, why would the master go through all of that trouble just to send you off somewhere else when he could have hired anyone to do it? Nay, he has plans for you himself."

Realizing she was not going to be sent into bondage, she calmed, though she did not like the reference to these still unrevealed "plans." She was led onto the boat and taken below to a small cabin.

"My name is Garven," the man said to her. "I'll bring you something to eat when we are at sea."

"Where are we going?"

"Lord Rogan will tell you," Garven repeated, and left her.

True to his word, it was not long before Garven brought her a modest meal. Lily devoured it, then sat stiffly on the edge of the narrow bunk, waiting for Rogan.

She was afraid.

Chapter Eleven

Lily reacted instantly to the rattle of the key in the lock of the cabin door. She was on her feet in a flash as Rogan ducked under the low transom and closed the portal behind him, taking care to turn the catch and pocket the key.

The room was too small to accommodate both of them standing, so she was forced to retreat onto the bed. Hating herself for a coward, she skittered backward, seeking the farthest point from his impassive face. The apex of the two walls stopped her and she wedged into the corner. She sat with her legs curled under her, as wary and tense as an animal at bay.

He seemed like a giant, his head grazing the low ceiling and his broad shoulders eclipsing almost everything else from view. Ignoring her, he stripped his gloves and unwound a scarlet sash, a remnant of his altar-server costume, and sat on the edge of the bed with his back to her.

"Let us clear up a few things before we begin, shall we?" he said. She could view his face in profile. His expression was stern and for all the familiarity of those features, he seemed almost unrecognizable. "I am not taking you to some foreign land to sell you into slavery. Garven told me of your fears." His lip quivered, as if in acknowledgment of a jest. "I am not going to beat you or harm you in any way. Of that, I give my word." He sighed, lifting a hand. "Now, you have nothing to be afraid of."

He was mocking her. Somehow, that cut through her dazed fear. "I thought you dead all these last months. Why could you not at least send word that you were alive?"

"I would have imparted the good news sooner, but what with organizing the men for the ambush and such, time slipped away. But I suppose there is no excuse. I could have at least sent a brief message. 'Hello, my darling, treacherous wife. I am not dead as you intended. I cannot wait to be reunited. Look for me at your next wedding.'"

Lily ignored his biting words. "How did you escape?"

"I have my brother to thank for that. We St. Cyrs are a resourceful lot. Combine that with our legendary stubbornness, and, well, there is not much that can hold us down. But, to your credit, you and your family almost succeeded."

Lily shook her head. "I never wanted your death, even when I thought you guilty. It almost destroyed me when I thought you had died."

Finally he looked at her, and she cringed at the coldness in his eyes. They seemed to blaze with icy ferocity. "How very touching. Not that I believe it, of course. You lied for your family's revenge and you are lying now. I wonder, Lily, if you are capable of truth.''

Lily closed her eyes against the condemning fire of his. "Elspeth cannot lie, and yet she did. I suspected it, but only after. You never hurt her, did you?'' She opened her eyes again, forcing herself to look at him.

"That is the first time you asked me.'' Rogan's voice was full of emotion. A flicker of pain passed over his features, gone before she knew if it had ever truly been there. "It was one of the things that gave you away. You were too quick to say me guilty.''

Rogan leaned back, wincing slightly as his back touched the wall. Gradually he relaxed in degrees. When he was settled, he gave her a lazy look. "My back, it still pains me. The scars are stiff.''

Lily looked away, swallowing hard. She could hardly bear to think of the pain of his stripped back, nor any of the other sufferings he had borne at the hands of her family.

"I had a great deal of time to think, these last months.'' Rogan sighed. "When one is confined to lie flat on one's stomach, unable to even raise one's head high enough to look at another human face for the pain that small action would cause, one generally has a great deal of time to give matters their due consideration. And, I certainly had sufficient topics to meditate upon.'' He stretched out his legs, flexing them to work away the stiffness and fatigue. "Need I say that you were chief among them?''

Lily was tempted to reach out a hand and touch his rigid shoulder. How she ached for his gentleness. "You think I betrayed you. But I was betrayed, too, that day. I knew nothing of their conspiracy! Could you not see how distraught I was? I wanted to die myself. And afterward, oh, God, afterward..."

"You play the part of doting lover so well, even now it amazes me." His lip curled. "No wonder I was so completely taken in. Lord, I almost blush when I realize how naive I was—me! After all I've done and seen, there I was, behaving like a bare-faced boy smitten with his first love, pleading with you to just listen to me." His eyes clouded to an unfathomable gray. "I suppose my pride can take the bruising if I confess that your betrayal stung deeper than the stripes on my back."

"What possible reason could I have for doing such a thing?" she asked.

"Why, revenge, my sweet."

"Revenge? What should I care about revenge?"

"For Alex's rejection of your sister." His perusal reflected only a vague interest in her protestations. "I hardly expect you to admit the truth," he said.

"You know nothing of the truth!" she accused, finding strength in venting some of her anger. "How can you blame me for this? Do you know what torture I went through, thinking you dead all these months?"

He sprang forward, his civility gone and his eyes wild with the ferocity of a wolf. "Tell me, Lily, was your torture anything like having the flesh flayed from your back with a razor-sharp strip of leather? Was it anything akin to being beaten within a breath of life and dragged into a stinking dungeon and left to die? Did you know that when my family's physicians got to me, one of them fainted dead away, like a woman.

Someone had tended me, but the wounds were torn anew during my escape. They marveled I survived.''

Lily's fledgling courage fled and she shrank away from his wrath. He did not relent. "So tell me about your tender regrets, wife, and move me to pity you. I can bear it, I assure you. After all, it can be nothing as terrible as lying in blinding pain that feels like it will take you over the brink of madness.'' He turned suddenly and leaped from the bed in a single, fluid movement. She could see he was shaking, struggling for control. "Such experiences can reduce a man to his most basic elements. Change him forever. I suppose I am changed, Lily. I am no longer the fool I was.''

With an effort, she pushed herself away from the wall. She stood, squaring her shoulders. In a calm, quiet voice, she said, "My crime is that I stood against you, and for that I am guilty. You say I never looked to you and asked you if you were innocent, and I confess, I did not. For those things, you have a right to revile me. I despise myself for such a terrible mistake. As for the rest, I never conspired against you. What should I care for Catherine's revenge? Aye, I stood with my family because I had good reason to think you the knave. Yet, on this you refuse to hear me. You do the same thing to me, Rogan, that you hate me so much for doing to you—condemn without hearing my explanation.''

His body was still for a long time. When he did not respond, the tension began to ebb from her as she thought perhaps he had finally realized the truth in her words.

His movement came in a rush. He whirled and leaped at her, his large hand grasping her chin and shoving her head up against the wall. His body held her pinned, a well-muscled leg on either side of her preventing the slightest movement. His face was only inches from hers.

Lily was terrified. He could crush her, break her easily with his untamed strength. His voice was low and coarse. "I said I would not harm you, and I am a man of my word. But I will not be responsible if you goad me beyond my endurance. I regret my self-control is not what it should be, but it has been tested mightily of late. So, I must give you fair warning," he said as he pressed her back harder, coming so close that their noses almost touched. "Never, never, simper about your innocence. I do not want to hear your lies again. Do I make myself clear?"

She bobbed her head. Just as suddenly as he had pounced he released her. She rubbed the bruised flesh where his fingers had been. When she looked up, he had his back to her again.

She was still frightened but, God save her from her impulsive tongue, she could not keep herself from asking, "Why did you come for me? If you hate me so, if you will not listen?"

"To give you exactly what you bargained for but never intended. You will live as my wife."

He turned his head, lifting his gaze from her feet to her head in a searing look and added cryptically, "But there are many types of wives."

She said carefully, "I do not threaten, but merely observe. My father will come looking for me."

"He will not find you."

"But he will know to come to Kensmouth."

"We are not going to Kensmouth."

"But you said that I am to live as your wife," Lily puzzled. "And your home is at Kensmouth."

"I also told you that there were many kinds of wives." He turned, standing with his feet braced, arms crossed against his chest, looking for all the earth like a smug satyr. "I intend for you to live at another place. I would not contaminate my own household with you."

Lily blanched. "You intend to lock me away?"

Rogan looked her over, the coldness in his eyes touching her skin and chilling her. "You will have a small household for yourself, an isolated place in Linden Wood. It is a pleasant enough place, a cottage really, with a small retinue of servants to help you, though you shall certainly have your share of chores. I imagine it will be much different from your privileged life at Charolais. There I will have you all to myself, so the better to serve my purpose."

Lily hated herself for the fear in her voice. "I do not want to be alone."

"Well, I did not want to be dead, but that made no difference to you."

"You risked your life just to take me prisoner?"

"I do not intend you to be simply a prisoner. I will live at Kensmouth, but I shall visit. You and I are legally wed, and I do not intend to cheat myself of heirs." His eyes flickered over her cruelly. "Though I have doubts whether I can overcome my revulsion of your nature to see the duty done. I suppose with the aid of darkness, some clever imaginings and a few cups of wine I could do it. I am hoping, anyway, since I do want children to carry on my name."

His words fell on her as if each one were of granite, crushing her under their cruel weight. She felt battered, no less than had he struck her with his fist. "That is no way to live," she whispered.

"Ah, yes, that is the point. You did not think I would simply allow you to go without retribution, did you?"

"You will leave me and our children alone and isolated away from the rest of your family, the rest of the world? Forever?"

He raised a brow. "I said nothing about leaving the children with you. I would not dream of allowing you to have anything to do with them. They will be removed immediately after birth and raised in my household at Kensmouth."

She felt a terrible wave of nausea rushing up from her stomach to lodge in her throat. "You would steal my babes from me?"

"I would no sooner entrust them in your care than leave them with a she-wolf," Rogan sneered. He took a step forward. "You see, I will control everything in your life. Who you see—which will be no one—what you do, what you wear, where you go. There is nothing that will come into your life without passing my approval. You will be my wife, but you will live only by my grace in all things. That is my revenge."

She felt dizzy. Her legs buckled and she collapsed onto the bed and covered her face with her hands. His voice floated above her. "When I was making my

long recovery, I came to this, the perfect vengeance."
He paused, his voice almost winsome. "Never-ending
penance for your crimes. It will go a long way to ease
my complaint against you."

Lily looked up and searched his face for some sign
of mercy. She said, "You could never be such a
beast."

He offered nothing more than a crooked smile. "I
have suffered beastly things, Lily, and most of them
at your hands."

Their gazes locked for a long moment, hers in anguish, his in triumph. Then Rogan shifted and looked
away. "Get some sleep," he said, rubbing the back
of his neck. "We dock close to noon and then we
have a long ride ahead. You will need your stamina."

He left her, locking her in behind him. It struck her
as almost funny. They were aboard a ship—where
was she to go? But the scraping metal sounded like
a death knell mourning her freedom forever more.

Chapter Twelve

The house sat in the midst of a clearing that was neither deep nor broad. In fact, it was barely enough space for the small dwelling and a narrow border of ill-tended gardens. The lacy canopy of intertwined branches overhead made it appear rather gloomy and forlorn all alone in the thick wood.

Lily had no idea where they were, indeed the only thing she did know was they were still in England, and that she had surmised only by the conversations she had overheard between Rogan's men. They had traveled north, she guessed, for it was colder here and the damp was biting.

They had ridden for three days after the ship docked, and each one was a study in torture as Lily had been made to ride with Rogan, enduring his silence, his implicit loathing. During the long hours, she comforted herself by mentally rehearsing long speeches where she would find the right words, blended with the exact degree of indignation, to break through his rigid contempt. The effectiveness of her righteousness would make Rogan understand his grievous error, followed by his great remorse, and finally there would be a blissful reunion as Rogan begged her forgiveness.

But these were only fantasies. She dared not give voice to the carefully plotted discourse she spun in her dreams, for this Rogan, the Rogan who had come back from the dead to punish and avenge, was a formidable man.

Now she viewed what was, she assumed, her new home with disgust. It had two stories, judging by the row of shuttered windows under the eaves of the thatched roof. Inside, she would later learn, the kitchens were attached to a large lower room that served as the gathering place, with two tiny chambers leading off for the servants. A wooden staircase led to an upper corridor where three plain rooms housed bedchambers.

This was where she was to live? And the only servants about were two rather grim looking persons poised by the front door. One was a severe-looking matron with small, intense eyes, the other a tall, awkward-looking fellow with a balding pate covered inadequately by a few precious strands of hair. The two stared solemnly as Garven lifted Lily down from the stallion and motioned her to go stand by Rogan.

"This is Sybilla, and her husband, Thomas," Rogan said.

The decayed house combined with the reticent faces of the servants snapped Lily into action. Her hands balled into fists at her sides. Never before had she endured such humiliation as the past few days.

Reckless rage possessed her, and it felt so good after the numbness of her fear.

"I am not going in there," Lily stated evenly.

Rogan studied her for a moment, his eyes narrowing.

She inhaled, drawing herself up to stand firm against his icy stare. "This is not a suitable house. I am not setting foot inside the door."

"Suit yourself." Rogan shrugged. He turned his back on her and called out orders to his men to join him in the stables. Before he left, he glanced back at her. "It matters little to me where you sleep. But this place—" he spread his hands to encompass his surroundings "—is where you will stay."

To her utter dismay, he turned on his heel and walked away, leaving her quite alone.

She looked around after the men had gone, pulling her mantle tighter about her shoulders. The thick press of bracken crowded in on every side, dark and smelling of earth and moisture, even in these barren months of midwinter. She was struck by the strange, alien feeling of the place, being used to the low grasses of the moors, the crouched, twisted forms of the trees that survived on tiny patches of fertile earth and the huge heaps of boulders that jutted up abruptly. Here, so far from Cornwall, she felt as if she were in some enchanted wood like the sort in the stories she had heard, where evil things dwelled in shadowed secrecy, watching and waiting to prey on the unaware.

She shivered, more from that last thought than the cold.

"It ain't no matter to me if you want to catch your death out here, but me and Thomas are frozen."

It was Sybilla, glaring at her hotly with those strange eyes. Beside her, Thomas's steady gaze made Lily cringe.

"Go on inside, then," Lily said sharply.

"Very well, mistress," Sybilla said deferentially enough, but her voice held no respect. She spun about and disappeared through the doorway. Thomas, however, continued to stare in silence a long moment before loping away.

Lily was surprised by the hot sting of tears in her eyes. Rogan would leave her with these two?

Rogan's men came back from seeing to their horses and filed past her. Feeling very much the fool, Lily wandered away from the house a bit, walking the narrow ribbon of path that wound through the overgrown herb garden. What was she to do now? She had said, within plain hearing of everyone, she would not set foot inside the house. Why had she been such an idiot? What had she been hoping for—that Rogan would suddenly say, "Oh, of course, let me take you to Kensmouth where you will be more comfortable."

She shook her head. Her temper would gain her nothing. Here she was, standing outside in the bitter cold, all alone, with no one to care about any of it.

Groaning, she became aware of another disadvantage. The aroma of soup reached her and her stomach heaved. So she was cold, alone *and* starving.

The soulful howling of a wolf cut through the still air just as the first flurry of snow began to fall.

* * *

Inside, Rogan's head snapped up at the sound.

Andrew caught his look and frowned as Sybilla ladled out soup for the men. His eyes slid to the door as if he were thinking of going after her.

"Do not," Rogan warned, but he was tempted himself to relent. No doubt his pigheaded wife would allow herself to be devoured before admitting defeat and coming inside.

"It is snowing," Garven said.

The comment annoyed Rogan. The old knight had a soft heart.

"Bread," was all Rogan said, jabbing a rude finger at the loaf farther down the table. But the tension was mounting within him. The wolf cry had him truly worried. Spiteful pride was one thing, but this foolishness would have to be—

The sound of the door opening was accompanied by a sudden draft that made the candles flicker. Several heads snapped up and were quickly brought down again when they saw Rogan's glare.

With her head bowed and eyes downcast, Lily came to sit at the edge of the bench. In the candle-light, her tumble of curls looked like a shimmering veil of gold and the soft curves of her face still glowed from the kiss of the cold air. Such a winsome sight, Rogan could not help but notice. A pity that fair facade hid such a corrupt heart. Hands folded on her lap, she sat in demure silence waiting for her meal as Rogan swept a quick gaze around to his men to make sure no one moved to go to her aid.

"Am I to eat, as well?"

The men shifted and cleared their throats and stared intently into their cups.

Rogan chose to ignore her, forcing her to ask, "Sybilla, where is my cup?"

Even Rogan was unprepared for the venom of his servant. "Lord Rogan is my master, and him is who I take my orders from. You can get your own meal, and this will be the last one you'll eat if you don't help."

"Thank you, Sybilla," Rogan said when he saw Lily coming to her feet. "I am too tired to enjoy a catfight just now. Lily, get your cup and fill it. Sybilla, show her where she can find the bread and broth." At Lily's shocked look, he explained, "In the future, you will not expect to be served by Sybilla or Thomas. As to your chores, we will discuss that later."

"Chores?" she squeaked.

He gave her a quelling look. "Later."

He finished his meal before Lily returned. Rising, he caught Andrew's eye. He read the unspoken question in his brother's glance.

"Even I have had enough for one day. I am going to bed. Have Sybilla give Lily the other room, and you take the third. The men can bed down in here after the table has been cleared away."

"I will take care of it."

Suddenly weary, Rogan stepped on the creaking treads of the old stairs. As an afterthought, he called Thomas over. "Bring up that old tub and fetch me some water."

The bedchamber was cold so he built a fire. By the

time Thomas arrived, Rogan had already stripped down to his underlinen. He prowled restlessly, alone with his thoughts, while Thomas fetched the water.

He was particularly infuriated. Lily had managed to appear completely ingenuous and, blast his weakness, pathetically appealing. Even with those cat eyes and lush mouth, she had a damnable way of looking like a lost child.

Rogan hunkered down in front of the fire and stoked the embers. The flames leaped to life, warming his skin, but he still felt cold inside. He had to be careful with the little flower, he decided. She could coax pity out of a demon.

A loud gasp hissed behind him. His head snapped up as he realized his shirt was off and his back was to the door.

The scars.

Whirling around, he found Lily standing in the doorway, holding a thick pile of linens. Her face was frozen in horror.

She had seen them, then. The ugly pattern of re-formed tissue would drain the color from a seasoned warrior. A woman, upon viewing them, might faint.

"Sybilla sent me up with these," she sputtered in an unsteady voice, raising up the stack of cloths in her arms. "She said you would need them."

A strange anger twisted its way around his heart. He had left Andrew specific instructions for Lily to be given another room. Apparently Sybilla had intercepted and sent her here to test his rage.

"So what do you think?" he said at last, grateful that his voice came strong, betraying none of the emotion suddenly swelling to life. "Not very beautiful, is it? I suppose it must repulse you to view it, but after all, it is fitting, I suppose, as you were the one who did it."

"I did not do that," she whispered vehemently, surprising him. The gleam of unshed tears made her eyes sparkle in the firelight. "Never say that!"

God in heaven, she was beautiful. In those months he had spent recuperating, he had almost forgotten just how much. Here, with the firelight glancing off her golden curls and her delicate chin set into a defiant line, he felt a familiar stirring in some hinter region of his soul.

Thomas's arrival just then with the bathwater was timely. On his heels, Sybilla appeared, pressing a chunk of soap silently into Lily's hands and giving her a meaningful look before following her husband out the door. Holding the soap as if it were some novel object she had never before seen, Lily turned to Rogan.

Sybilla wanted them together tonight, Rogan realized, wondering if the servant knew that having Lily view his wounds, touching them and feeling the uneven ridges of the scars as she washed him, would make him almost mad with outrage. Good God, did the woman wish Lily dead?

"Get out," he told her, turning his back on her again. Trying not to think of what it was she was seeing, the repulsion she must be feeling at the sight of the ruined flesh, he dropped the linen and stepped into the tub.

"Wh-where should I go?" she asked with uncertainty.

"Give me that soap and leave. One of the other rooms should be free."

She came forward, her slim fingers brushing against his palm as she dropped the soap into his hand. It was as if that slight touch changed him, for all of the sudden his fingers closed over hers.

He felt rather than saw her surprise, for he was staring at a large knot of wood on the far wall. "On second thought," he said, "I will need someone to wash my back."

If she had hesitated but a moment, Rogan truly did not know what he would have done. He supposed this was some kind of test. If she had failed, he might have leaped up out of the water and taken her slim neck in his palms. He might have, for the hurt and pain were balled up so tightly inside he was doubtful he could have controlled it. As it was, she made no protest, but dutifully dipped the washcloth in the water and worked it against the slab of lye to form a lather.

He braced himself for her touch, but when it came, featherlight and untroubled by its subject, it was worse than the recoil he had imagined. Her hands glided easily across his back, unconsciously sensual, as she smoothed the lather over his ruined skin. She gently massaged the tired muscle and left him surprisingly relaxed in the wake of her ministrations. Yet another tension began to build, a blending of resentment and unwilling desire. He found himself clenching his teeth, working his jaw with a vengeance until his temples throbbed. Her hands moved down his back, to his waist, spreading out to circle around to his sides.

Suddenly he could bear it no longer. Grabbing her hands by the wrists, he pushed her away.

"Go to your bed now," he said gruffly. "Tomorrow we will speak about your duties. As you can see, the servant staff is small and you will have to do your share in the running of the household."

She paused. Refusing to look at her for fear of losing his thin veneer of control, Rogan casually picked up the soap and cloth and began to wash his hair. His eyes were closed, but he heard the soft click of the door latch clearly enough to tell him she had gone.

The tension in the room receded as he finished washing and emerged from the tub. He would have to speak with Sybilla. He did not want any more surprises. And as for Lily, why should it bother him if his scars repulsed her? In fact, they *should*. Not because they were ugly, though they were that, but for the treachery and betrayal they represented.

The whole incident was strangely disturbing, leaving him raw and aching as he climbed into bed and doused the light.

His back!

Alone, in her room, Lily sat in darkness, unaware of the cold, not feeling the hardness of the pallet upon which she perched. Her mind reeled with the haunting vision of those scars. Huge strips of puckered flesh, still red and looking startlingly new, crisscrossing the living flesh. She had seen them before, those awful welts, but somehow she had thought they would fade.

They would never fade, not the wounds on his back nor on his heart.

She closed her eyes and swallowed hard at this harsh truth. Lord, she was miserable. She had no one. A family of deceivers, a husband who despised her, servants who held her in contempt. A life without promise, lonely and bereft of love.

What was worse, she was almost sick with worry over Elspeth. The memory of her stricken face loomed in Lily's mind, haunting her and bringing tears to her eyes. Was that what ate at her—her own duplicity? Lily wished she had ventured to query her little sister, but she had been too afraid to dare it, Elspeth's nerves were so delicate.

What had made Elspeth lie? It was Catherine, to be sure. She could only assume her eldest sister had threatened something ghastly to force Elspeth to cooperate with her. Poor, poor Elspeth. Lily remembered her little sister's anguish after Rogan was imprisoned and felt a fresh clutch of grief. How Elspeth must have suffered. Rage chased the sadness as she seethed against Catherine. Because of her, Elspeth was in shambles and Rogan was irrevocably changed, consumed by hate and bitterness.

And Lily's life was ruined beyond measure.

As she leaned her head against the bedpost, she wondered what she had done to deserve it.

...

Chapter Thirteen

"So, you plan to make a servant of your wife?" Andrew said as he cocked his crossbow. They were out in the forest, hunting small game, an easy task since the tracks were clear in the freshly fallen snow.

"It will not harm her to learn how to cook and to help with the serving," Rogan answered with a shrug.

Andrew took careful aim and sent the arrow flying. "Ah, that makes ten hares." He paused. "Sybilla hates her. She is a vicious hag, you know. She might try to harm Lily."

As they walked to retrieve the felled animal, Rogan thought of her sending Lily to him last night. He said, "I can handle the servants."

Andrew glanced at him. "I wonder at this course you have chosen."

"This course is not one I have chosen. It is the only one I have."

"Have you given no thought on what Marshand will do now that you have abducted his daughter?"

"She is no longer his daughter, but my wife. And there is nothing the old fool can do without exposing his own treachery. How would it look to have it known that he had a fellow noble all but killed for nothing more than injured pride? Enguerrand had the upper hand once, but he played it and now he has lost the advantage.''

"And this is what you want, to live with a woman you despise, dedicating yourself to her punishment to the end of your days?''

Rogan did not answer as they bagged the game and mounted their horses. Andrew's words stirred in Rogan's heart. Once, he had thought that the elusive prize of happiness would be his. He had thought he had found a woman with whom he could share a life of contentment and desire and the kind of sharing a man yearns for with a woman. It was a bitter medicine to be reduced to this: a jailer, a tyrant. But, as he had said, what else was there?

Rogan growled, "You think I make too much of all this, do you?''

"Of course not!" Andrew answered sharply. He sighed, shaking his head. "I just wonder what it will cost you. And what you hope to gain.''

Sighing, Rogan asked, "What exactly is it that has you so troubled?''

"Your soul, brother," Andrew answered without hesitation. "It is your immortal soul which has me so troubled.''

Lily was in the kitchen when the brothers returned from their hunting. Andrew, who had not spoken a word to her since their flight from Charolais, dumped his pouch on the table and went upstairs. Leaning his shoulder against the doorjamb, Rogan slung his pouch up beside his brother's and waved a hand at Lily to open it.

Gingerly picking up the first sack, she peered inside to find the carcasses of several small animals. Letting out a shrill cry, she flung the offensive contents on the floor.

"Is that how you treat your supper, wife?"

She gaped at him. "Supper? You give me a pack of disgusting…dead things?"

"Have you never eaten rabbit or squirrel?"

"Yes, of course. But it was merely bits of meat in a stew. You cannot expect me to touch those!"

"I most certainly do," he drawled. "In fact, you are to skin and gut them, then cook them for the evening meal."

"But I do not know how!" she objected, eyeing the stiff corpses strewn at her feet.

"Sybilla will tell you," he said. He leaned his back against the wall, a slight twinge of pain registering on his face. Lily thought of the tender wounds, remembering he had said they trouble him sometimes.

"You had better pick those up," he said casually, indicating the game.

Lily stared back at him, considering her options. Up to now, she had obeyed his orders, except when she had refused to come into the house. That had been foolish. If she were to indulge her wounded pride, she would have to choose her battles more wisely.

But she could not bring herself to touch those hairy creatures, not even for fear of him. Acting on impulse, she grabbed a large flat spoon and slipped the bowl under a rabbit, balancing it cautiously. With infinite care, she brought it back up to the table and dumped it.

Turning back to Rogan, she smiled smugly at her accomplishment.

"You do enjoy your petty triumphs, do you not?" he said. "Take comfort in whatever duties you can manage to avoid." In a sudden movement, he pushed away from the wall and stood before her, his whole body only inches from hers. His hands stayed at his sides, but she was caught just the same by those gray wolf eyes. "You will not be able to evade all of them so easily."

The spoon fell from her limp fingers, clattering onto the wooden floor. There was no mistaking his meaning—the insinuating closeness of his body, the searing look all made clear to what he was referring. Lily felt as if the breath had been knocked out of her. With his smirk back in place, Rogan sauntered out of the room.

She trembled with rage, finding it difficult to refrain from the impulse to pick up the spoon and send it flying at him. Paling at the realization that should she do it—though, of course, she never would—the wooden missile would hit him squarely on the back. The thought of aggravating his wounds made her feel ashamed.

She could not even indulge in a pleasant fantasy without guilt! Well, she decided petulantly, she would imagine the spoon hitting him on the back of the head, then. The image made her smile, and she played it over and over in her mind as she scooped up the rest of the animal carcasses.

Sybilla came in, looked at the pile of game, and said, "Take the large knife and cut the throats. Then, pull the skin away from the meat and slice it off. Try to keep the pelts in one piece, we can use them." Picking up a bag of peeled turnips, she poured them in the pot hanging over the fire and left again.

Lily stood still for a long moment. *Cut the throats? Slice away the skin?*

Enough. She had played the docile role for too long. Summoning up her courage, she daintily picked up the small corpses with her thumb and forefinger and plopped each one, fur and all, into the pot of boiling turnips.

Brushing off her hands, she smiled to herself with great satisfaction. There, she had made supper.

Rather surprised when Rogan did not appear to drag her downstairs by her hair, Lily curled tighter under the rough blanket. The warmth from the tiny fireplace was sufficient, though she missed her furs. But the setting was cozy enough, and surprisingly, she was being allowed to enjoy it undisturbed.

With a surge of mischievous glee, she wondered how they had enjoyed their stew and how long it had taken them to finish picking the fur out of their teeth.

Her pleasure was short-lived. Rogan pushed her door in and stood on the threshold. "Come to my room, Lily," he said.

"I—I am already abed."

"Do not force me to say it twice." He turned and disappeared, presumably to his room.

Lily stood on trembling legs and followed. In the dim light of his chamber, Rogan was just a shadow by the bed.

A taper flared and he touched it to a torch, bringing the place to light. Silently he moved to the hearth and knelt down to stoke the fire. It was a long time before he spoke.

"You ruined good meat, which is hard to come by in these cold months. What is more, you wasted what took Andrew and I an entire day to hunt. You did not think I would overlook that, did you?"

"Sybilla told me to skin them. You saw how I could not even touch them. She wanted me to chop off their heads!"

"You are to do as you are told."

"I am to take orders from a servant?" She stamped her foot down in indignation.

"Sybilla has my authority. She will let you know what it is I expect from you."

"And what will you do, beat me if I refuse?" she shot back, her chin jutting out defiantly.

"I may," he said threateningly, straightening and advancing toward her.

"Well, then do just that!" she exclaimed, taking a step forward as if openly pronouncing she was willing to meet this fate.

"Take care, Lily, you do not want to provoke me."

"Spare me your threats. If you will beat me, then go ahead, for I truly do not care any longer because *nothing matters*. You will do what you will. What can be worse than what has already befallen me? You have taken me to this awful place, with only those who revile me as my companions. I have not one stitch of clothing other than this torn gown—my wedding dress at that. I have not bathed in days. I am exhausted, having been woken up by that harpy you call a servant before dawn to cook your meals. I am tired, Rogan, and I am filthy. If I get a few bruises along with it, so be it.''

Rogan stared at her for a long time before moving slowly to close the gap between them. Lily braced herself, a sudden lapse of courage making it hard to stand in front of his heartless gaze and wait for the first blow.

''You have no other clothes.'' It was not a question. Rather it was as if he had only just realized his oversight.

Lily blinked in surprise. ''I have been wearing this for almost a week.''

''Why did you not ask me for something suitable?'' He sounded irritated.

Lily was too struck by disbelief to speak. Rogan brushed past her, knocking her back a step as he stomped to the door. ''Thomas!'' he yelled down the corridor. ''Heat some water for the tub!''

Lily could hardly believe her luck. Here she was, ready to take the worst of punishments, now being treated to a bath.

''Take that off,'' Rogan said, coming back into the room and closing the door. He waved his finger at her gown.

''Wh-what?'' Lily stammered.

"Get that thing off. As you have just called it to my attention, it's covered with filth."

"It is all I have."

"I will find you something else. Take it off now."

Since he obviously had no intention of leaving, or even turning around to afford her some privacy, Lily stood awkwardly before him.

He offered a lopsided smile as he struck a cocky pose, arms crossed in front of him, shoulder against the wall. "I have seen it all before, wife."

"Matters were different between us then."

"What difference is it?"

She stuck her chin out. "It makes a difference to me."

"I am having that thing burned, so if you want, I will cut it off for you," he suggested, pulling out the small dagger in his belt and showing it to her.

"No!" she said. Pushing aside her modesty, as well as her outrage, she tore off the offensive garment, trying not to think of his gaze sliding down her form.

"Thomas is coming," she said. "Is he to view me unclothed? Is that part of your *revenge?*"

He scowled at her, but drew a blanket off the bed and held it out. As he wrapped it around her shoulders, she thought how strange it was that the brush of his fingers along her bare skin should seem so warm. He held her for a moment, arms snug around her, the length of his body pressed lightly against the back of hers. The tickle of his breath was at her ear, making tiny currents of pleasure ripple through her.

Thomas arrived with the water. Lily ducked behind

Rogan, but she needn't have worried. Thomas did not dare a single glance. As soon as he had gone, she quickly dropped the blanket, lifted her shift over her head and nearly leaped into the steaming tub.

She knew Rogan watched her, but she could hardly have cared now she was immersed. She washed leisurely, taking time to soap and rinse her hair twice.

She would have liked a longer soak, but the gray gaze trained on her every movement eventually made her self-conscious. She rose and grabbed one of the drying linens. Wrapped tightly in the plush cloth, she sat by the fire and combed her hair out with her fingers. Rogan frowned at her from his seat on the bed.

"I have no comb for my hair. It will get tangled. And I have no clothes," Lily said.

"You will not need any tonight."

Lily felt her heart give a lurch and lodge itself in her throat.

He continued, "I will instruct Sybilla to secure something suitable. Tomorrow."

Lily thought of the kinds of gowns Sybilla was likely to deem suitable, but said nothing. She was far too concerned about his comment regarding her not needing clothes tonight.

He had said he wanted children. She should have prepared herself for this. But night after night during their long journey here, he had rolled her into his blanket without giving the slightest suggestion of desire. What had he said on the boat? If he could overcome his revulsion, he would see to getting children from her? But if he indeed felt repulsed, why were

his eyes so dark and why did they linger almost long-
ingly on her body?

She stood, gathering the ends of the linen around
her. "I should be going back to my room."

His hand shot out and grabbed her arm before she
could get by him. "There still is the matter of the
'stew' you made for supper."

So, it was that on his mind, not desire. "Now that
I am clean, you wish to beat me?" she asked innocently.

"I will not beat you. You will find out what your
punishment will be when the time comes."

"Then, I shall go to my room."

She made to leave again, but his grip held her fast.
In a soft voice that brooked no argument, he said,
"You will stay here tonight."

Her heart leaped in panic. She could not do this.
The cruelty, the humiliations, even abuse she could
take, but not this intimate touch when it brought so
much back, so much she could not bear to remember.

She did not move as he stepped behind her, his
hands on the linen where it lay against her shoulders.
Gently he clenched his fists, gathering the cloth into
his hands.

"Please, no. I—I'm not ready."

His voice came soft and clear at her ear. "It is not
like this is the first time. I told you I intended this."

"Why? You hate me!"

He did not answer. Turning her around to face him,
he slipped his hand around her waist and drew her
close. "Yes, I hate you. But you are my wife."

His head dipped down and his lips captured hers,

stealing her breath away. The feel of his mouth stunned her for a dizzying moment. She stiffened, jolted to the core by her body's almost violent reaction. Then, incredibly, he gentled the kiss. Somewhere in the back of her brain was a dull awareness of her intention to resist, but she did not heed it. A sensuous longing sparked to life, powerful enough to rob her of her will.

A low moan escaped, sounding passionate and mournful in her own ears, a testimony to the torment of that kiss as it deepened. He caught her tight up against him, parting her lips and slipped his tongue inside, touching it to hers.

This was what she had feared. The feel of his body was like a drug, intoxicating and able to lull her into sensual abandon. But for him, this was merely his duty. Not a pleasant one at that, he himself had said.

The thought brought her up short. In a single burst of resolve, she pulled back, stumbling a few steps when he let her go.

He looked furious. He looked glorious. His eyes smoldered, his lips parted as his chest rose and fell heavily.

"Please," she said. Her voice sounded meek, pleading. She tried again, this time forcing her tone to a stronger level. "Not like this, Rogan."

"How would you have it?" he growled. "You dare deny me?"

She couldn't speak. She simply shook her head.

He raised a single finger before her. "I could command this of you if I had a desire to do so."

"Yes," she acknowledged. "But I beg you not to."

He glared at her, as if he could scarce believe her gall to ask so much. Suddenly he dropped his hand. "You plead so prettily, Lily. A man would have to possess a heart of stone to be deaf to it. And though mine is no longer the tender member it once was, even I cannot bear to force you."

His expression grew fierce as he reached a hand out and cupped the back of her neck. "I told you on the boat what I expect. Tonight, you learned that I meant it. I shall be requiring you in my bed. Prepare yourself, for this is the last time I will be patient."

She bit her lips and nodded, wishing he would let her go. Tears were brimming and she did not want him to see her cry.

Staring into those gray depths, she feared she would be lost. So much of her hungered for the very things she denied him.

It seemed an eternity before he released her. "Go to your room," he said simply.

On winged feet she fled without a moment's hesitation, slamming the door to her small chamber behind her and leaning against it while she tried in vain to steady her thundering heart. She squeezed her eyes shut, refusing the tears. They slipped out all the same, silently running down her cheeks and onto her hands where the slim band of gold Rogan had long ago placed on the second knuckle of her index finger gleamed dully in the candlelight. Throughout all that had passed, she had never removed it, not even for her wedding to de Aignier.

The next time he took her in his arms, she would have to submit. Be taken without passion, without love. A chore, a duty it would be. Nothing more.

If Rogan had wanted to keep her in hell, he had found an excellent way to do it.

Chapter Fourteen

Sybilla woke Lily just before dawn the following morning.

"Here's a dress," she spat, throwing a rough woolen garment onto the bed. Lily sat up.

"Put it on and come to the kitchen. There's work to be done. Lord Rogan's gone, and I'm to make certain you don't be lazing about just 'cause he's not here."

Lily dressed quickly and went downstairs.

Sybilla was waiting. "After you are done with the pasties, there is laundry to be boiled. You will find the cauldron outside. Make sure you stir roughly. Thomas has built the fire for you but you will have to light it when you are ready."

Lily did not bother to respond. Resigned, she turned to the chore of baking the meat pies.

She kneaded the dough and rolled it out with the heavy pin. Placing a dollop of spiced venison in each small round, she folded the pie in half and pinched the edges, just as Sybilla had taught her. She could barely lift the heavy baking tray and several pies slid into the fire while she was struggling to put them over the hearth. The flames reacted violently, shooting up a shower of sparks that singed her sleeve.

It was only a short time later when the acrid smell of charred food caught her attention. Too late, she dove for the tray, burning her hand. Her efforts were in vain, for the pasties were blackened beyond hope. With a vengeance and some entertaining thoughts of Rogan doubling over when her fist connected to his stomach, she began again, cutting the fat into the flour to make the crusts and mincing and spicing a new slab of meat.

When these were cooked and put on the flat sill to cool, she hurried to see to the laundry. Her hands were covered with tiny cuts from her misuse of the knife and the burn on her palm throbbed. But she was running too far behind, so she put the discomfort out of her mind while she vigorously stirred the boiling cauldron.

She was scalded once or twice, then had to repeat the agitating action again when she realized that she had forgotten to add the soap. By the time she wrung each piece and spread them on the rocks to dry, she was in agony. There was not an inch on her body that didn't hurt. Shivering in the cold, she hastily stoked the fire, too preoccupied with wanting to return to the warmth of the house to notice when her hem caught on fire. She was beating out the flames when the first sounds reached her ears.

She stopped, lifting her head. All at once, she became acutely aware of the gloominess of her surroundings. The day was overcast, and the thick cluster of tree trunks around her made it dimmer. When another screech came, her first thought, she was ashamed to admit, was of spirits.

Her second, after picking up the distinct rustle of the dead bracken, was of animals. She remembered the cry of wolves that first day and wondered if they would be so daring in daylight as they were purported to be at night. Almost immediately, however, she detected high-pitched voices and knew that it was no ghost or beast who stalked her, but only children.

She could see them now, hunkered down behind a piling of boulders halfway up the hill. The trees were not so thick, nor were the little ones so clever for them to be invisible.

Her aching body and dispirited soul had put her in a foul mood. "You better come down here and tell me what you are about," she called crossly.

"See, I told you not to go so close. She smelled us!" came a loud whisper as the three faces ducked under cover.

Far from amused, Lily shouted, "You had better tell me why you are spying on me!"

Tentative heads poked up once again. "We have the cross of our Lord to protect us, witch!"

"Get going, then, you silly twits!" she snapped, turning her back to them. The cold was seeping clear into her bones and she had no time to fuss with the pack of waifs.

Indistinguishable whispers hissed from behind her, which she promptly ignored. After a space, she heard them scurry off. She did not know who they were, and didn't much care. Hauling up some of the sodden garments that had slipped into the snow, she gave the fire a few vicious pokes and hurried indoors.

She noticed the missing pies immediately. With a cry of rage, she flew to the open sill to stare dumbly at the empty tray.

Those devils! They stole her pies!

Plopping down onto a nearby stool, she fought the wave of anger curling in her chest. The halt of footsteps behind her brought her attention up to the frowning countenance of Sybilla, standing just inside the door.

"You lazy girl," she hissed, her beady eyes glowing like twin dots of fire. "I leave you alone and find you resting. Where is dinner? Have you been sitting there this whole time? Well, if you do not see fit to follow my instruction, then you simply will not eat today. Now, take the cart and go into the woods to gather some firewood. And don't be all day about it."

"I am soaked to the bone," Lily said dangerously. "And I am exhausted. I am going upstairs to my room. I will remove this wretched garment and hang it up to dry and while I am waiting, I think I shall have a nap."

Sybilla took a menacing step toward her. "Get out in the woods, I say, and do what I have told you."

Lily stood, and without any forethought to the foolishness of her actions, sauntered brazenly up to the woman. Sticking her chin out, she stared into the pinched face.

"No," she said simply. Sybilla's mouth fell open. Grabbing a handful of raw beans, Lily brushed past her and climbed the stairs.

* * *

Andrew St. Cyr stood in the doorway of Rogan's chamber and stared at the hunched shoulders of his brother. It was one of those times Rogan wanted to be left alone, Andrew knew, but he had too many questions to quietly retreat and leave him in peace.

Andrew said, "All went according to plan. I would have expected you to be strutting about her like a smug cock. Do not tell me you have doubts?"

"Do not be ridiculous!" Rogan exploded, coming to his feet to pace before the hearth.

"Then what is it?"

He stopped, resting his hand on the stone lintel. "It is just that it is more complicated than I thought. She acts one minute like the suffering martyr, then the next she is a spiteful vixen."

"You had feelings for her once," Andrew prodded. "She is quite beautiful. It seems she is adept at inspiring sympathy. All the men refer to her as 'the little flower.'"

"Truth, she excels at it," Rogan growled. "I half expected a rebellion on my hands. She has this quality of innocence. The damned creature pouts as if she were the wronged one. As for being referred to as 'the little flower,' I believe I have you to thank for that." Whirling, he held up a finger as if scolding his younger brother. "If you are suddenly so concerned with the saving of souls, then you had better start with hers, and quit your troubling over me."

Unperturbed at his brother's temper, Andrew exclaimed, "An excellent idea. You are so right!"

Thoughtfully, he rubbed his jaw. "But how to go about it? It will not be simple..."

Puzzled, Rogan watched him as he hurried away, all but rubbing his hands together over his mysterious revelation.

Three cooked, fat partridges sat on the windowsill, filling the glade with their luscious aroma. Lily was crouched down behind the scrubbed oak table.

It had been almost a sennight since the little thieves had struck, and she had become near obsessed with catching them and giving each a turn over her knee. Every day, she had set out enticing treats to tempt them, but the little demons did not appear.

One benefit of her newfound mission was Sybilla's approval of Lily's show of industry. Combined with Lily's defiance, it was quite effective in discouraging the dyspeptic servant's abuse. As much as Lily was able under the circumstances, she was enjoying herself.

Ah! At last her patience was rewarded. Lily watched triumphantly as a grubby hand reached up and closed around the tantalizing bait.

Lily crept to the door. Ignoring the cold blast of wind, she emerged just in time to see the small trio disappear around the corner of the house. She smiled grimly as she slipped unheard along the wall, pausing to listen.

"Go ahead, Lizzie, take it," the boy's voice said.

"But you are hungry, too."

"No, take it. I'll get another."

Oh, no, you won't, Lily thought. Her hand itched to slap their impudent little behinds.

"But the witch baked it. What if she poisoned it?"

Now, there was a thought. Nothing deadly, mind you, just something to have made them regret their boldness.

"Nonsense, Lizzie, why would she poison her own meal? She din' know that Oliver would snatch it." This from an older, steadier female voice.

"Witches know things. Maybe she saw it in a spell."

"Are you going to eat it or not?" the boy demanded.

"Go on, I know you're hungry," the oldest urged.

Now, thought Lily. She peeked her head around the wall.

She was taken aback at the sight before her. They stood in a circle while the smallest one bit voraciously into the little bird. The boy, whose back was to her, scanned the woods for any threat of discovery while the oldest, the girl with the soft voice, watched the youngest eat. Her grimy face was enraptured by the sight of the succulent meat, but she made no move as it was devoured before her eyes. And the child, the littlest girl who guiltily partook of the feast, was only four years old. If that.

Gone was Lily's thirst for revenge. As the tot's clumsy fingers shoved bits into her mouth until her cheeks bulged, Lily thought, *My God, when was the last time they had eaten?*

The little girl, Lizzie as they had called her, suddenly stopped. She thrust out the half-eaten carcass. "Here, Anna, you have the rest."

The older girl could not withstand the temptation. Reaching for it, she tore off a small leg and smiled, "Just this little bit. Go on, Oliver, you take it."

Lily could not have moved if the angel Gabriel had appeared at that moment and bade her take flight. She watched as the boy shook his head, turning away bravely in silent command for his sisters to finish the feast.

That was when they saw her. Anna was the first, glancing up, then staring wide-eyed as she met Lily's gaze. Seeing her alarm, the boy snapped his head around, and last, the little Lizzie looked over with a mournful "Oh!"

"The witch!" Oliver exclaimed.

"Wait!" Lily cried. "Do not run!"

In unison, they whirled and, in a flash, they were gone into the thicket.

"I have more partridges," Lily called desperately. She was surprised at the sudden need to get them back. But it was no spanking she was thinking of now. Those wretched faces, so hungry, so grave. It struck her how frantic they must be to dare the wrath of a witch to get some food. She tried again, "I am not a witch!"

But they had flown. All that was left was the torn remainder of the partridge on the muddy ground.

The next day Lily stepped out into the cold sunshine, basket slung on her arm, and sauntered into the woods. Behind her, as if forgotten, the door gaped open and the scent of sausages wafted out to permeate the forest with its tantalizing aroma.

Once beyond the tree line, she cast off the basket and hunkered down, crawling under cover until she had rounded to the front of the house. She dashed inside, running through the gathering room to the kitchen, there to wedge between two great casks of flour and wait for her guests.

It was not long before the sound of whispers alerted her that they had arrived.

She heard the faint tap of their footsteps on the wood floor as they stepped cautiously toward the food placed on the tabletop above her. Once they were safely inside, Lily sprang forward and dove to the door, slamming it shut and throwing the bolt.

Ear-piercing screams sent her halfway to the ceiling. She whirled, waving her hands at the three panic-stricken faces to shush their awful wailing. "Quiet! Quiet! I am not going to hurt you!"

Oliver grabbed a nearby mallet and held it steadily before him. "Let us out, witch, else I cleave you in two."

It was not funny, really it wasn't. The poor things were truly terrified. And though the boy was only of an age of perhaps eight or nine, he could do damage with the tiny hammer if he wanted. Still, Lily could not help herself at the sight of his bravado.

"Listen to me, you little dolts," she said between giggles. "I am not a witch. I tried to tell you that before."

"Oh!" Lizzie wailed.

"Yes, you are, now stand aside. I have the cross of the Lord Jesus Christ, and I know how to use it!"

There was no help for it. Lily dissolved into laughter once again.

Lizzie started wailing, which made Oliver more agitated. "Hush, girl!" he ordered.

"Now, everyone calm yourselves. I brought you in here so I could talk to you."

Burying her face in her sister's skirts, Lizzie's sobs grew louder. "Lizzie!" Oliver admonished again.

"I can't help it," she wailed, "the witch is going to eat us!"

"I said hush!" With that, he delivered a sharp slap to her little cheek.

Lily stepped forward, and in one motion took the mallet from the boy's hand and pushed him away from the girl. "Do not treat your sister like that, stupid child!" Turning to Lizzie, she said, "Truly, I am not a witch. Why would I eat you when I have made these delicious sausages?"

They all looked amazed at this logic. To illustrate her point, Lily grabbed one and began to munch.

"Who are you, then?" Anna asked with wonder.

"I am the Lady Lily, Lord Rogan's wife."

"Ha!" Oliver exclaimed. "A lady!"

It was true she looked more like a serf than anyone remotely associated with the noble class. "Well, I am," she said defensively. "But that is not the point."

"You look ugly," Lizzie said.

"Well, I daresay you three are hardly a vision of

beauty yourselves," Lily answered irritably. "Why have you been stealing my food?"

"Da's on a drunk, so we had to get outa there," the boy said aggressively.

"What did you do? Some mischief, no doubt. You seem a questionable trio."

"We didn' do nothin'!" Lizzie exclaimed. The older girl hushed her before her brother could cuff her again.

"Then why in the world would your da hit you?"

"'Cause he's drunk his ale. Golly, and you call us stupid."

Lily was shocked. "You mean he just hits you? I find that unlikely."

The boy crossed his hands in front of his chest and refused to say another word. The other girl, the older one, stepped forward. "I do not think you are ugly at all. I told them so. They saw you doing your chores and said you were a witch. But I thought you might just be a bit tired."

"I am at that." Lily smiled.

"Why are you tired? Why don' you jus' go to sleep?" Lizzie ventured.

"I have a lot of work to do."

"See, she is no lady. Ladies don' do the launderin' or the bakin', you fools." The boy glared at Lily. "She's lyin'."

"Well, I am a kind of a lady who has fallen on hard times. Enough! I think it is you three who should be doing the explaining."

Undaunted, Oliver challenged, "Then why do you

not simply call up your knights and ride away to your castle?''

Lily glowered at him and was thinking of a suitable answer when the older girl said quietly, "Because she has to wait for a prince, Oliver."

Lily looked at her appreciatively. "That is correct," she said primly. "I was put here by a cursed man, and I must wait for someone special to take me away."

"Who is it? Who brought you here?" Oliver demanded. "If you really are a lady, I can fight, you know. I could rescue you."

"You are not a prince," the older girl objected.

"Shut up, Anna!" Oliver yelled, falling upon his sister and pummeling her with his fists.

"Hey!" Lily yelled, pulling the boy away from Anna. She held him by his soiled collar, giving him a shake. "You are quite a disagreeable fellow, do you know that?"

"What do you know?" he cried, and Lily was surprised to see the sheen of tears in his eyes. "You are just a girl, and you are not a lady!"

He broke away from her and ran to the door. Struggling with the bolt, he managed to lift it, disappearing into the forest.

Lizzie narrowed her eyes and stuck her fists on her little hips. "You are mean!" she said, and ran after her brother.

Amazed at this remonstration, Lily looked to Anna. The girl just stared back at her, hesitating for a moment before slowly heading out the door herself.

"Anna," Lily called. When the girl turned back,

Lily handed her a square of cloth containing the sausages. Taking them, Anna gazed at her benefactress in wonder.

"I really do think you are beautiful," she said quietly, then left.

Alone, Lily stared after them, marveling at the strange encounter. What odd children. The whole episode left her puzzled and...strangely moved.

Something kept nagging at her. She unbolted the door to the great room and went upstairs. She found the small hand mirror in Rogan's chamber and, for the first time in weeks, took a good long look at herself.

She did look ugly. Her face was pale, with dark circles under her eyes and blistered lips, and her skin was covered with dirt smudges. Her hair was dull and unkempt, pulled back unceremoniously in a utilitarian knot. She could see why the young Oliver had such a difficult time believing her rank.

They had thought her a witch. Did she then so resemble a hag that she frightened little children? It was a sobering thought.

Rogan had taken away her freedom. Had he also taken away her youth, her beauty? Did she have anything left of herself anymore, or had he taken that, too? She had been ready only days ago to beat three starving children for stealing some food, when it had not meant more than inconvenience. Was she changing so much that she could be so small hearted? My God, she was becoming like Catherine! And was that Rogan's fault—or hers?

A hard resolve began to form in the pit of her stomach. No, he would take those things that defined who she was only if she let him. And she would not. No matter what, she would fight to the end to keep her soul safe from his vengeance.

She would stand for this humiliation, this *degradation* no more.

And she would start by becoming mistress of Linden Wood!

Chapter Fifteen

Rogan rode through the forest, fighting the mounting anticipation trilling in his veins. Linden Wood was just ahead. It was the first time he would be seeing his wife since that shattering night when he had discovered she could still command his passion.

Whatever had led him to show mercy then, he could not fathom. He cursed himself for it, for his body had burned ever since, and he had been deeply afflicted by all manner of erotic images. Holding Lily, feeling her supple body writhe under his as soft cries of pleasure tickled his ear...

Good God, he had never thought she could effect such a response after all that had passed, but he had found his body as vulnerable to her uncommon beauty, her artless sensuality, as it ever had been.

It had taken some time to reconcile himself to the fact. In the end, he had decided he had best accustom himself to the powerful attraction between them. Purely physical, of course. It was, after all, not so bad considering he was to sire a parcel of St. Cyrs with this woman. It made his job much easier, and was it so wrong if it were more than a bit enjoyable?

And today, he could wait no longer. He would have her, her reservations be damned. She was his wife, curse it all.

There was a strange, possessive thrill at the thought. Aye, Lily would have had time to accustom herself to his demands. There would be no excuses.

In the clearing, he called for Thomas. That man was like a ghoul, Rogan reflected as the lanky form of the servant suddenly materialized. He always seemed to appear out of nowhere at a moment's notice. It was as if he were always hovering about, almost always on hand wherever Lily was to be found.

Handing him Tarsus's reins, Rogan watched him speculatively as he disappeared in the direction of the stable.

He heard Lily's voice from the side of the house. Tamping down the surge of excitement, he headed that way.

He spied the slim form of his wife in the vegetable garden, leaning against a long-handled hoe. He was all at once acutely aware of her ill-fitting dress stretched taut across full breasts. It hung almost a foot above her ankles, showing too much of her shapely legs. Her hair was caught back off her face, but the rebellious mass escaped in spiraled tendrils around her face and neck. Even with her skin smudged with dirt, the florid sensuality of her features was unmarred. All this he took in in an instant, as well as the curious tableau she presented with her unlikely partner.

To Rogan's utter disbelief, Sybilla was on her hands and knees in the dirt before Lily, listening patiently as her mistress spoke authoritatively. "I do not know much about peas. Do you think that is too much sun? Perhaps we should do the beans there, the turnips here, and then the peas. Yes, so go ahead, and I'll turn these beds here."

She saw him, freezing in midmotion as she was about to take up the hoe.

"Rather early for gardening," he said casually, stepping further into view. He was distinctly aware of a discomfiting heat, though the March wind blew cool.

She took a long time to answer. "We are merely getting the beds ready. I thought we might try an early crop. My father sometimes did that, but of course the weather is much milder in Cornwall."

He nodded. Sybilla had come to her feet, brushing off her skirts and looking somewhat embarrassed.

"Fetch the spiced wine I made," Lily said to her, then turned to Rogan. "I did not know you were visiting today, but I have some pork roasting which will soon be ready. Are you hungry?"

The transformation was incredible. She stood across from him, the poised and gracious hostess receiving a guest. The damnable flash of heat that had come upon him was distracting. He had spent weeks preparing to take command the next time he was with her, and here she was receiving him as if she were the grand lady of the castle and he a mere visitor.

A cruel resentment curdled in his gut. Narrowing his eyes, he drawled lazily, "As a matter of fact, wife, it is a matter of hunger that has brought me to you for the day, though I am not a particular admirer of your cooking.'' He let his gaze roam insolently up and down her form, lingering at her breasts and her naked ankles.

Heaven bless her, she did not fail him. The flash of fury in her eyes came at him like green-blue fire, but she said nothing. Dropping the hoe into the dirt, she stalked off into the kitchens. Judging by the loud clanging going on, she was working up a temper.

Rogan whistled as he followed her inside, feeling much better. But the damnable heat did not abate.

He watched her as she moved about in the kitchen, wielding the knife well enough to cut off several neat slices from the shank of pig skewered on the spit. Sybilla, who avoided his eyes as if she had been caught in the act of some unmentionable crime, handed him his cup of sweet wine and disappeared.

Rogan sipped it gingerly. ''No fur?''

Lily had the grace to blush as she pushed a trencher loaded with the meat toward him. ''Do you want some dried apples? There are some in the bin.''

''Yes,'' he answered, poking suspiciously at the proffered meat.

Upon tasting it, he decided it was quite good. ''There is a bag out around the side of the house, by the road. I left it there when I dismounted. Fetch it for me.''

She gave him a long look, so long in fact he thought she was going to refuse. But after a moment she rolled her eyes and stomped off.

As he chewed his food, Rogan reflected that things

were going much better this time. She was used to her place already, controlling her temper. And though she had obviously asserted herself with Sybilla in his absence, she was not refusing to work for her keep.

Lily returned, dragging the heavy parcel behind her. "If you are only staying for today, why have you brought so much?"

"Take it upstairs and unpack it," he ordered.

"I cannot lift this up the steps. It is too heavy."

Rogan cocked a russet brow. "That is your problem."

He heard the annoyed tapping of her foot before she went to the back door. "Thomas!" she called.

As usual, the servant appeared with surprising speed, giving Rogan cause to suspect he had been lurking just outside the door. Lily instructed him to take the parcel upstairs. Thomas loped away with Lily following.

With her gone, he felt the tension drain out of him. He stretched, realizing how taut his body had been.

The shrieks from the second level brought him to his feet. Diving for his scabbard, which he had unbuckled and set on a table, Rogan had the weapon drawn in an instant and began charging up the stairs when Lily appeared before him, holding up one of the gowns he had brought for her.

"Thank you," she said breathlessly, hardly able to speak. Her eyes glittered like brilliant gems, her face flushed with pleasure. His jaw dropped at the sight of the high spots of color accentuating her finely wrought cheekbones and the dazzling smile that spread her luscious mouth to show even, white teeth.

The parcel, as she had discovered, contained a pair of gowns and various necessities for a woman. They were castoffs, hardly anything grand, but Lily's unabashed gratitude would have made one think they were trinkets fit for a queen.

Rogan cleared his throat and lowered his sword. "One of my knight's ladies sent them. She said that you would need such things. If there is anything she has forgotten, tell me and I will see that you get it."

"Tell her I appreciate her sacrifice," Lily said. "I will take this peasant robe off at once."

Like a child delighted with an unexpected gift, she spun on her heel and scampered back up the stairs. Rogan could not keep his gaze from drifting to the shape of her derriere as he was afforded a generous view of that particular asset.

He thought of the half-eaten meal cooling in the kitchens, then promptly dismissed it as unimportant. With a new purpose, he followed her into his chamber.

Thomas had already gone and Lily had the hem of the brown wool lifted to her waist. Seeing him, she dropped it back in place.

Rounding on her, he sat back on the bed, never taking his eyes off her. "Go ahead," he urged.

She hesitated, her gaze locked with his. A deep blush stained her cheeks.

A flash of defiance passed over her features before Lily turned her back to him and removed the garment, casting it heedlessly onto the floor. But when she reached for the new gown, he caught her hand and turned her around.

With a sense of detached amazement, he found he was trembling. Her hand was slim and warm in his. There was a slight pressure as she resisted his taking it, but the effect of that merest of touches was like a sliver of lightning searing its way up his arm. Memories of their last encounter flooded through him, leaving him breathless.

Resisting the urge to toss her onto the bed, he let his eyes travel slowly over her form, taking in the womanly curves not quite concealed under the transparency of the light shift. The undergarment came only to midthigh, leaving her long legs bare for him to admire. His gaze came up to view her slim waist, small enough for him to span with his two hands. Farther up, her breasts strained against the inadequate cloth, rising firm and round with their pink nubs tight. His hand ached to feel the shape of them, to graze those aroused peaks against his palms. Shoulders graceful, sculpted like a Greek statue, long arms that were lithe and slim—

He stopped. A sudden knot formed in the pit of his belly, for the skin on her arms was mottled with dark bruises and one large red blotch. He turned her hand over, seeing the cuts and abrasions that marred the smooth, feminine lines.

Of course, he scolded himself, she was no longer a lady of leisure. She worked alongside Sybilla, doing chores no woman of her class ever had to perform.

"What are these?" he snapped, as if it were her fault her lovely skin had been ruined.

She gazed at the wounds and answered in a matter-of-fact tone. "That is a scar I received from scalding water. These are just bruises, mostly from trying to lift things. The cuts on my hands—I am afraid I was terribly clumsy with the knife at first.''

An irrational rage gripped him. ''See that you take better care,'' he barked. ''I am not accustomed to taking scullery maids to my bed.''

Even as he said it, he knew it to be cruel. The sharp intake of breath, the recoil of her body told him the comment had stung. Damnation! One moment he was cursing himself for being too soft, and the next hating the sound of his own viciousness.

''You beast!'' she spat. ''How dare you insult me. You make me labor like a serf, then revile me for it. You have no right to abhor a single scar, for on my body, these marks attest to the proof of your abuse!''

She was right, of course, though it did not improve his temper to know it. ''If you force me to give a whack to your backside, you shall see proof of my abuse!''

''You would not do it!''

''You know better than to try me, Lily. I am capable of many things you dislike.''

She tossed her head. ''What could be worse than you have already done?''

Looking wild and unbelievably desirable, she faced him, her hair cascading about her like a golden waterfall and her hands fisted on her hips. Like some Amazon, or an irate goddess…

This was all too much talking anyway. He had not come here to converse with her. With a jerk, he pulled her into his arms, giving in to what it was he had wanted all along.

Whether from fear or passion, she melted into his arms, instantly inflaming his fevered senses, and kissed him back.

"You have decided to play the willing wife," he murmured. "Is this a ploy? I shall have to be on guard."

She made to yank back, but he held her fast, chuckling at her sputtering rage.

"Why must you insult me? It speaks ill of you, Rogan. You have the upper hand, yet you seek to humiliate me further. Do you always prey on the weaker sex? It is not very sporting."

He disliked her gibe. Yet her eyes sparkled and her lips were red from his kiss and he could think of nothing but touching her.

"No," he stated gruffly. "It is not. Shall you have words of love from me, then? Shall I ply you with mention of how your hair gleams like spun gold? How your eyes glitter like gems of the rarest quality?"

He pulled her down with him onto the bed, hitching his leg over her limbs so as to better feel the full length of her body against his. "How your breasts are full and ripe for a man's hand. *My* hand, Lily." He cupped the swell of flesh and watched her lips part, her eyelids grow heavy. He dully became aware that his tone had lost its mockery. Yes, he could speak every compliment sincerely, for even with everything else between them, she was still the loveliest woman he had ever seen.

It was only when he heard her gasp, felt her arms curling around his neck and her lips press fully on his, that he realized he had spoken this last thought aloud. He groaned, then let it pass as his tongue parleyed with hers. His hands moved boldly, feeling the lean curves that had fed his fantasies for these lonely months.

"It is day," she gasped, more in wonder than a denial as his lips traced a path to her breast. Rogan merely nodded before tugging open the neckline and baring her to the waist. She lay unmoving as his eyes took in every detail, savoring, feasting. As he lowered his head to take the rose-colored nipple in his mouth, she arched to meet him, her soft cry sending his blood pounding through his veins at a frantic pace.

His arousal strained against the confines of his leggings. It had been so long, he feared he would not be able to wait, yet he did not wish to take her roughly. Why this was so, he didn't stop to ponder. He only knew that in this realm, he could not be cruel.

His hand moved to the cleft of her legs and she parted for him, willingly, eager. The feel of her slick heat made his head swim and he worked off his garments quickly. The need to drive into that tightness was robbing him of his ability to reason, to think, to exercise his will.

He rid them of their clothing quickly while his hands roamed. He was impatient and she was ready...

When he entered her, she thrust her hips up to take him in deeper. He managed to withdraw, pausing to steady his resolve, then drove in again. His mouth claimed her cries, his hands held her tight as he thrust again and again, losing himself in the tide of sensation surging through his body.

This time the intensity of his passion did not take him by surprise. He gave himself over to it without hesitation as the exquisite feeling built, carrying him higher. He had only to feel the tight spasms of Lily's sheath, hear her soft groan to know she had found her fulfilment. The knowledge spun him out of control, and he buried himself deeply as he was overcome with shattering ecstasy.

Spent, exhausted, he leaned on his elbows. There were no more tender words. His hands ached to caress her, but he willed them to be still. He rolled to his side, laying a possessive hand across her stomach to signal that she was to stay.

Despite what they had lost, there was still this unfathomable passion. It was all he had left of a union he once thought would be the fulfilment of the secret dreams he had not dared admit, even to himself. It was not much, and, if he were honest, it left him aching. But for now, in the aftermath of pleasure, it was enough.

Chapter Sixteen

After Rogan left, hardly deigning to speak to her as he quickly dressed and quit the room, Lily lay perfectly still atop the crushed furs and welcomed the numbness that stole over her. Unfortunately, the state did not last.

She didn't bother to examine the passion he had displayed. Assuming men were different, that they could function physically with almost any woman, she dismissed the tender, sensual interlude. She had seen for herself the many couples who could barely exchange a decent word surrounded by a brood of sullen children, and knew it was no great feat that a man bedded his wife.

Months passed, during which Rogan visited frequently. Their encounters were lusty but it was always the same afterward; he was distant, cold and hard.

She had a fright when her monthly flow was later than usual. She could not face bearing a child to have it taken from her—no, that would drive her insane as nothing else could. Despite her desire for babes, she wished more than once that Rogan's seed would forever find her barren.

There were the three ragamuffin children, of course, Anna, Oliver and Lizzie. They came now almost every day. She was becoming fond of them, too much so, she often thought. But they were company, the only other souls she was allowed to see outside of Rogan and the dour-faced pair of house servants.

It was one fine day in early summer when she sat in a small clearing near the house. It was a favorite spot, and the children had often found her just so, enjoying the freshness of the new day as she worked on some chore or other.

She had come to love this new land, working outdoors as much as possible. The sounds of the forest were now familiar, as were the telltale signs of the small visitors' approach.

Lizzie ran forward, bursting out of the underbrush and shouting a hello. She helped herself to a handful of dried peas from the bowl on Lily's lap.

"I hope you are planning to help me and not simply stuff them into your belly," Lily said pleasantly.

With her fist halfway to her mouth, the child paused. "Do I have to?"

"I spent the morning making tarts for you, and now I am behind on my other work. What do you think is fair?"

Anna came up and took the bowl from Lily. "I will do these for you, my lady."

"Wash up first," Lily said automatically, standing up to peer back into the woods. "Where is Oliver?"

The two girls exchanged an incomprehensible look.

"He is not coming," Anna said softly. "Da's got work for him."

Lily frowned. She knew the three lived alone somewhere in the woods with their father, but could glean little else about their home. "And what of you, do you not have chores?"

Anna only shrugged and said, "Where do you want me to put these when I am done?"

She motioned for the peas to go into the pot she had brought along. It did not escape her how the older girl imitated her speech, enunciating her words in the manner of a noble, nor did she miss the adoring way the dark eyes watched her, and little by little, she mastered each one of Lily's mannerisms. With a pang, Lily was put to mind of Elspeth, who was often in her thoughts. Many a lonely hour she spent worrying over her little sister's welfare. If she dared, she would have asked Rogan of news, but the subject of her family was not one she could broach with her husband.

The children were a sufficient substitute for her affection. Again she regarded the pair of girls fondly. If it weren't for the filth covering them, one would never know they were peasants.

Which gave Lily an idea. Crossing her arms in front of her, she eyed them speculatively. "Since you two have come to help me, I wish to do something to reward you."

"What?" Lizzie said with her mouth full.

"You will see. It will be a surprise."

The delight on the small face immediately fell to suspicion. "Do we still get the tarts?"

Lily laughed. "Yes, yes, but *after* the surprise. Finish up, Anna. Here, Lizzie, take this and follow me."

The walk back to the house was dominated by young Lizzie's chatter. It seemed that Oliver had been clever enough to snag a rabbit with his slingshot and, according to both girls, the family had dined like kings.

Lily was less than enthusiastic at their boon, however, reflecting on the paltry supper compared to what she had grown up with. Five courses, with desserts and cheeses and fruits to follow, were the norm at Charolais. Even at Linden Wood, she could never claim to have gone hungry. Still, the pair were delighted their brother had supplied such a feast and were still talking about it when they reached the house.

"What about the other woman, the mean one?" Anna asked, hesitating.

"Pay no attention to Sybilla, just follow me."

"We are going inside?" she asked with awe.

Lily nodded. "Of course, it is my house. Now, come."

They followed, shrinking behind her skirts as Lily led them into the gathering room and up the stairs. Calling for Sybilla, she took them into the small chamber that was hers.

The arrival of the servant sent the girls skittering to the corners, cringing as if a jackal were at the door.

"I want the tub filled, Sybilla," Lily ordered, "and bring whatever cloth you can spare. Oh, and fetch my needle. I will have some sewing to do."

The woman narrowed her eyes at her mistress. "You mean to put them urchins in the master's tub?"

Drawing herself up, Lily peered down her nose at the other woman. "I do. Do you have something you wish to say in objection?"

She looked as if she had plenty to say, but after a moment facing Lily's formidable expression, she shook her head. "You go too far," she muttered, but did as she was told.

"And fetch my soaps and comb," Lily called after her, smothering a giggle at the way Sybilla cringed at the command.

"You do not mean to dunk us in the water!" Lizzie cried.

"I most certainly do!" Lily said, whirling around to two terrified faces. At their appalled expressions, she raised her eyebrows at them, a gesture that brooked no argument. It was effective at quelling their resistance. Well, it should be, she mused, realizing she had learned it from Rogan.

"All ladies bathe—regularly."

"It is unhealthy!"

"I wash all the time, and look, I am no worse for it. And what's more, I have special soaps that smell glorious. You will look like a pair of young princesses, and smell like them as well."

The word *princesses* hit the mark and their dubious expressions were replaced by nervous interest.

When the large tub was filled, Lizzie hung back as Lily marched them into Rogan's chamber. "Will it hurt?" she asked in a quivering voice.

Lily sighed. "Elizabeth, when have I ever done

anything to harm you? Now, remove your clothing. Anna, help her.''

It was a testimony to the older girl's faith that she obeyed, each stiff movement speaking of her uncertainty. When at last they were completely unclothed, Lily succeeded in coaxing them into the water.

As she lathered up the cloth for washing, Lizzie watched in horror. ''Are you sure it will not hurt?''

''No, no, child. What in heavens is this, I cannot get it off? I swear, I have never seen such grime—''

''Ahh!'' Lizzie screamed. Lily gave her an impatient look, thinking her protesting the scrubbing. ''Hold still. Lizzie!''

Standing up, the tiny child opened her mouth and let out a terrible wail. ''You hurt me! You promised, ahh!''

''Shh! Lizzie! Where did I hurt you?''

But it was Anna who gave the answer. Slowly the other girl poked a slim finger at the darkened area Lily had been washing. '''Tis not dirt.''

Frowning, Lily bent closer to inspect the dark patch.

A dizzying sensation came over her all at once. No, it was not dirt. It was an angry weal, fresh and raw. And it was not the only one. Yanking the child around, she saw the small legs and arms were similarly covered with long discolorations.

''Is this what you meant when you said your father was on a drunk?'' Lily's voice came low through her clenched jaw.

Lizzie was still bawling, and Anna just stared silently. Looking her over quickly, Lily saw the older girl had similar abrasions.

"All right, calm down, sweetling," Lily said gently. She grabbed a soft linen that had been set to warm by the fire and wrapped it around Lizzie. Lifting her out of the water, she carried her over to Rogan's bed and laid her down. "I am sorry I hurt you. I know I promised, but I did not know what those marks were. Hush, now, it is over and I will not hurt you again. Come now, you do trust me?"

Limpid brown eyes awash with tears stared unwaveringly at her. Lizzie bobbed her head and sniffed. Lily left her for only a moment to bring Anna out of the tub and sit her down beside her sister.

Her mind raged with questions, but she knew the children would give her no answers. Yet the truth of their abuse was abundant.

"Is Oliver still with your father?" she asked.

"Da says he has to hunt from now on, he ca't come wi' us no more." Anna's carefully learned speech was reverting back to its previous pattern under stress.

"Tell me where you live. And I want no evasiveness from you this time, miss! Tell me!"

"What do you mean to do?"

"I mean to fetch him here where he will be safe."

Anna gasped, her eyes wide with terror. "But Da—"

Standing, Lily gave her hand a squeeze. "I will handle Da. I have a few choice words for a grown man who brutalizes children. Now, you stay here. When I get back, we will see about some clothes for you."

There would have been more protests, but Lily waved her hand impatiently. Reluctantly Anna explained the way to their cottage. Lily gave each a quick hug before leaving. To Sybilla, she said, "Find something for them to wear and see they get the tarts, and—" this added with a single finger held before her to punctuate her words "—be kind to those girls. They are dear to me."

Stopping to pick up her table knife, she slipped it into her pocket before she left.

Rogan rode toward the cottage, wondering why he had bothered returning to Kensmouth when all he had wanted to do since he arrived home was head back to Linden Wood. And Lily.

He gave up trying to analyze it, for it had made his head ache attempting to reason out his single-minded desire for his wife. And fighting it was futile. So he simply surrendered to it and told himself it meant nothing.

The appearance of Thomas on the path couldn't have been more surprising. The large man looked ridiculous astride a brown mule, his toes dragging on the ground. When he saw his master, he began waving his huge hands.

"She be gone!" he yelled. "She went to get the boy!"

Rogan reined in the startled stallion. "What the devil are you talking about?"

"My lady, sire. She went to their cottage. She be in danger."

Rogan heard two important things: *My lady*—meaning Lily—and *danger*.

"I followed her. I watch over her. No harm come to her with Thomas around, but I got afraid. I come to get you."

Rogan realized the man's constant presence near his wife was his way of protecting her, keeping guard. Good Lord, she had managed to charm even this simple soul, with his brutish face and soft heart. "Where is the cottage?" he snapped.

Thomas supplied Lily's location, and Rogan dug his heels into the stallion's side. He knew the woods well; he had no trouble finding his way. He spotted the hut from the top of a small ravine. Seeing he would do better on foot, he dismounted.

No sign of Lily. As Rogan crept closer, a large figure lumbered into view, a big brute of a man. Unseen, but close, Lily called, "Oliver!"

Just then, she rounded the house and came face-to-face with the man. As Rogan neared, he could hear their voices. It was not a long conversation, but it was a heated one. Lily whirled away and called for Oliver again.

Rogan began to sprint. The man was moving behind Lily, his big ham fist raised.

Rogan ran like a madman, letting out a keening war cry. Alerted, Lily whirled and saw her attacker, but not soon enough. Her scream blended with his own voice and still, Rogan knew it would not be sufficient to save her from the blow. The large man swung, and with a considerable distance still between him and his wife, Rogan saw Lily crumple.

The man looked up, searching for the owner of the bone-chilling cry. As quick as such a large man could, he dove toward one of the walls of the hovel and retrieved a scythe.

Standing over Lily's unconscious form, he cried, "Get outa 'ere, an' leave me an' my kin alone!"

Rogan never broke stride. He careened out of the tree line, and ran headlong toward the huge oaf, who had hunkered down with his weapon in a defensive stance.

Rogan knocked him down, tumbling with him on the dirt. He rolled, springing to his feet. The man stood, still clutching the scythe, staggering and squinting to focus on his attacker.

Rogan drew his sword, displaying it to discourage the man. Lily was so close. With a flicker of his gaze, he saw she had not moved. He could barely stave off the need to rush to her side. "Move away or I will cut you down, man!" he growled.

The red eyes glared, and large, liverlike lips curled in a snarl just before the lout charged forward. Rogan moved aside, smacking him smartly on the backside with the flat of his sword.

Confused, the man stumbled past. A new voice distracted them both for an instant.

"You killed the lady!" a young boy yelled, running straight at the large man. Ignoring the gleam of the scythe's blade, the tyke launched himself at the man, pummeling his small fists against the beefy legs. "You killed her! I hate you, I will kill you myself!"

The man seemed hardly perturbed. He merely kicked and sent the boy tumbling away.

Rogan's muscles hardened as he braced himself for full battle. "You do quite well with women and children. Let me see how you do against a man full grown."

The other stomped, pawing the ground like a bull, and snarled an incomprehensible reply. Rogan lunged, cutting swiftly with his sword. He connected with the scythe, which the man used like a staff to defend himself. With a vengeance, he swung blow after blow, knocking the man backward. His opponent had phenomenal brute strength, which he brought to bear in retaliation.

Rogan saw his opening and quickly slammed the butt of his sword into the man's forehead. He looked at Rogan for a moment in dismay before he toppled to the ground with a thud.

He had barely hit the earth before Rogan was beside Lily. His vision seemed to blur for a moment when he wondered if he was too late. Then her eyes fluttered open. "Lily," he said softly.

"Rogan." She smiled, her hand coming up to brush his cheek. Then her gaze slanted away to a spot just behind him. Her smile widened and she said, "Oliver."

Rogan looked over at the boy who had dropped to his knees beside Lily.

"He di'n kill you," Oliver whispered.

Lily giggled. "You should know that you cannot kill a witch that easily." Reaching out, Lily drew up the boy's tunic to show the bare flesh underneath. Rogan glimpsed a collection of welts before Oliver snatched the clothing back in place, and snapped, "Hey!"

Lily's eyes caught Rogan's. "I came for the boy. To take him home."

"I'm not goin' wi' you! When Da wakes up, 'e's gonna be terrible mad!"

Lily sat up, pausing and holding a trembling hand to her temple. "You will not be here, and you are not coming back to this place ever again. And do not talk that way, you know better."

Just then, Thomas arrived, puffing hard from having come so far on foot. He must have run the entire way. He stopped, then grinned. "Ye got 'er."

Rogan nodded, then jerked his head to the unconscious lummox. "Take care of him. I will bring your mistress home."

Lifting Lily, he spoke to the boy. "Get the reins of the horse. And I hope you are as fearless with beasts as you are with your father, for Tarsus despises the spineless."

The lad shot him a resentful look before obeying.

Settling Lily on the saddle, he looked down at the boy. "I do not know why she wants you to come back to the house, but she risked a lot to get you. Until I have some answers, you are coming with me."

The boy looked at him with awe, nodding. Even more amazing, he allowed Rogan to lift him atop the stallion.

"I know," Rogan muttered to Tarsus as he took up the reins to lead him back to Linden Wood. "Women and children are not your preference. You long for the simplicity of battle, where you can know what to expect—and from what quarter!''

The beast snorted in agreement. Casting a puzzled look behind him, Rogan nodded. ''Me, too, friend. Me, too.''

Chapter Seventeen

"**W**hat the devil were you thinking?" Rogan asked, not unkindly, as he lay Lily down in her bed. He had insisted on carrying her up the stairs, despite her emphatic claims she was fine. She looked at him now, a touch of wariness in her face. However, she was wisely silent as he slipped off her shoes and drew the woolen blanket up to cover her. "The man was a brute, senseless with drink. He could have killed you without a thought."

Nervously her fingers plucked at the rough wool. She looked like a penitent child. No, not a child. Never could this woman look like that, with her hair unbound and spilling every which way like a lion's mane, the clear sea blue of her eyes cutting through to a man's soul, and the sultry mouth that made his stomach tighten just to look at it.

"And who is the boy?" Rogan demanded, drawing up a stool to settle down next to her.

"Oliver," she answered in a small voice.

"Yes, I am aware of his name. Why did you go to him?"

"His sisters told me that he was with his da, I mean father, and I had to get him away."

"Then you knew the man was a sot?"

"I knew he mistreated his children. I never dreamed he would deal with me likewise."

Rogan sighed in exasperation. "Are you such an innocent, or merely a fool? If Thomas had not followed—"

The downward flutter of her eyelids cut off his tirade. She looked too pathetic to scold just now. Rising, he said, "You will want to bathe. If you are hungry, I will have Sybilla bring you up some food. I will be back."

The aftereffects of fear made him gruff, but God save him, he was not truly angry with her. He still did not understand the entire episode, but he was far more amazed by his own reaction to pursue it just now.

He was not the kind who was much fazed by battle. Renowned for his chilling calm when facing an enemy, he had felt completely different seeing Lily mauled by that insane idiot. He had fought for his life more times than he cared to remember, but never had he fought as he had today. For another. For Lily. And for the first time, he had felt an unfamiliar emotion. Panic.

Such were the thoughts troubling him as he stepped into his chamber. He was met with a startling chorus of high-pitched squeals. Whirling, he cast about for the source of the ear-shattering noise to find a pair of small faces peering at him from the bed. Two little girls, terrified by the looks of them, clutched each other as they scrambled from under the blankets.

"What the—?" he began, then shouted, "Lily!"

The girls had wrested themselves free of the blankets and shot to the door, almost knocking Lily down as she raced into the room.

"Anna, Lizzie." They flung themselves against her, burying their faces in her skirts. Looking up at him, eyes shining in amusement, Lily said, "Rogan, these are Oliver's sisters."

"What are they doing in my bed?" he thundered, sending the children into renewed fits of terror.

"Lower your voice, please!" she snapped, surprising him into biting back his next remark.

As if the situation were not confusing enough, Sybilla arrived just at that moment with an irate Oliver in tow.

"Stop being such ninnies!" the small boy commanded. "This is the man who saved the lady!"

Anna was the first to respond. "Saved her from who?"

"From Da. He hit her. Would have killed her, too, but the man took him down."

"He took down Da?" Lizzie said in amazement, turning back to Rogan with a look of awe.

It was ridiculous, the warm feeling that look of admiration gave him. "He was just a drunken fool," he said more curtly than he had intended.

"Whacked him on the arse with the flat of his sword!" Oliver declared, and the three erupted into delighted giggles.

"Oliver!" Lily scolded, pretending to be offended.

"Well, he did," Oliver said sulkily.

"Yes, well, this is all very interesting, but it does not answer the question of what they were doing in my bed."

"Sleeping," the tiny one said simply.

"I could see that for myself," Rogan growled. He was getting mightily annoyed with all of this. Especially Lily, standing among the trio like a mother hen. "What I wanted to know is why?"

The small girl's bottom lip popped out, trembling as her eyes filled with fresh tears. "You don' like me!"

Raking his hand through his hair, Rogan turned away with a groan of frustration.

Taking command, Lily said, "Nonsense, Lizzie, Lord Rogan is just surprised. And confused. I will explain it all to him, but you must go with Sybilla and she will warm some milk for you."

"I don' like her. She is ugly!"

Lily saw Sybilla bristle. "That is not a mannerly thing to say," Lily said sternly, "and I want you to obey me. I will be down in a little while."

"Come, Lizzie," Anna said, though she herself seemed not at all sure of the sour-faced woman who waited to take them away. "The lady would not send us to any harm."

When Oliver made to follow, Lily caught him by the scruff of the neck. "Not you, Oliver. You will take a bath first, then you may join your sisters."

The look of outrage on his face was enough to tell what he thought of this plan, but Lily held up a single finger to stem the tirade before it began. "Unless you

wish me to stay here with you and make sure it gets
done. You will not sit at my table unless you wash
that filth off you."

The boy stomped over to the tub and peered suspiciously into the water. "It smells."

"I will fetch you some new soap, one that is not
scented. And wash your hair and behind your ears.
Leave your clothes for Sybilla to collect and she and
I will mend and clean them for you."

He rolled his eyes eloquently but said nothing.

She looked as of she would have fussed over the
boy some more, but Rogan had reached the limits of
his patience. Seizing Lily by the elbow, he steered
her out of his room and into hers. "Now, I will hear
all of it."

She told him everything, from the first stolen pie
from the windowsill to how the girls had come to be
in his bed. Through the tale, he listened patiently,
finding his anger receding with each word. In its
place, a strange amazement grew and, with it, a
grudging admiration. She had shown remarkable
courage on behalf of these waifs.

"And what do you intend to do with them now?"
he asked when she had finished.

"I really had not thought of it. I suppose they
should stay here with me."

He frowned. "That is hardly a practical solution."

If the story of how she had rescued the children
surprised him, then it was an added shock to see the
hard, determined look come into her eyes.

"I am not sending them back to their father. You
saw him—he is little better than an animal."

"What of their mother?"

"Anna told me she died several years ago. The children live alone with that beast of a man."

"No, they mustn't return," he agreed.

"They would be no trouble here. I would teach them their chores. They would not be a burden to anyone."

The strength of her determination impressed him. "All right, but I want no problems from all of this," he began, but the rest of the statement was cut off when she launched herself at him with such force it nearly knocked the breath out of him.

"Oh, thank you, thank you!" she cried. She was on tiptoe, her arms flung around his neck, her body pressed against the whole length of him. With her arms still wrapped around him, she leaned back to look up into his face. "I will give you no cause to regret it, I swear."

The effect of this unexpected display was like the weight of a ton of bricks slamming into his gut faster and harder than an Arabian mare at full gallop. Her eyes danced, the clear blue-green seeming to glow from within. And it had been a long time since he had seen her smile like that. Not since Charolais...

He wanted nothing more than to kiss her right at this moment, but as pressing as that desire was, there was an equal amount of resistance. This was what he had lost, this Lily with her shining face and merry eyes filling him with a feeling he had not thought himself capable of anymore.

As if of their own volition, his hands came around her waist. He wanted to say something cruel to wipe the unguarded delight from her face, for he couldn't bear it. But a part of him was fascinated by it, as well, and the words didn't come. Instead, the urgent need to topple her onto the bed and ravish her screamed in every nerve in his body.

If he made love to her now, as he so longed to do, he would lose everything. It wouldn't be as the husband taking the wife, it would be as a lover.

Slowly he extricated himself from her embrace, gently peeling away the graceful arms from his shoulders. With a pang of regret, he watched the veil come over her features again, melting away her happiness and replacing it with the familiar reserve.

Lily stepped away. She smoothed her skirts and cleared her throat. "I will go tell the children they are to stay."

He was glad when she was gone. It took several moments to get his breathing even again. When that was done, he went to hurry Oliver out of the bath so he could have his solitude.

Rogan spent the rest of the day in the stable. There was not much to do there, but even restless boredom was preferable to the domestic confusion going on inside the house. From time to time, he heard an outburst drifting from the upper windows. The young buck, Oliver, voicing his displeasure with something or other, he assumed. Later, a clash of pottery from the kitchens and Sybilla's angry tones indicated some problem with the evening meal.

He had not liked his reaction today to his wife's spontaneous embrace, not one bit. If he were honest, he would have to admit it had shocked him that the old infatuation could be rekindled. Passion he could understand, for she was the most desirable woman he had ever laid eyes on. But tender emotion—that he could not comprehend. How could he forget for an instant what she was, what she had done?

With a heavy sigh, he decided he was too tired to sort it out tonight. It was late to go back to Kensmouth now, and things had been quiet enough in the house to assure him that the situation has settled down. After a good night's rest, it would be clearer in the morning, he reasoned as he headed into the cottage.

Someone had lit a fire in his room, and Lily's door stood open, revealing it empty. Beyond, a small crack in the third bedroom showed a sliver of light.

He could not resist. Careful not to make a sound, he crept down to the door, inching it open to peer inside. The room was dimly lit by a single rushlight. In the bed, Oliver lay asleep, his head thrown back, mouth agape. Beside him, the serene form of the older girl lay curled up prettily, hands folded neatly under her chin. On a straight-backed chair, Lily cradled the youngest child. She was rocking her, and singing some soft melody in a low voice. The flushed face of the girl was relaxed, her mouth pursed with her thumb poised at the lips as if she had just lost the comfort of it in the relaxed state of sleep.

Slipping inside, he grimaced as the board groaned under his foot. It sounded impossibly loud in the quiet. He cringed, and stopped. Lily looked up and pressed a finger to her lips. He nodded.

She tried to stand and was having a difficult time doing it while holding the child. Rogan took Lizzie from her and laid the child next to her sister.

Beside him, Lily tucked the blanket around the girl, who had not stirred one bit. "She was afraid," Lily whispered. Before folding the last of the coverlet into place, she lifted the hem of the girl's dress and frowned at the bruise on her side. "How could anyone harm an innocent child?"

Rogan's head snapped toward her. She wasn't looking at him, but he could see her face in profile. Her expression was a blend of pity and anger as she gazed down at the sleeping girl. She was unaware of him, lost in troubled thought.

Something bitter and hard knotted in his stomach. In this moment, he could almost believe he was wrong about her. It was an extraordinary thing for her to say, she who had used him, seen him beaten and almost burned alive. Yet it was said so sincerely, with no effort to effect a response from him. There was no sideways look to gauge his mood, no dramatic sighing and moaning about it all. Just that simple comment, though the cleverest of speeches could not have moved him more deeply.

She looked at him then. Without thinking, he brushed a stray curl from her cheek. She smiled back, and he could see her as she had been in the garden the first night they met, awkward and blunt and achingly innocent.

The knot in his gut tightened. God, he was a fool! How he missed her—that Lily, the woman who had caught his eye and then his heart. He would never admit to another soul that he had loved her. But he had. Oh, he truly had. It was what had made the rest of it so wretched, like a living nightmare from which there was no waking.

She slipped silently to the doorway and paused, waiting for him. Rogan wondered for the hundredth time what was happening to him. The cold, sterile luxury of his rage was slipping away, yielding to...what? A need. A need for Lily.

He walked rapidly to the door, closing it softly behind him. His wife waited for him in the hall.

Wordlessly he took her by the elbow and steered her into his room. She opened her mouth to say something, but never had the chance. He kissed her, hard at first, then more slowly, letting the tension ease as desire kindled to life. As always, she came to him willingly, melting against him. It felt like a homecoming and his arms tightened around her.

There was a sense of slipping away. There were words inside of him, but he didn't know what they were. He wanted her, wanted to make love to her and bury himself inside of her in the mindless taking and giving that they found together. But even that was not enough.

A surge of fear, like a man drowning who finds the energy for one last lifesaving kick to the surface, made him pull away. His breath rasped in his throat, belying the casual way he turned his back on her.

"I will not press you tonight. You have been through much today. Go to your room."

She didn't move to go. "But—"

"Leave me," he barked, raking his hand through his hair with a vengeance.

When he was alone with his thoughts, he wished she had stayed. He was not fit company tonight, not even for himself.

Lily woke. A vague feeling of something not being right was her first awareness, and then she remembered. She knew he would be gone already.

The familiar emptiness lodged in her breast, and she felt close to tears. It was silly, she should be glad he was gone. But it was always this way after his visits. When he was here, it was almost agony to be near him, to have him hold her, yet still keep so much from her. But when he was gone, it was worse. A terrible sense of failure pressed down on her like the weight of the world.

A slight stirring beside her caused her to start and made her aware of the press of a small body against her back. Turning, she saw Lizzie's eyes flutter open and a sleepy smile spread across her face.

"I had a nightmare," she said.

"Did you? What was it?" Lily shifted and gathered the small, warm body into her arms.

"I don' 'member."

"Well, it is over now, and the sun is up. Nightmares are not real, remember that. Dreams cannot hurt you."

The irony of her words hit her, and she buried her face in the clean, sweet smell of the girl's freshly washed hair. She had lied. Dreams *can* hurt.

Chapter Eighteen

Andrew cringed at the sight of the house. He had forgotten just how gloomy it was, such a dim, dingy place. He wondered how the little flower fared here. Just the thought of her set his heart to racing with doubt. Was he being a fool? That is what Rogan would have said.

That weird servant, Thomas, came to take his horse and instructed him that he could find the mistress in the great room. Hitching his packet over his shoulder, Andrew headed indoors.

Lily sat alone in a corner, curled up by the small fireplace with a pile of sewing on her lap. He had to stop to let his reaction settle. He was uneasy enough without such a scene as this. She looked so lonely, so much the outcast. It was exactly as Rogan had intended, and he himself, God help him, had agreed.

But then, much had changed for him since the beginning of all this. It was nothing anyone would notice from the outside, but his soul was slowly undergoing a transformation. And at the heart of it was the distinct guilt over Lily.

He had prayed for answers and found none save a sudden urge to come to his sister-in-law. And a purpose, though he hardly understood it, became imperative.

Well, he had better hope it was divine direction, for if it were anything less it would be trouble if Rogan ever caught him. His brother had made it clear no one was to interfere with Lily, and Andrew doubted his offhand comment about tending to Lily's spiritual needs meant he would be pleased to find Andrew here.

Drawing a steadying breath, he started over to Lily. The sound of his footfalls brought her head up, and she seemed startled to find him standing before her. She rose, a fluid movement, and stood as if braced for some bad news. Watching him warily, she nodded a careful greeting. "Andrew."

"Relax, my lady," he said, moving forward to take the seat opposite her. "I come not as your brother but as a priest."

"A priest?" Her tone was mildly disbelieving.

"I am one, you know, although I have not much acted like it. To be truthful, I never much cared for any of it. But lately, I have become aware, rather belatedly, of the responsibilities of my calling."

"And so you have come here to be my priest?"

The unworldly color of her eyes flashed. She more than likely thought him sporting with her. After another sigh, he explained, "I was promised to the church at birth, not such a strange thing. It is the normal custom, to pledge certain children to the priesthood or to a nunnery. Except I had no inclination to go, you see. I rather preferred hunting with my brothers and the secular life I was used to. But, money can buy anything, and so it was easy to secure a relatively unhindered existence with my family, living much as I did before. It never bothered me, my lack of attention to my profession. Until now. It seems I cannot abide the fact that you have been made to live here without benefit of spiritual…guidance.''

She sat, perching on the edge of her chair like a bird poised for flight. ''And what makes you think I am in need?''

''We all have spiritual needs, my lady.'' Lifting his bag, he began to remove its contents. ''I will use that trestle over there,'' he said, indicating a table near the wall. With reverent hands, he removed the altar cloth, candles, chalice, cross and Bible.

Lily watched impassively as he set up the makeshift altar. When he was finished, she asked, ''Does Rogan know you are here?''

''No.''

''Why should I believe you? You were as much a part of all of this as he.''

''You have absolutely no cause to trust me, I know. Except that I am vested.''

''I know many priests whose spiritual loyalty is much impaired by their human nature. You are still Rogan's brother.''

''True. But I am, if you do not know this already, an honest man. And I have never followed Rogan with blind loyalty.''

''So, Rogan did not send you.'' She nodded, then gave him a slanting look. ''God did?''

Andrew smiled and spread his hands out in silent apology.

"So, what is it you want?"

"I will say mass. I shall eat luncheon before that, but otherwise, I will be unoccupied. I will be available for confession."

She stood bolt upright, feet planted apart as she faced him like an inflamed fury. "Is that what this is about? You will have my confession. I suppose you are eager to hear how I betrayed my husband, how I laughed with my family after we thought him dead. What a disappointment, I should think, that I will tell you none of these things."

She spun on her heel and was about to stalk off when Andrew reached for her arm. "Lily, listen to me. I told you I came here as your priest, not Rogan's man, and I meant that. You know I am forbidden to speak of another's solemn penance. Nothing you will say shall go beyond the two of us.

"Even more, I cannot allow anything you tell me to affect me as a person. If you do speak of guilt, then I must forget I heard that admission from your lips. And if you are innocent, I can do nothing to aid you in your present situation."

He saw she was listening. "Lily, I cannot help you with Rogan, that is not why I am here. But I cannot hurt you, either. Nothing you tell me in the sacrament of confession can make any difference, except to God."

"You believe me," she said suddenly, and her lips trembled as her eyes filled with tears. "You know the truth."

He released her, turning away. "I told you, that is not why I am here."

"But you do!"

He looked at her again, forcing himself to view that shining hope light her face. Did he believe that ingenuous expression hid a cold and calculating heart? "Very well, I admit it. I thought Rogan was right at first. But you have been steadfast in the face of Rogan's vengeance, with a nobility of spirit that has persuaded me we were wrong to accuse you."

With a gut-wrenching cry, she flung herself into his arms. He recovered quickly from the surprise of it, holding her and feeling an odd kind of peace as she clung to him like a drowning woman who has just been saved from the clutches of the sea.

"Now," he said softly as her outburst subsided, "go and reflect on your sins, and I will hear your confession when you are ready."

Disentangling himself, he retreated to the small chamber on the second level that had been his. He hoped she would take a while, for he needed much time to pray.

A mild breeze wafted pleasantly through the hall of Brenton Castle, stirring the many candle flames into jangling points of illumination. Shadows flickered along the high stone walls in a grotesque dance of dark images. Catherine Marshand Craven narrowed her eyes at the playful specters as her husband belched.

"Damnation!" he exclaimed, wiping the back of

his hand across his lips. The other hand rubbed the roundness of his belly.

Catherine gave him a withering look, of which he took no notice.

"Fine meal," he commented to no one. One of his sycophants, a wiry fellow with a gaping hole in his smile, laughed in an annoying high-pitched manner.

In disgust, Catherine threw her meat onto her trencher and stood. Sagramore Craven, Earl of Brenton, gazed up at his wife, his bloodshot eyes taking a moment to focus on her. "Off to bed, my love?"

"Yes," Catherine answered tightly. Her eyes lifted, peering over her husband's head for the one she sought. Phillippe nodded in answer to her silent signal.

"Perhaps I'll join you," Craven said, hoisting himself up from the chair. Beside him, his toothless crony giggled in salacious glee.

"I was going to walk a bit in the garden first," Catherine said quickly, knowing how Sagramore hated exercise.

"Humph," Craven grunted, falling back into his seat. "In that case, I'll have another ale."

Catherine hurried away, weaving among the people seated on the trestles with a rage smoldering in her chest. Darting her eyes over to Phillippe, she saw he was already making his way out of the room.

"Madam," a voice said, cutting into her awareness.

Catherine's head snapped around.

"Someone to see you," a young servant said. "He's waitin' over there."

Catherine's gaze followed the direction indicated. A dark, rangy man stood by an arched alcove. Dorvis. A trill of excitement rippled through her.

Motioning for Dorvis to follow, she turned and quit the hall. By the time she reached the corridor, Phillippe was already waiting.

"Ah, *chérie,* you—"

Catherine held up her hand for silence. Behind her, the stranger stepped through the threshold.

"Lady Catherine," he said, and smiled, showing a row of pointed teeth that were badly stained a brownish yellow.

"You have some news?" she demanded.

"Lord Rogan remains at Kensmouth. The Lady Lily is still secreted away."

Catherine smiled. "Ah. Good." She paused a moment, as if savoring the great news. Casting her eyes to Phillippe, she said, "Is it not delicious? Imagine their misery."

"So you will leave them be?" Phillippe was surprised.

"For now," Catherine purred. "But not forever. I must plan carefully. I was too rushed before. This time, I shall plot at my leisure, and act in due course." She turned to Dorvis. "Return to Kensmouth and wait there. If anything of interest comes about, report to me immediately."

The man bowed and headed out the door. Phillippe lowered his mouth to Catherine's ear. "What do you have in mind, *ma petite?*"

Her eyes glittered coldly as she stared after Dorvis.

"I do not yet know, Phillippe. But when I do, be certain it will be *glorious*."

"Bless me, father, for I have sinned."

Lily knelt before Andrew, her head bowed and hands clasped before her. She dragged in a long breath and began, "I almost did grievous injury to a trio of innocent children who needed me. I am ashamed at how cruel I was to them at first. I have been unkind to Rogan. I have had evil thoughts, fantasies, of revenge. I know that he oppresses me, but he thinks himself just. If I were guilty of the betrayal he believes of me, I would deserve all he does and more. But I do not deserve it at all. I have tried to understand, to excuse him, but sometimes I..."

She paused. "I want his forgiveness, and I want what existed between us before the treachery of my family destroyed it all. There is something inside me that rails against the injustice. A quiet rage. Sometimes it is directed at him, sometimes at myself. Sometimes—and please forgive this!—I am so angry at God for letting this happen. A saint, as we are all called to be, would accept their lot and live in holiness no matter what their circumstances. But I cannot."

Lily again paused. Andrew sat unmoving before her, head bowed. She finished her confession. "I am weak, and prone to self-pity. I am ungenerous. And I have bullied Sybilla."

When she paused, Andrew murmured, "Is that all, Lily?"

"For these and all my sins, I am heartily sorry."

There was a long silence as Lily awaited her penance. She had not realized how much she had needed the cleansing of mind and soul until she had knelt down and begun talking. She feared Andrew would rebuke her. And if he did, was it God's wrath he would be speaking, or pure human disgust?

Andrew reached out and took her folded hands in his. His expression was so kind, so full of pity that the well of emotion that had formed her words burst like a swollen river flooding its shores.

"Hush," he said softly, "you have made a good confession. But, Lily, I cannot do anything as a man to help you. I am bound, as I told you before, to keep the sacrament in secrecy."

"I know," Lily sniffed, "but you have already helped me. Having no one to talk to, no one to share my thoughts with, it made everything confused and…jumbled up inside. Now, I understand, at least myself, much better."

Looking down at their intertwined hands, Andrew thought for a long moment. "I am going beyond my duties as priest, but if that is a sin, then I will answer for it. Lily, listen to me for I will give you some advice." When he looked up at her, his boyish face was composed in grim lines. "Do not stop fighting. For yourself, and for my brother. Never accept the guilt that is not yours, but also show my brother, by your actions, the kind of woman you are. Make him doubt himself."

"I cannot," she protested. "He will not allow me to speak of it."

"Keep loving him, and be patient. But be strong."

He smiled at her. "You are, you know. Very strong. Accept what he has done to you, but strive to move past it. And take everything he gives, then press for more."

Lily shook her head. "It sounds like a riddle. I do not know what you are asking of me."

Letting his hands fall away, his shoulders slumped. "I do not know, either. I suppose the truth is there is nothing I can say to make a difference." Andrew sighed, his jaw working in agitation. After a moment, he said, "For your penance, make a sincere act of contrition and pray the Lord's Prayer thrice each night."

It was a heavy penance, and Lily gave him a startled look. "Not as punishment," he explained. "For strength. For God to help you."

"My thoughts precisely," Rogan's voice cut in. "I was just saying to myself, God help these two."

Lily saw Andrew stiffen just before they both turned to face the angry visage of her husband. His eyes, burning like twin beds of white-hot ash, contained all one needed to know of his mood. She had never seen him look so dangerous. That first night on the ship, perhaps. It had cowed her then, but this time, strengthened by her confession and the knowledge of Andrew's support, she felt no intimidation.

"I do not suppose you wish an explanation?" Andrew said.

"On the contrary, I am looking forward to it. But you I will hear from later. For now, leave my wife and I alone."

Andrew hesitated, seeming reluctant to do so. Lily smiled, silently reassuring him. Nodding, he said, "I will be just down the hall. And Rogan, keep in mind that it was I who came to Lily. The fault, if there is one here, lies with me."

Rogan glared silently until Andrew had gone. Turning back to Lily, he said quietly, "I could kill you right now."

"I am sure you are quite put out," Lily shrugged. "It must be simply galling to have others acting outside of your sovereign will."

His expression changed from shock to amazement. "Are you scolding me?" he asked incredulously.

Andrew's advice had settled inside her, making a difference, somehow, as she faced the man whom she had both loved and feared for so long. "You surprise me with your foolishness, Rogan. You waste your strength on this pointless quest to make me pay for what I never did——"

"I have told you," he growled, "I never want to hear those lies from your lips again."

"Then you ask the impossible, for I can either lie or I can speak my innocence, but I cannot do both. You are so accustomed to bullying your way into victory, you have lost your appreciation for the truth. You are not Almighty, Rogan. You can not insist on your will and have the stars and sun line up in accordance to it. Neither can you insist on your beliefs and make them facts. So, instead of telling me how you wish to murder me, for whatever reason you are convinced is adequate, why do you not simply ask me what it was Andrew and I were doing? You may find it enlightening."

"Have you formulated a lie so quickly?"

"You are a sad man," she said, and sighed. "You have let this hate consume you."

Like a wolf, he lunged forward, snarling, "A hate nurtured and grown from your family's good teaching."

Again, as so many times before when he wished to physically intimidate her, he loomed over her, bringing his face within a hairbreadth of hers. This time, however, Lily did not cringe. Instead, she reached out her hand and laid her palm against his cheek. "I know."

It was as if the power of that touch drained him, for his fierce mien faded and he stared back, pain flooding his eyes. "And you betrayed me."

"No, Rogan. I never did."

"And now you have taken Andrew from me."

That startled her. "What?"

A sad, bitter smile played on his sensuous mouth. "Must you always play the innocent? Could you just not once admit your perfidity?"

"What did you mean—take Andrew from you?"

"I find you practically in his arms, alone, and you have the nerve—"

"Well, had you come but an hour earlier, you would have seen me actually *in* his arms. He came here as a priest."

His snort of derision communicated his disbelief. "My brother was never much of a priest."

"He heard my confession and is preparing to say mass. It is true, whether you believe it or not."

"I never knew you were so devout," he said with a sneer.

Her eyes narrowed. "There is much you do not know about me."

Lapsing into silence, he glowered at her for a moment. "Tell me about you being in his arms," he demanded suddenly.

"I was crying. He was comforting me."

"The fool."

Lily shook her head. It was hopeless to try to reach him. "I am taking the children to mass, now. We can resume this afterward."

"I have not dismissed you," he warned.

Lily paused, turning her head to look at him over her shoulder. "Yes, you have. You dismissed me a long time ago."

Chapter Nineteen

Lily shot Oliver a warning look, willing him to sit still. On her other side, Lizzie drooped over Lily's arm, ignoring Lily's nudges for her to sit upright. Lily sighed, casting a glance heavenward with a prayer. In time, she would teach them proper behavior for church.

Anna, however, sat in rapt attention. She stared straight ahead, eyes on the makeshift altar. She had mastered much of Lily's mannerisms, imitating a girl of good breeding so much so that one would hardly have known that she was of such humble stock. Oliver, too, with his proud, blustering temper, was not so unlike the spoiled sons of the noble class. He certainly had the bravado of the bravest of knights, which was not always a blessing, but he heeded Lily's gentle corrections, dropping the crude speech he had learned from his father in favor of a more cultured vocabulary, and tried to behave.

And Lizzie was young. So easygoing, she simply went the way the wind blew, fresh and excited about the least little thing. In quiet times, one could always hear her humming. She never walked anywhere—it was either skipping or running even for short distances. Her exuberance was infectious, as fascinating and precious as Anna's goodness and Oliver's pride. All three, each so unique and dear, had won a place forever in Lily's heart.

When Andrew entered, Lily indicated to the children that they should stand. As he spread his hands over the altar and called out the beginning phrases in Latin that drew them all to worship, Lily saw Rogan slip opposite Lizzie. Meeting her eye, there was, for once, no mockery or challenge in that gray wolf's gaze. He bowed his head toward her and muttered, "I never saw him say the mass."

Lizzie shifted and, to Lily's horror, draped herself against Rogan's leg, using it to prop herself up as she lolled about.

"Stand up!" Lily hissed sharply. Rogan's large hand came down to pull the child's head back to rest against his thigh. Lily looked up, surprised. The gesture was almost affectionate.

"I was bored at her age myself."

Lily could scarce believe it. Turning back to the mass, she felt a warmth suffuse her insides.

Andrew turned his back to them, addressing the cross that had been set behind the altar. Like a balm, the familiar phrases comforted as Lily sang out the prayers on cue, her voice mingling with Rogan's rich baritone. At communion, she took the cup and the bread, sampling each before handing it to Rogan. It was as if she had come home again after a long voyage in a foreign land, for daily services were a part of life at Charolais. It was one of the few things she had missed.

And Elspeth.

She dearly missed her little sister's reverent and joyous presence by her side.

After the final prayer, Andrew came to her. "Thank you," Lily said, tugging on each of the children's shoulders to prompt them.

"Thank you, Father," they said dutifully. Lizzie made no attempt to stifle a yawn.

Andrew only smiled at her, ruffling her hair. "I can come again in a week or so, and we can make it a regular ritual."

"That will not be necessary, Andrew," Rogan said.

Andrew frowned, looking sideways at his brother. "This has nothing to do with you, Rogan. I am simply doing my duty, for Lily and these children."

"I did not mean that I would forbid your coming. It is just that Lily will not be here. Come for the children if you wish."

Lily's head snapped up. "What?" Shock, dismay and blistering hope rang out in the word.

Turning to her, Rogan explained, "You are coming to Kensmouth with me."

Was this some cruel joke? "When?"

"Now. Today."

Lily shook her head to clear away her confusion. "I do not understand—why?"

"It is only temporary. Alexander is coming to visit and he wishes to meet you." Rogan spread out his hands, offering a quirk of his brow. "I can hardly ask him to come here."

Her heart soared. Then another consideration stopped the rise of joy in her breast. "But the children…"

"They will be safe here. Sybilla will care for them."

All at once, Anna, Oliver and Lizzie cried out and clung to Lily's skirts.

Lily drew a long breath. "I am afraid that is impossible. Sybilla has no affection for the children. They are afraid of her. I cannot leave them in her care."

"She can hardly be worse than their father, and they managed to survive that," Rogan said impatiently.

"That is precisely why I will not leave them. They have endured quite enough."

"You have no choice. They cannot come with you, so they will have to stay here."

Lizzie began to wail, softly at first, but it grew in volume.

"No," Lily said firmly. Rogan's look was thunderous, but she could not back down. "They could come with us. They would not be a bother."

"I said no."

Steeling herself, Lily tried again. "Please, Rogan."

"I am not taking a pack of ill-bred urchins to Kensmouth. Would they be content to sleep with the servants, do you think, after all of the pampering you have given them? It is impossible, Lily, and there can be no other answer. You might as well resign yourself to it, because they are not coming with you. And no amount of sullen pouts or argument can change my mind.''

For the hundredth time that day, Rogan cursed himself for a fool.

The caravan of travelers moved slowly along the path to Kensmouth. The road was riddled with deep ruts and gnarled roots that impeded their progress enough to try his patience. In addition, the poor conditions made the advance of the wagon clattering behind him a bone-jarring ride for Lily and the children.

Not that they complained. By God, she better not utter one word, Rogan thought darkly. How she had gotten him to bring them along, let alone agree to put out the story that they were her kin, he would never understand.

"We need to stop," Andrew called up to him.

Rogan expelled a heavy breath. "We are not stopping," he growled.

"The child has to—"

"Again? We have let her out three times already!"

Andrew explained, "She is nervous. Nerves affect children like this."

"Did she drink a whole skin before we left?"

"It will only take a moment."

Muttering something about peasant children dictating to the ruling class, Rogan swung his horse around and cantered back to the wagon. "Hurry up!" he called.

The older girl and Lizzie clamored out of the back and ran for the cover of the trees. Lily, looking serene and poised, smiled tentatively at him.

She looked incredibly lovely. The sun on her hair made it appear like gold. Soft, curving lips drew his gaze, making him linger and think of crushing them to his. Something inside him eased, robbing him of his irate mood.

"How much farther?" she asked.

"Perhaps an hour or slightly more. Depending on how many stops we need to make."

Her smile deepened, causing the corners of her eyes to crinkle. In the light, the color of them paled to a limpid aqua. "It is good of you to be so patient. Thank you."

The vague realization he was being charmed occurred to him, but he didn't pursue it. There was a difference in her, a poise or self-assuredness. Why did it not annoy him?

"Where are they?" Rogan said after a pause.

"Do you want me to go and find them?"

"No, then I will have to search for all three of you before long." Calling to one of his men, he said, "John, go and see where they have gotten to."

"Rogan, no!" Lily cried. "They will be terrified if your man routs them out. I shall go." Swinging her legs over the boards, she was about to leap to the ground when Rogan stopped her, grabbing her tightly by the arm.

The feel of her skin under his fingertips was like touching fire. His horse skittered close, and his thigh grazed her hip. Their gazes locked briefly just before he looked away. "Here they come."

Rogan kicked his horse to the fore and they set off again. His hand burned where he had grabbed her; his thigh throbbed, and an unsettled feeling followed him all the way home.

The handful of soldiers and rickety trap that straggled in just before sunset was hardly an entourage befitting the master and mistress of the castle. Rogan took note of the curious glances they drew as they pulled to a stop before the keep.

Dismounting, he handed Lily off to a servant, instructing her to show his wife to his chamber. Then he disappeared without so much as a farewell.

Lily insisted in seeing the children to their quarters first. Only after they had been properly settled did she agree to be taken to her room.

Once alone, Lily took in her surroundings. Rogan's chamber was definitely masculine, boasting only a few well-made furnishings. There were even some touches of comfort, a thick pile of furs on the carved bed, a set of cushions by the window seat and a cozy grouping of straight-backed chairs by the hearth. Wandering aimlessly, she touched this thing and that, curious about the man who was her husband.

Lifting the lid of a chest, she drew out a padded tunic for winter wear. No doubt it had been laundered before being stored away, but she could still detect the faint smell of him on the wool. She buried her face in it, closing her eyes for a moment as she savored the clean, masculine scent.

"I never thought you a thief," Rogan said. "Besides, I doubt that will fit you."

Her head snapped up. He was lounging in the doorway, arms folded and shoulder against the frame to balance his crossed ankles, looking far too amused. Blood rushed through her, heating her cheeks and making her stomach flop sickeningly. How humiliating, to be caught *sniffing his clothes!*

Folding the tunic neatly, she placed it back in the trunk and closed the lid. She could feel him grinning, though she dared not glance his way.

To her surprise, he did not mock her. "Where are your things?" he asked, entering the room to sit and remove his boots.

Lily pointed to where her two gowns, one comb, one spare shift and remaining sliver of scented soap lay neatly on a bench.

He scoffed. "Find somewhere to put those away. I detest clutter."

She did not point out that he had several items out of place. "I did not want to disturb your belongings."

"They are only belongings, how can they be disturbed?"

"I meant disturb you."

"I am already disturbed."

He was being cross apurpose. "Very well," Lily said innocently. Opening the lid of the chest, she mashed his neatly arranged clothes until there was a bit of space. Then she tossed in her things and sat on the lid until it closed.

He was staring at her, trying to look serious. But the quirk at the corner of his mouth gave him away. "You really are a piece, do you know that?"

"Piece of what?"

"Piece of aggravation, that is what!"

"Why did you put me in this room? With you, I mean."

He stripped off his tunic and undershirt. "Better to keep you close, where I can watch you."

The sight of his bared chest made her mouth dry. "Watch me do what?"

He looked at her as if she were a supreme nuisance. "Crush my clothing and suchlike. It amuses me." He took a step forward in a move that was almost threatening except for the dancing light in his eye.

"How easily you are amused." Lily, not to be daunted, took a step toward him.

"Not for most. But you do, when you act the silly child." He took another step.

"But I am no child. I am a woman." What was this game they were playing? She moved closer.

He raised his brows. "I have noticed, I assure you."

Excitement began to build inside her. He was only inches away, and with one final step he closed the distance. She waited, hardly daring to breathe. The air between them crackled as if lightning were about to strike. Her gaze dropped to the hard, broad chest just before her and her hands itched to touch. What would he do if she slipped her arms around his neck and kissed him?

The light died in his eyes and he turned away.

Disappointment almost crushed her. Biting her lip, Lily spun toward the bed. The game, whatever it was, was at an end. Feeling as if she had just been dancing on the edge of a cliff, she knew she should feel relief. Rather, a wretched sense of defeat weighted her shoulders as she doffed her clothes and slipped into the thick bedding.

Rogan was more than a little angry at himself, though for what, exactly, he was not certain.

No fire tonight, though the room was cool enough for it. He preferred sleeping in the cold. So, when he doused the candles, the chamber was cast in utter darkness. He peeled off his leggings and carefully climbed under the furs. Lying on his back, he stared into the uninterrupted black with his hands behind his head, trying to concentrate on something other than his naked wife lying within reach.

"Rogan," she whispered.

"What?"

"Am I to live here, or will you take me back after Alexander leaves?"

"This is only temporary, Lily."

She did not argue or complain, though Rogan almost wished she would. The silence after his statement was empty. He felt a pang of regret.

It was the children, that was what was troubling him. Not them, really, but Lily when she was with them. Why would a woman like her—a liar, a betrayer—take lovingly to a band of forlorn peasant waifs? She had thought his life worth nothing, yet she cared for these three with the fierceness of a lioness and the gentleness of a Madonna.

It had changed things somehow. For Lily, and for him. The cool, brittle shell of hatred was cracked, crumbling. Would a traitoress act this way? Risk his wrath, which she had never dared on her own behalf, for others? For peasants, even, children or no?

And if he held her, took her in his arms and made love to her as he so longed to do, the crack would widen. If he so much as touched her, the shell would be split wide-open, and his soul with it.

He marveled at such poetic thoughts. *Look at me,* he thought, *a warrior, a man of action and purpose, playing the philosopher—examining too closely the meaning of every little thing.*

God, but that woman was trouble. Even when she was being no trouble at all.

Chapter Twenty

It was the following morn, as the castle assembled to break the fast, when Lily noticed the woman.

She was struck right off by the flaming hair—a rich, luxurious red—and the wide, blood-hued mouth. Dressed in a gown of softly woven wool that clung provocatively to her voluptuous form, the woman moved through the hall, exchanging greetings with those she passed. Lily watched, at first only envious at the easy way this confident beauty was able to walk and converse among these folk who only stared at Lily with antipathy.

Seated beside her, Rogan was deep in conversation, paying no heed to the woman's approach. Thus it was only Lily who witnessed how her pouty mouth curved slowly into a sly cat's smile as her large eyes settled on Rogan.

"My lord, I had heard you returned." Her voice was low, almost a purr.

Rogan looked up and smiled pleasantly. "Alyce. I did not see you yesterday."

Alyce slid her gaze to Lily. "And you have brought

your wife this time. What a pleasure it is to finally meet you."

"And you, Alyce," Lily answered cordially. She didn't like this woman. Some instinctive reflex told her, despite Alyce's pleasant demeanor, she was no friend.

Alyce returned her adoring gaze to Rogan. "And with a pack of children in tow, I hear."

"Yes, my wife's cousins."

Lily noted her husband seemed not to notice how Alyce had a manner of speaking as if the two of them were having an intimate conversation.

"I had hoped to ride today and heard you were going out. Do you mind if I join you, or is it too important a business to have a woman along?" She sulked prettily.

"As a matter of fact, I was going over to Albermarle today. If that would suit you, you may come too. He will enjoy seeing you."

She rewarded Rogan with a bright smile. "That would be lovely. I will enjoy trading barbs with that old warhorse." The smoky gaze shifted again to Lily. "What a shame, I shall not be able to visit with you today. I so wanted to. Perhaps tomorrow you will come to the solar."

As if she were the lady of the castle, inviting me to join her, Lily raged silently.

Shrugging, Lily said perhaps she would.

Alyce turned back to Rogan. "So, I shall meet you in the stables." With a sideways flutter of her eyelashes, she sauntered on.

Rogan excused himself, leaving Lily to ruminate over Alyce and their planned outing.

The three children and Lily were sitting together in the hall nearly a sennight later, Lily trying to supervise their manners. In truth, she was not being very attentive. She had not noticed Oliver sulking on the end of the bench or Anna's troubled look.

With her brows drawn down, Lizzie said, "You are not listening to me. I *said*, Father Andrew gave me this doll, and Robert said I stole it. Oliver knocked him down and the stable master boxed Oliver's ears."

"That is nice," Lily murmured, craning her neck to glance over the crowd in the hall. Ever since she had met the beautiful Alyce, Lily had been hard put to keep her mind on anything else. She was obsessed with knowing where she was—and where Rogan was—at all times.

Anna's giggle brought her attention. "Lady, who are you looking for?"

"No one, I am not looking for anyone. What were you saying, Lizzie? Oliver gave you a doll?"

"No! I *said*, Father Andrew gave me the doll and Oliver got his ears boxed."

"Father Andrew boxed Oliver's ears? Oliver!"

"Nooo," Lizzie said, completely exasperated.

Lily groaned. Sighing, she held up her hands for everyone to calm themselves. "What happened?"

The boy shot her a sullen look. "That Robert was making Lizzie cry."

"So he boxed your ears?"

"No, the stable master did after I whupped Robert."

Lily put a hand to her forehead. "Oh, Oliver, will you never learn? You cannot afford to be drawing attention to yourself, or what will Lord Rogan do? He could send you back to Sybilla. I will not have you making trouble."

"Lady," Anna interrupted softly, "Robert is mean. He *was* making Lizzie cry."

"Well, avoid him in the future. You must keep yourselves out of harm's way."

Oliver sprang to his feet, jamming his fists on his hips. "He is a bully. He hates us! He says that you are a murderer and we come from a bad family."

Lily's throat tightened. She had not thought of this—that the children would be subjected to the resentment against her. Everyone in the castle knew of her "betrayal," and had made no secret of their lack of affection for their new lady. It seemed they were equally scornful of her "kin."

"No matter," she said, recovering with aplomb. "We will spend the day together. Perhaps a picnic. Would you like that?"

"Oh, yes!" the girls chimed. Oliver looked hopeful, but he was still steeping in his mood.

"Very well, let me go to the kitchens and pack up some things and we will be off."

"Can Lord Rogan come?" Lizzie asked, jumping up and clapping her hands together at the idea.

"Lord Rogan is busy, sweetling. Now go ahead and wait for me at the gate. I will be along presently.

And Oliver,'' she called, ''I am not cross with you. You did well to protect your sister.''

This finally did the trick to cheer him. He gave her a smile, and Lily felt her heart swell. She wanted to throttle this Robert herself for picking on a little child. If it had not been for her fears of Rogan becoming impatient with the children, she would have applauded the young boy's bravado from the start.

It did not take her long to gather together some cheese and several apples. She added a few strips of salted beef and managed to steal away one of cook's mutton pies when he wasn't looking. Stuffing them into a pannier, she slung it over her shoulder and went to meet the children.

''Now, we must not go far. Perhaps just into the forest. It would do no good to get lost.''

''Oh, an adventure. Hurray!'' Lizzie squealed, skipping merrily ahead of them as they set out across the meadow.

Oliver picked up a stick, acting officious as he scouted out their path. They were lucky enough to come across a stream just inside the tree line, where they settled on the rocks to have their meal.

Oliver and Lizzie were anxious to explore. Lily allowed them to climb over some outcroppings.

''There is a waterfall up there!'' Lizzie called back excitedly.

''Take care not to fall in!'' Lily answered.

''It is shallow,'' Oliver said, shaking his head disgustedly at her solicitousness.

Next to Lily, Anna clicked her tongue. ''I am sorry he is so much trouble.''

"Do not be," Lily said. "Oliver has a harder time of it in some ways than you girls. He has appointed himself the head of the family, and in so doing feels very grown-up. It chafes his pride when I treat him like a child."

Anna nodded, adding shyly, "Oliver sees the knights and he thinks he should be a great fighter someday. But he is only a peasant, and after this visit, we will return to Linden Wood. And when he grows up, he will be a farmer, like Da."

Lily smoothed the girl's sleek dark brown hair affectionately. "It is a hardship. Perhaps I was not right in bringing you here." She paused. "And what of you, Anna?"

The girl's gaze flickered away, and Lily saw her wince. "I know it can never be different, for any of us. I know what we are."

Lily drew her close, her arms around her slight frame. Anna looked up at her face. This child, almost a woman, with her pretty nose and wide eyes looked no more a common waif than Lily herself had at that age. And she was not much younger than Elspeth. The thought of her sister sent a pang of grief through Lily's breast. How she missed her.

Looking back down at Anna, Lily said, "Whatever you are, I love you just that way. You cannot know what a joy you all are to me. You *are* my family."

"I love you, too," Anna said, squeezing Lily tightly.

A squeal brought their attention to Lizzie, just in time to witness her teetering on the edge of a rock.

Lily stood up, ready to call out a warning when the tot lost her balance and fell into the stream.

Lifting her skirts, Lily was about to jump in when Oliver catapulted himself into the water after his sister and dragged her up by the collar. Lizzie was sputtering, but a wide smile showed under the wet veil of hair. "That was fun!"

"Oh, honestly." Lily sighed, sitting back down.

"There is Lord Rogan!" Anna exclaimed, pointing off in the distance.

Lily's head shot up. Indeed, it was. He was visible on a bluff that rose above the far bank, the telltale color of his hair catching the sunlight and turning the auburn a burnished copper. That, and the unmistakable way he carried himself made it certain it was her husband and no other. And he was not alone. A brighter gleam of red came from the woman who walked next to him. Even at this distance, Lily could see that Alyce had her hand lightly on Rogan's arm.

Her throat suddenly went bone-dry. "Yes, well, Lord Rogan has many duties that take him to all reaches of his lands. I suppose he is on some mission or other." The forced lightness in her voice sounded false in her own ears, and Lily could see Anna was not fooled.

"I do not like that lady," Anna said. "She is always talking to Lord Rogan. And she laughs strangely." Lily knew what she meant. Alyce's laugh, when it was for Rogan, had a deep, seductive sound to it. Anna continued, "And the other day, she gave Lizzie some honey cakes and started asking all kinds of questions about you."

"Did she?" Lily glanced back up to where her husband and Alyce stood. Just then, Oliver shouted out to Lizzie, and the sound of his voice must have carried to the crest of the ravine for Rogan turned his head. Lily saw him pause and then turn back to Alyce briefly before setting off down the steep path toward them.

Alyce stood for a long moment as the breeze lifted her fiery hair. Even at this distance, Lily could almost feel her frustration. Finally Alyce whirled, skirts billowing out gracefully, and disappeared down the other side.

Turning her attention back to her fast-approaching husband, Lily braced herself. He was probably going to be furious. Tucking her hair into place, she rehearsed her defense.

Lizzie spotted Rogan. "Hallo!" she called out cheerily. Lily grimaced when Rogan did not return the greeting.

"Before you scold me like a wayward child," Lily called as soon as he was close enough, "let me first say you have never commanded me to stay within the castle walls. I did not think you would mind if we did a bit of exploring."

Rogan stopped. He stood with his legs braced wide, his hands resting lightly on his hips as if he were assessing her. His face was unreadable.

"Lord Rogan!" Lizzie called. "I am all wet. I fell in—it was fun!"

Rogan shook his head as if the whole business were too unbelievable.

"Come sit in the sun, then, Lizzie, so you will not

catch cold,'' Rogan answered. ''Summer illness is the worst kind.''

He waited for the child to pick her way carefully over the stones to him, then hoisted her up, exclaiming at the coldness of her wet clothes against his skin.

''Here,'' he grunted, depositing Lizzie on a sun-drenched rock.

''I saw a deer a moment ago,'' Oliver announced, coming up to join them.

Rogan rewarded him with a grin. ''I hope the hunting party will be as lucky. We have to stock our larders for the big feasting.''

Lily could scarcely keep her eyes from her husband. He was not angry! In fact, he seemed quite amicable. He sat down on one of the rocks, his one leg drawn up with an arm slung over the knee.

''We are having a picnic!'' Lizzie declared happily.

''Really? Do you have anything left? I am starving.''

''Oliver, see what is left in the pannier,'' Lily ordered quickly.

The boy rifled through the leather pouch, pulling out wrapped parcels. ''There is an apple left. Not much cheese. Oh, here is the mutton pie.'' He held up the offering reluctantly. They had been saving that.

After only a moment's consideration, Oliver held out the pie. ''Here.'' Oblivious to his sacrifice, Rogan took it and began to eat.

''What were you doing?'' Oliver asked. He settled himself down facing Rogan. Lily noticed the attentive way the boy looked at him, with the blatant sheen of worship in his eyes.

"I was just walking," Rogan said easily, "something I enjoy doing occasionally. It clears the head."

"Was that Alyce I saw with you?" Lily asked, trying to make her query as casual as possible.

"Yes. She was out for a ride, then joined me."

"I thought she did not like to go out without you."

Rogan shrugged. "It is close to the castle wall. Safe enough. I keep up the patrols."

"Are there any wild animals about?" Lizzie asked.

"Or thieves?" Oliver chimed in, his face alight with anticipation.

Rogan leaned back on his elbows and stretched his long legs before him. Lily could not help but admire the lean form. The thrill of pleasure low in her belly reminded her of his long absence from her bed.

"Not now. But there used to be. We called him the daevil rider, which is an old word meaning 'devil.'"

"A devil!" Lizzie's eyes were round with awe.

"He used to like to ride into a village or onto a farming cottage with his band of men. He was a real gentleman, they would say, taking only what they needed, offering his apologies, then riding away. Some say he left them gold later, in the manner of payment for what he had stolen."

"What happened to him?" Anna asked breathlessly.

"The truth is he just disappeared one day. Many boasted they had caught him and seen him hung, but nothing could be proved. No, I think he was just a fellow down on his luck. It was after the Great War, you see, and the Conqueror had taken away many lands, turning folk out of their homes."

"Imagine!" Anna sighed, clearly thinking this a very romantic story. "Did he have a love?"

"No one knew much about him. His identity was never revealed, though there were rumors that he did indeed have a lady, a noblewoman, who was devoted to him."

"I wish I could have caught him," Oliver declared. "I don' care how polite he was, he was a thief! I'd o' smited him with my sword and hung him from a tree."

They all fell to giggling at Oliver's boastfulness, which made the boy grin sheepishly.

"Warring is not a glorious thing, Oliver," Rogan said, his voice steady and quiet. "It is ugly. It should be avoided at all costs."

"Tell us more stories," Oliver demanded.

"Yes, please," echoed Anna.

Rogan obliged, his soft voice relating the folklore of the woods. As he spoke, Lily watched him in wonder. He was such a gentle man right now, tolerant of the children, indulgent even. And so handsome it made her mouth dry. Yet, even the sharp pain of longing could not mar this moment, for they were together. It seemed so right to have him here, completing the circle, a part of them.

A part of her. She would never be complete without him.

They stayed much later than they had meant to. The sun was already dipping below the horizon when they set out for home.

The children ran ahead, gay with abandon, and Lily knew a similar joy. She felt like skipping and laughing herself. She even thought of slipping her hand into Rogan's as they made their way home. But some distances, no matter how remote they might feel at a given moment, could not be spanned so easily.

There was a chill in the air that night, but Lily did not call for a fire. The soft glow from the wall sconces flickered lazily on the stone walls of the chamber. Rogan, seated by the empty hearth, was looking over his clothing, examining it for rips.

He had been preoccupied all evening, quite unlike the carefree, charming man he had been this afternoon. It was as if a pall had fallen over him the moment they passed through the tower gate.

"Do you need me to sew that?" Lily asked, seeing him poke his finger through a hole in a tunic.

"Is that a talent of yours?"

"Actually, I am atrocious with a needle. But good enough to mend a hole."

Wordlessly he handed it over.

"I have no thread here," she said. "I will see to it tomorrow, if that is all right."

Rogan shrugged. He was in a quiet mood. Pensive.

"Thank you for today," Lily ventured.

"What about today?"

"With the children. You were so good with them, they were delighted. I am glad you were not angry that I took them into the forest."

"I was a bit at first. But there was no cause."

"Your stories were wonderful."

Rogan smiled. "I believe I stirred young Oliver's

blood. He was all set to smite the daevil bandit with his sword!''

''And hang him from a tree!'' Lily laughed. ''I fear he is a bit bloodthirsty.''

Rogan chuckled.

''He is a spirited lad,'' Lily said. ''He admires you. His father was a rotter, but in you he sees a good man to emulate.''

''He is extraordinarily fanciful. I am certainly glad he has come under your influence, else I fear I would find him in ten years raiding my forests, and *he* would be the bandit being smitten!''

His eyes rested on her for a moment. Lily thought she saw approval in his expression.

His gaze slid away, and he stood. ''I think I will go back to the hall.''

''Oh.''

He hesitated, as if unsure. Lily thought of what she could say to make him stay, to utter some clever phrase that would cause him to laugh, come over to her, slip his arm around her and draw her close.

''Well, then, wife, good night,'' he said finally.

''Good night, Rogan.''

He went out the door, leaving the room empty and quiet in his wake.

Lily fingered the tunic she would repair tomorrow. The sting of tears blurred her vision as she wondered if it were his men whom he went to join, or did he seek the company of a lush redhead with a throaty laugh and welcoming smile?

Chapter Twenty-One

Andrew sauntered into Lily's chamber with his trademark grin and a warm embrace.

"Brother," Lily exclaimed happily.

He gave her a serious look. "Tell me, how is it between Rogan and yourself?"

She forced a smile. "It is fine. Much the same, but no worse." Andrew continued to look at her in his steady way. It was no good. She was never much of a liar. "No, that is not true. I am much afraid he is growing further from me. Before, at least he hated me. Now, I doubt he gives me much thought at all."

Andrew looked confused. "I don't know what has happened to cause you to think such a thing, but I do know Rogan is not indifferent to you."

How could she confide in him her fears about Alyce? If she were wrong, she would look ridiculous. And if she were right, did she want him to inform her that her worst dread was true? "I am not so certain," she said simply.

"Lily, listen to me. I am going to go away for a while. I hate to leave you, especially when you look so miserable. But there is something important I have to do." He paused. "There is a favor I must ask of you. I was mistaken about you for a long time. Can you forgive me?"

Lily was surprised. "There is nothing to forgive. How could you have thought otherwise?"

"You are too generous. I am afraid I cannot be so charitable with myself. I am going to try to make this thing right, though I swore to remain neutral. If it be wrong of me, then I will take that chance."

He held her briefly before saying a curt farewell.

Alone, Lily could not spare him a second thought. What she had said to Andrew was true. She was losing Rogan. She had to fight, to try—something.

Then, she got an idea, an idea that nearly terrified her.

But she would do it. She had to. She had nothing else.

"What news?" Catherine demanded.

Dorvis did not hesitate. "Lily is living at Kensmouth. Lord Rogan is softening toward his beautiful wife."

If not for Phillippe's arm coming about her waist, Catherine would have crumpled. *No! No!* she thought, *it is what I have feared!*

"I bring some other news, something interesting. I have met someone who is as displeased with this event as you are. That one offered to be of service, but wishes to remain secret. I am to ask if you cannot alert your father so he can fetch Lady Lily home."

Stunned, Catherine stared at him for a moment before exploding in gales of shrill laughter. "Is that what you think?" she cried when she caught her breath. "That we wish to *rescue* her? Ah, it is too funny, is it not, Phillippe?"

Dorvis's eyes flickered from her to the swarthy Frenchman. "I do not understand."

"She is his wife, you idiot," Catherine snapped. "She belongs to him. My father would have no right to take her back even if he wanted to."

Phillippe stepped forward. "There are other measures which could benefit both our new friend and the Lady Catherine. We are most interested in punishing Lord Rogan for his crimes."

Dorvis's face creased as he looked at her in utter disbelief. "You are not thinking of harming Lord Rogan?"

"No, no, of course not," Catherine said smoothly. She shot Phillippe a warning look, and the swarthy Frenchman retreated. "Go back to Kensmouth. Relay anything of import. Come only when I summon you. Tell our new friend we wish but to make mischief."

"Yes," Phillippe agreed, his eyes locked on hers.

The man was obviously relieved the plan was no more sinister than this. He bowed and took his leave.

"He will not forgive her, *chérie,*" Phillippe said. "Rogan shall never be reconciled with Lily."

"No, Phillippe, he shall not. We will make very certain of it."

Riding his lands was a duty Rogan usually enjoyed. Today, however, he was restless, impatient with delays and longing for home. But once inside the castle gates, the familiar diffidence took over. It was typical of late: he longed for his wife, but when he was with her he was at a complete loss, inventing reasons to take him away again.

He did not tarry with his men, but made his way to his chamber. The torches in the hallways burned softly and he began to strip off his scabbard before he reached the door. He exhaled a long breath as he entered the room, deciding that it was good Lily was probably asleep. He did not know what to say to her anymore. Where he had once been so sure, now he questioned everything.

As he stepped inside, he stopped, gaping at the scene laid out before him.

Lily stood in the middle of the chamber. Like a Greek statue, she was draped loosely in a soft linen towel that left her sleek shoulders and an alluring glimpse of leg bared to his view. Beside her was a large tub with steam rising out of it.

Dully he was aware he should shut the door behind him but he couldn't seem to move.

Seeing him, his wife appeared startled. "Rogan, I did not hear you." The play of the torchlight on her naked skin made a tantalizing display. "I was just going to bathe. I did not know you would return so early. Would you like me to fetch you something from the kitchens? I can do this later."

"No," he answered quickly, his voice almost a croak. "No need. Go...go on."

He should leave. Not for the sake of her privacy, but for his own sanity. Instead, he swiped the portal shut with the heel of his boot.

She let the soft linen float to the ground and stepped daintily into the tub. The glimpse of rounded breast, gently curving hip and flat, narrow waist was not nearly long enough for Rogan's liking. She settled into the water and leaned her head back gracefully with a sigh.

Good God! Her swift effect on his body made him grit his teeth. A cautioning voice in his head urged him once again to retreat.

"How was your ride?" she asked. Taking up the soap, she began to lather her arm.

"Fine," Rogan muttered. She spread the foam over her shoulders and neck, tilting her chin back. He moved to a stool and sat.

"Were there any problems?"

"Nothing of importance."

"Did Alyce enjoy her day out?"

"Alyce was not with us."

"Oh, I thought she had gone, too."

Rogan swallowed convulsively as she sat up a bit so that her breasts were clear of the water and in full view. He could not tear his gaze from them, wet and shining in the soft light. He let out a soft growl, almost a groan, when she smoothed the lather over each perfectly formed mound, the chill from the air on the moist flesh tightening each pink tip to excruciating tautness.

"I suppose you know Andrew has left?"

"He told me." His voice was barely a whisper.

This was torture! He almost breathed an audible sigh of relief when she settled back, the temptation of her breasts safely out of sight, but then she immediately drew a leg up and began on it, starting with her toes and progressing in slow, agonizing circles upward to each lithe thigh.

"Oliver is upset at having to sleep with his sisters—he wants to bunk with the other boys. I told him this was impossible since we are only guests. 'Tis regrettable he cannot be fostered, he would put the other pages to shame."

He could follow nothing of her conversation. When she was done with one leg, she started on the other.

With an effort, he rose and turned his back, trying to find something on which to concentrate. He took off his padded tunic and untied his undershirt. Pulling off his boots, he stood and stretched, trying to ease the tension from his muscles. His leggings, he left on. He didn't dare remove them and make so obvious to Lily what effect she was having on him.

His mistake was glancing up when he heard her rising from the water. She stood in full view, her face turned away as if completely unaware of his presence, and began rubbing the linen in unconsciously sensuous movements over her skin.

That was it. It was all Rogan could bear. He was upon her in three long strides before she could even get out of the tub.

"Oh, thank you," she said simply, and laid her hand on his shoulder for balance as she stepped over the rim. A quick smile she shot over her shoulder as she wrapped the damp cloth around her again.

"Oh, no," he growled, grabbing her arm to bring her back. "What game are you playing now, Lily?"

"Game?" She was all wide-eyed innocence, but he could sense her tension.

"You are an accomplished seductress, I will admit.

So tell me why you wish to lure me to bed. Do you think it will win you a permanent place here in my household?''

Her eyes clouded, becoming a deep aquamarine. "You always look for the evil motive from me. Do you not remember, it was you who came upon me at my bath, husband?''

"Oh, aye. But this—" he waved his hand at the tub "—was quite a display.''

Something came into her expression just then, a deflated look. To his amazement, the corners of her mouth trembled as if she were fighting to keep them from turning down. "I am sorry if I disgusted you.''

Damn! "Did I say I was disgusted, you little vixen? Quite the opposite. And do not look so surprised. You are quite tempting, I assure you.''

"Oh? I am glad to see that you are not too exhausted from your tryst with Alyce to notice," she flung back.

"Alyce? What the devil are you talking about?''

"Today. Every day. I see her with you, riding, walking in the woods.''

"I did not walk in the woods with Alyce!''

"I saw you! The day you came to the stream with the children and I. You were with her!''

"Is that what this is about?" he said with a laugh. "You think I am bedding her?''

"She is beautiful, and she wants you! And you never touch me—''

She broke off, and with a stamp of her bare foot, turned away in a huff.

He was mad to do it, but the impulse came over him, tearing away all reason, all pride. With a jerk on her arm, he spun her around and pulled her up against him in one motion. "If I take Alyce, if I take a hundred women, it is only of concern to me. You..." The words drifted away, for she looked at him with such blatant longing that the need to hurt her died in his breast. He knew what she felt, for he felt it inside, too. A need was what it was, a need to let go and crush her to him and kiss her.

The linen came loose and dropped to the floor. Neither one of them made a move to retrieve it. They just stood, caught, until Lily whispered, "Rogan," and all but leaped into his arms.

With a low growl, Rogan enveloped her. His lips descended on hers in a rough kiss. He splayed his hands across her back, roughly running them down over her buttocks to cup the smooth, naked flesh and pull her full up against him. He was aroused, inflamed beyond imagining, making the contact a heady, dizzying maelstrom of sensation, but it wasn't enough. Suddenly nothing was enough. He swept her into his arms and carried her to the bed. Together they toppled onto the lush pile of furs. His hands could not stop, questing, teasing, touching her everywhere, exploring her secrets, and it still was not enough. It was unbearable to break away in order to strip off his leggings, but when he came over her again, there was no gentleness, only a mad abandon.

And when he entered her, plunging deep inside in one thrust, it was not enough even then. It would never be enough, for the wanting of her body, to touch and hold her and go with her to the brink of sanity and beyond, was not what he yearned for. The fears of being destroyed were there, but they no longer mattered, for the great need had taken him over. The need for Lily, all of her, not just her body but her soul, as well. Until then, even the ultimate explosion of unimaginable pleasure was not nearly enough.

Exhausted, Rogan rolled away, lying on his back and staring at the ceiling as his breathing returned to normal and his heart calmed. A thick dread saturated his limbs as he thought, *Dear God, what have I done?* He made to sit up, but was prevented from doing so when Lily flung herself on him. He could have easily pushed her away, but her words made him pause. "Do not leave!"

She was crying, he saw, a fact that took him completely by surprise. Confused, he struggled to concentrate on her distress, for the acute awareness of the pointed tips of her breasts pressing against his naked chest was disconcerting.

"Do not leave me," she whispered again. "Whatever you believe of me, I pray you will listen to me now."

She adjusted a fur to shield her nudity. It was a good thing, he supposed sullenly, for he could hardly have paid much attention to what she was saying with so much of her naked flesh in full view.

The tears had subsided. Now her eyes were a cool aquamarine as she spoke, voice steady and calm. "I did a terrible thing to you. I stood against you, I condemned without hearing you, but I never conspired. It is the truth, whether you believe me or not. But what I did...I let them hurt you. I ask you—I beg you to forgive me."

Her eyelids fluttered as she lowered her gaze,

speaking in a voice so soft that he could barely hear it. But he had no trouble understanding her words. "I still love you. I have never stopped."

Rogan closed his eyes, feeling the weight of her, so light, as she lay against him.

In his mind's eye, he saw her. Laughing with the children, scolding Oliver in a gentle, loving voice. Standing up to him, a passionate spitfire with flashing eyes and stubborn chin. In his arms, melted against him, head thrown back, mouth slightly open as her teeth sank into the fullness of the bottom lip.

This was what he had feared. His bitterness had run out. God help him, if she were the very Medusa, he could not push her away from him now.

Neither could he speak the words that burned in his soul. It was as if a part of him were frozen, refusing to be thawed in the warmth of this tenderness. He stared for a long while at the exposed timbers overhead. What now? He could not hate her. But could he forgive? And how could he ever forget?

And love. She had spoken of love.

He had no answers. Really, he never had. He eased her head against his shoulder, liking the warmth of her pressed against him. After a while, the soft sound of her even breathing told him she slept.

The night was old when he finally closed his eyes.

Chapter Twenty-Two

Alexander St. Cyr, fourth Duke of Windemere, arrived with all due splendor on the appointed day.

Lily stood with Rogan on the massive outside steps of the hall, feeling a bit awed by the elegant retinue that filed through the gate. The knights were gathered in straight lines, their armor well polished. Behind, a train of wagons loaded with goods lumbered, attended by a large number of courtiers and servants, all outfitted with the livery of the duke: bright red for courage, green for peace and purple for nobility.

Last in line came a covered carriage draped with satin curtains, which were pulled back to allow a glimpse of a petite woman seated on a cushioned seat. She peered out, looking a bit round eyed and apprehensive even with the presence of the imposing man riding beside her.

He could be none other than the duke. Alexander, at first glance, was a giant of a man. He was broader than Rogan, barrel-chested where Rogan was lean. His coloring and features put Lily to mind of Andrew, but with an unmistakable arrogance. He looked about him as his men halted their procession and dismounted as close to unison as could be managed.

"You forgot no one, did you?" Rogan called. "Is there a servant or knight left behind to watch your gate?"

"I shall send for them if your staff here is lacking," came the response. "Where is Andrew?"

"You shall have to make do with the friar saying mass. Andrew has gone on some mysterious mission, one he has not seen fit to confide in me."

Alexander frowned. He swung his leg over the rear of the horse and leaped to the ground in a move surprisingly agile for one so large.

He came over to Rogan. The brothers grasped each other's arms in greeting, then embraced. Lily winced at the rib-crushing force of it. "You look well," Alexander commented, examining Rogan critically. "You have gained your strength back. I shall look forward to a challenge, and we shall see how strong you are."

"Why do you constantly seek to humiliate yourself?" Rogan asked dryly. Alexander chuckled, then turned to hold out his hand to the woman in the carriage.

"Carina, come, my love."

The lovely woman rose and extended her hand to her husband. Alexander rushed to perform the duty of handing her safely to the ground. His solicitude was all the more striking considering his bullish form, but the reason became evident when Carina's slightly swollen belly came into view.

"My wife is tired. We were delayed at the river."

Rogan's upper lip curled. "I am surprised the very waters did not part for you."

Alexander smiled. "Ah, water has no wisdom, else it would have."

"Hello, Rogan," Carina said. Her voice was like a song, lilting with a musical accent. Lily saw the wariness in her, not sure of her reception. The family must have been upset indeed when their eldest sibling wed a merchant's daughter, and a foreign one at that. By the inflection of her words, Lily would guess Italy was her native country.

"It is an honor to see you again, sister," Rogan said pleasantly. "May I present my wife, Lily."

Alexander looked at Lily, giving her the full brunt of his perusal, his dark eyes burning in their assessing sweep from her head to her toe, touching every inch. Lily felt as if she had been scalded.

"Your grace," Lily said, sinking into a deep curtsy.

Alexander peered down his nose at her. "There is much I wish to say to you."

Lily rose on trembling legs. There was a slight pressure at her hip and she realized that Rogan had slipped his hand about her waist. Her heart swelled at this small sign of caring.

It was Carina who broke the tension. "The sun is hot, Alex. Should we not go inside?"

Immediately alerted to his wife's discomfort, Alexander broke off his glare. "Certainly, let us go in."

Rogan kept Lily close to his side as they entered the hall. She felt as if a surge of invigorating power flowed through that touch, bracing her against the threat of his elder brother.

Inside, they assembled around the head table. Lily was subdued as the family fell into easy conversation. Lily was fascinated by the duke and his wife, who made no secret of their deep devotion to each other. Carina was just the type of woman one would expect to dote on a husband, but Alexander resembled an ox. The look of affection on his large-featured face was…well, rather touching. But even Alexander's dotage did not detect the lines of fatigue in Carina's features, for he was too distracted with the reverie of being reunited with his brother.

"Perhaps the duchess would prefer to rest," Lily interrupted. The St. Cyrs turned toward her. To Carina, Lily said, "You must be tired, your grace."

Carina smiled. "It seems I always am these days."

"You are a brute to bring her on this journey when she is so advanced with child," Rogan said.

"Oh, I would not let him leave me," Carina defended. "Since he was insistent on coming, I made him take me with him." With a sideways pout at Alexander, she added, "But I did not know he would force me into that ridiculous…conveyance."

"She wanted to ride!" Alexander boomed.

Lily went to Carina's side. "Perhaps some refreshment sent up to your chamber would be more in order," Lily suggested as she led the way.

Carina laughed. "Yes, that would be wise. That is another state that seems to constantly afflict me as well—hunger!"

* * *

"I ask you again, brother, what the devil it is you have in mind?" Alexander took a pull from his flask then slapped it down on the table. Across from him, Rogan heaved a sigh, weary of the argument.

"I told you of my plans," he said.

"Plans? What plans? Is this Linden Wood? Is she suffering? No! In fact, she looks quite content."

"She is hardly that."

"And neither are you."

"Now you sound like Andrew," Rogan groaned. Coming to his feet, he began to pace, sweeping his hands in the air to illustrate his words. "He besets me that my vengeance is too much. You are not satisfied it is enough."

Alexander followed Rogan to his feet. "Good God, man, have you forgotten so quickly the stripes on your back? I, for one, am not so anxious to forgive the sight of you lying two breaths away from death, your flesh such a bloody mess it horrified even me. How can you forgive that?"

Rogan whirled. "I have not forgiven," he said through clenched teeth.

"Then where is the payment you swore you would exact? In the pretty clothes—"

"They are castoffs, for God's sake."

"They should be rags!" Alexander thundered.

Rogan squared off across from him. Though the elder brother was taller and had more bulk, Rogan was the recognized champion of their rivalry. It went back as far as they could remember. Alexander's blustering way of taking control of everything and everyone and Rogan's quiet refusal to capitulate clashed.

There was, however, genuine love and concern between the brothers, and knowing it was for this reason Alexander was challenging him, helped Rogan keep his temper.

"You defend her," Alexander accused.

Rogan gave a quick shake of his head. "No, I defend myself."

"Why you did not simply put her aside, I will never know."

"You need not understand me, brother. Just do not oppose me."

"Oppose you?" Alexander exclaimed, as if to deny it. Then his eyes widened as he realized that was precisely what he was doing. He relaxed, blowing out a long breath and said, "Sit down," in a conciliatory tone.

"I would like very much to be done with this conversation. We seem to be saying the same things over and over, with no avail." Rogan did not take the seat. Leaning against the wall and crossing his ankles, he regarded his brother gloomily.

"That is because you will not listen to me. You always were stubborn."

"No, it is because you cannot stand it when someone does not obey you without question. And if I am stubborn, which I do not deny, than you are insufferably overbearing."

Alexander gave a short laugh, waving his hand in the air. "I know that. If not from the many times you have said so, then from my wife, who tells me more gently."

"You can keep me here until the sun rises, tonight

and the next and the next. But nothing will get accomplished until it is you who listens to me.''

Alexander glared at him. ''You throw all away, perhaps endanger your life, for this woman? Did it ever occur to you that she may yet again plot against you?''

Rogan could not resist a laugh. ''Ah, brother, you are quick to condemn me, but is it so long ago you yourself risked all for love? In your case, the stakes were no less dire, for you put family honor on the line, the duchy itself, and if Richard had not been appeased, imprisonment and execution could have been your reward as easily as not.''

Expecting Alexander to anger at this reminder, Rogan braced himself for the tirade that was sure to follow. Instead, his brother lifted a thick brow in speculation. ''So, you are in love with her.''

The impact of the question rocked Rogan to the core. ''Of course not!'' he snapped reflexively. ''Do not badger me with the absurd. I am simply saying that you and I are not likely...'' He could not seem to find the correct words to explain himself. ''Ah, blast!'' he shouted, turning his back on Alexander and stalking out of the room.

Lily could hear the faint sounds of their argument from her chamber, though their voices were too muffled to make out the words. She was shamelessly curious, for it was most certainly about her they quarreled. She even opened her door and leaned out to try to better hear what it was they were saying, but a strolling guard sent her back inside.

When her husband finally came in, she pretended to be asleep. She heard him yawn and stretch before undressing. Peeking beneath her lashes, she saw him rub the back of his neck—a telltale sign of tension.

The bed sagged as he lay down next to her. "Lily?" he whispered in the darkness. "Lily?"

Trying to decide whether a person truly asleep would waken at the call, Lily lay still and forced herself to breathe evenly despite the pounding of her heart. She felt the warmth of his hand on her arm, but he did not shake her. After a while, she could resist no longer, and rolled onto her back, lifting her arms to welcome him.

Chapter Twenty-Three

Dorvis shifted uncomfortably before Catherine. She held the torch higher, giving him her sternest look and watching him wriggle under the glare.

"That is distressing news," she said.

The darkness in the tower chamber refused to be banished, licking greedily at the lone torch as if it would swallow its struggling light. The slow drip of water echoed against the stone walls. She was alone with this man, but she was not afraid. There was only one man she feared—the man of whom they now spoke.

"They share a chamber. And her cousin is being fostered there."

"Cousin? We have no cousin."

"The three children who live with her. She brought them with her, and they are being given lessons. Lord Rogan is instructing the boy himself."

Dismissing this nonsense as unimportant, Catherine prodded, "The Lady Lily, she seems content?"

"No, but the rift between them closes every day."

"What of the weasel, Andrew?"

"He is gone. No one knows where. Some say he and Lord Rogan quarreled, and he has been banished."

"Ah, that would be lovely, but impossible. Those two will not be apart for long. Tell me, is she to return to her hovel?"

"Some say yes, some no. The gossip is all people want to talk about. News of them is spread about anxiously."

"No doubt my sister has wound her claws about their simpleminded hearts," Catherine muttered. She walked a few paces, thinking. She must act wisely and strike with cunning. This time, she must finish the tender lovers for good.

There would be no peace while those two lived. She could no longer bear the torturous visions of the sweet ecstasy her sister shared with the man that should have been hers. Even Phillippe's skilled hands could not banish her obsession with Rogan St. Cyr. Now, this latest report of the two of them growing closer...

Impossible, but true. What to do?

There was really only one thing.

Whirling back to the messenger, she said, "I know you are a bit squeamish, Dorvis, but Rogan must be destroyed."

Dorvis paled. "Our friend at Kensmouth is specific about that matter. Lord Rogan must not be harmed. And I will have nothing to do with it."

"There is no choice," Catherine declared, circling behind him.

Dorvis eyed her warily. "No, you'll not do it! I shall warn them. I am no murderer!"

Catherine's fingers curled around the dagger secured in the folds of her skirt.

"Of course I shall do nothing to Rogan if you do not wish it," Catherine lied. "We must think of something else." Dorvis was not clever enough to conceal the fact he did not believe her.

Pretending to pace, Catherine tapped her finger against her chin. As she passed close to him, she went into action, moving with the speed of a snake. She struck out with the torch, catching him off guard. Dorvis screamed, throwing up his hands to cover his face.

The blade came easily out of its sheath with a smooth, slicing sound. The hilt was solid and cool in her hand. Dorvis was still cringing as she brought it down to bear. The first blow glanced off his shoulder. He roared in pain and outrage. She pulled her hand back, this time slicing upward and catching him in the chest.

Then he whirled, summoning his strength to hit her with the back of his hand. The force of the blow flung her backward to slam full force into the dank wall.

The knife fell from her hand and skittered across the floor. The torch sputtered out beside her.

The burns and blood loss were taking their toll on the man, but now Catherine had no weapon. She let out a scream that rebounded crazily in the damp cavern. Dorvis lunged forward, his hands closing around her throat to cut off the sound. The crushing grip of his fingers closed off her air. Catherine clawed at him, reaching desperately for his eyes. The man held fast, pushing harder until she felt the soft crumple of her throat as her windpipe collapsed.

Her blood roared in her ears and her vision was ebbing fast. Dimly she was aware of the easing of the pressure at her neck, of the man, now just a shadow in her faded field of vision, snapping his head up. Then, the sounds. Someone coming.

He let her go, and she dropped to the floor. She heard his retreating footsteps, the growing din of men approaching. Catherine tried but couldn't lift her head. Blood filled her throat and mouth.

She clung to consciousness, desperately fighting the black tide threatening to engulf her. "Phillippe," she groaned as her husband's men lifted her off the floor. Her head flopped helplessly, and there were shouts of alarm.

Let me live, she prayed defiantly. *Let me live to speak to Phillippe.*

"Get the earl!" someone shouted.

No, it is Phillippe I want! She could not speak, but with the force of her will she sent out this last request.

The lull of sleep eternal was almost too much to resist, but she clung to life. The men were confused, speaking quickly, arguing. She heard her husband's voice demanding an explanation. Distinctly she saw him lean close and murmur, "My God!"

Not much longer. She could stave off death no more. And then Phillippe was there, his voice calling to her as she slipped backward and away.

At last! She could smell him, the scent of sandalwood he wore. She must speak, must tell him. Summoning her last reserves, Catherine issued her final bloody breath. "Kill Rogan."

The children were extremely excited about having an honest-to-goodness duke in their midst.

"Does he have a coat of ermine and a crown of jewels?" Anna asked.

"No," Lily answered, laughing. "But he does have a tunic sewn with gold thread." In fact, Alexander, like Rogan, eschewed the gross overornamentation that his class usually favored. Nonetheless, it was true he did allow a modest pattern of gold thread to be sewn into his clothing, a small concession to his position.

"Gold!" Lizzie exclaimed.

"Don' be stupid, gold is nothing to 'im," Oliver spat. "'E's got trunks of it!"

"I'll thank you to remember your manners. Sisters are people, too." Lily reached out and tousled his hair. In response, he pulled away angrily. "And mind your speech."

Rogan's voice cut in, "Good morn." Lily started. She had not heard him approach.

His auburn hair shone in the sunlight pouring through the windows, throwing off glints of gold. Dressed simply in a tan tunic, with the lacings left open at the throat, he was cool and at ease, but there was heat in those gray eyes when they fell on Lily.

"Good morn, my lord," Anna said. Lily smiled at the worshipful gaze she leveled at her benefactor.

"Lord Rogan, tell us about the duke," Lizzie begged. "Is it true that he eats ten plates of meat at each meal? Is it true that he has a hundred trunks of gold and jewels and he never wears the same tunic twice?"

Rogan chuckled, pulling the small girl onto his lap as he took a stool. He looked at Lily over the blond head, his eyes glowing. "Alexander is my brother. Imagine Oliver grows up to be a great king." To this, the girl dissolved into laughter. Rogan continued. "Would you think him grand, or would you remember him as he is now, with currant juice showing at the corner of his mouth and a rip in his hose?"

"Oliver a king!" Lizzie shrieked, not able to get past this unbelievable imagining.

"There you have it. I can only think of the duke as he was, a loud bully with a huge heart and a nasty temper."

"Is he mean?" Anna asked softly.

"No, not at all. Just a bit full of himself."

Lizzie swung her gaze to Lily. "Do you have a brother?"

"No," Lily answered evenly. "I have two sisters."

"Like Oliver."

"Yes." The reference to Catherine and Elspeth hung like a cloud, obscuring the happy moment. Nervously, she looked to Rogan. His expression was inscrutable. Her eyes dropped to her lap.

"What are they like?"

Bracing herself, Lily did not raise her head. "My younger sister is much like Anna. The other...the other is very mean."

"Like Oliver!" Lizzie exclaimed.

Oliver flushed angrily. "No, not like Oliver," Lily

scolded. "Oliver is a fine boy, if a bit impulsive at times."

Rogan said, "He shall make a great soldier one day."

Lily was surprised the mention of her family did not cause Rogan to grow irate. Gathering the children together, she ushered them upstairs for washing up before supper. As she departed, she cast a lingering glance over her shoulder, wondering what unimaginable thoughts were hidden behind Rogan's implacable facade.

The following morning, Lily woke to find herself in a restless, irritable mood. She gnawed on a crust of bread at the morning meal, and later when she was about her chores, the rich smells emanating from the kitchens made her stomach heave.

Just before supper, she felt fatigued. Thinking to find a spot where she could rest in solitude, Lily headed toward the master's solar, which was rarely used. Thanks to the six feet of stone wall, the room was perpetually cool while the large shutters could be flung open to allow a flood of late afternoon sunlight.

Crossing the room, she headed for one of the tall windows overlooking the private yard. A small sound caught her attention and she whirled about, surprised to find Carina rising from a deeply cushioned seat.

"You startled me!" Lily exclaimed.

"As you did me." Carina was, as usual, guarded.

"I am sorry."

"You look pale," she said, advancing toward Lily. "I have some cool cider if you wish."

Lily never ceased to puzzle over the lovely woman's timid manner. She was the wife of the duke, for goodness' sake. Whoever had opposed her marriage could do nothing now, for the union had been accepted by the crown and she was with child, hopefully the heir to Windemere.

"Would you care to sit?" Hesitating for a moment, Lily nodded. Carina took another chair.

They were uncomfortably silent for a span.

Carina said in her soft voice, "You seem troubled."

Lily let her head drop back and sighed heavily. "You must know the story, your grace."

"Please call me Carina." The duchess flushed. "And you, no doubt, have heard mine. I see in your eyes you wonder what to make of me. After all, I am Italian, a foreigner, am I not? A member of that inferior race, and a merchant's daughter."

"No!" Lily protested. "I was thinking something quite different. I was wondering what you thought of *me,* the wife who is supposed to have betrayed her husband after only a day. Surely, you must despise me as all the rest do."

Carina was startled, then began to laugh. After a space, Lily joined her.

"I suppose we both have reason to suspect others will judge us," Carina smiled. "Did you?"

"Pardon me?"

"Did you betray Rogan after only a day?"

Surprised, Lily recovered and offered a vehement "No."

"Strange," Carina mused, but said no more.

"You may be of humble birth, but at least you are beloved by your husband."

"And despised by everyone else. And you have won the hearts of all, though you know not where your husband's affection lies," Carina countered. Frowning, she added, "Are you certain you are well? Your color is so pale."

"I am tired today."

Carina nodded. "The heat is taxing."

"I suppose it is a small illness."

Carina looked at Lily thoughtfully. "Could you be with child?"

Lily froze. The room, the delicate woman sitting across from her, the light streaming through the windows all receded as the blood drained to her feet, leaving her a cold, hollow shell with the liquid sound of her own heartbeat pounding in her ears. "With child," she whispered.

"Have you missed your flow?" This Carina asked with a slight blush. "When was the last time?"

Lily knew she was right. Her last monthly course had been too long ago. She had not noticed with everything else happening around her. "Oh, dear God!"

"But this is excellent! You are to give your husband a child of his own!"

"No!" Lily moaned, jumping to her feet. "You do not understand! I cannot be with child, I cannot!"

"What? Why?"

"He'll take my child. He told me so. He'll take my baby and I'll never see it again!"

Carina's delicate brow furrowed as she regarded Lily. "You must tell me everything. Here, drink this.

It is cool, it will relax you. Now, take a deep breath, and begin.''

Under Carina's gentle command, Lily did as she was bade. In between sentences, Carina prodded her to sip from the cider. When she was finished, Lily sat staring at her hands clutched around her cup. Carina gently took it away and folded her hands in hers.

"We must take time to think of what is best to do,'' Carina said at last. "I will speak to Alexander.''

"No!'' Lily insisted. "Alexander hates me. He believes all of those wretched lies.''

Carina nodded, unperturbed. "True, Alexander does believe you conspired against Rogan *because* it was what Rogan believed. Can you not see how Rogan has softened toward you?''

Lily shook her head emphatically, hardly hearing her. "Rogan has not forgiven me. We have a truce. That is all.''

"But there is gentleness—I have seen it. In fact, it makes Alexander positively livid. If you but speak to him, perhaps he will relent.''

Lily pondered this for a moment. "Perhaps. Or perhaps not.'' A single tear raced to her chin. "I cannot take the chance.''

"Then, what will you do?'' Carina challenged softly. "It is not as if you can keep this matter private.''

"I do not know,'' Lily whispered. Her eyes were wide as she looked imploringly at Carina. "May I ask you to keep my secret until I can think of what to do? It may only be postponing what is inevitable, but I cannot face Rogan yet.''

Without hesitation, Carina nodded. "Of course, you must decide what is best. I shall promise not to interfere if you will pledge in turn you will not act rashly."

"Agreed," Lily said, offering a shaky smile.

Carina sighed softly as she said, "My dear friend, you must hold fast."

The weather was fine, the kind of day that makes a man feel like he has the world all to himself, Rogan thought. A crisp wind brushed away the heat of the sun and there was not a cloud to be found. The new greenery of the forest shimmered in the breeze, undulating in a sultry dance and casting dappling patterns over those below.

He urged Tarsus into a run. They cleared the gatehouse at full gallop and headed straight for the stables where he dismounted. He was anxious, impatient and single-minded. He wanted Lily.

"Rogan." A feminine voice cut into his thoughts. He looked up, blinking away the clinging reverie.

"Alyce. Hello."

"I was just on my way to the ladies' solar when I saw you and remembered we had a wager."

Rogan frowned. Damnation, but his brain was fogged. "Wager? I do not recall."

She made a pouty face in mute umbrage. "You really have forgotten? You insisted my horse would never clear the fallen tree. And she did."

"Ah. I remember now." It was difficult to concentrate on the conversation.

"Well," she said with a smile, "it is a gorgeous

day and you *do* owe me an afternoon ride. That was the wager.''

He shook his head. ''I just brought Tarsus in. And now is not a good time. Tell me, have you seen Lily?''

He thought he detected a flash in her dark eyes. ''Yes, actually. She seemed rather cross. I saw her duck into your solar.''

''Thank you,'' he said, and stepped around her. Calling over his shoulder, he added, ''We shall take in that ride soon.''

Alyce's smile was tight as she answered, ''Of course.''

Whirling, Rogan set off down the corridor only to collide with someone heading in the other direction. His left shoulder glanced off the man's right side, knocking Rogan sideways. He snapped his head around just in time to see the fellow duck and turn, as if he were hiding.

Ridiculous, Rogan thought, wondering whether the other was afraid Rogan would berate him for his clumsiness. Anyone who knew the master of Kensmouth knew short-tempered abuses were not his way. Had he been thinking clearly, the oddity of the encounter would have registered a note of interest. As it was, Rogan merely cast a curious glance at the hunched, retreating form before hurrying on his way.

When he arrived at the solar, he entered without warning. To his utter shock, his wife was standing with his sister-in-law, their heads bowed close together. Both faces swung toward him, eyes wide and mouths open in a perfectly matched set of *O*s.

At this somewhat guilty reception, Rogan's keen instinct tweaked somewhere in his gut. He cocked a jaunty brow. "Wife." Turning to Carina, he said, "Sister."

Carina inclined her head regally. Rogan had to admit her lack of breeding did not show. In fact, it never had. "I am feeling fatigued," she said in her faintly accented way. "I shall take my rest."

Rogan bowed respectfully as she passed, waiting until she had closed the door before turning back to his wife.

Her pallor, if it were at all possible, had increased. "What is it?" he said, concerned. Moving toward her, he extended his hand. "Are you unwell?"

She skittered away. "I am a little ill. It is nothing serious, just a touch of fever, I fear."

"Come sit," he offered. She seemed to float slightly beyond reach.

"I think I will take to my bed," she murmured.

Rogan was mildly surprised. Lily, as long as he had known her, was not inclined to midday rests. Then he noticed her hands clutched in front of her, knuckles white, and his eyes narrowed. She was upset, nervous. She was keeping something from him.

He made his tone conversational, with a hint of solicitude as he moved closer. "Are you certain you are well? Would you like me to call for the physician?"

"No!" she exclaimed, cringing from him again. Her lips jerked into a poor attempt at a reassuring smile. "No, I am fine. I simply need rest."

He swept his hand toward the door. "Then, by all means, allow me to see you to bed."

She stared at him, seeming as if she would object. In the end, she put her head down and complied without protest.

Wordlessly he ushered her to their chamber. She was up to something, he could *feel* it. *What the devil was she hiding?*

A cold, hard feeling was winding its way around his aching heart.

"Undress," he said in a low voice as he shut the door behind them.

"Please call my maid," she said.

"*I* will be your nursemaid."

"Rogan, I am not so ill as all that." Again, the forced smile. "I refuse to keep you from your work."

"Not at all, my lady," he said.

Hesitant, she finally kicked off her slippers and, with Rogan's aid, shed her gown. He could not suppress a shudder of desire as he viewed her lithe body draped only in the thin gauze of her chemise. Resolutely he turned his mind away from such temptations and settled down in a chair as she nestled onto the furs.

Crossing his arms over his chest, he waited, wanting to see how far she would take her playacting. To his utter amazement, his wife was asleep within a pair of minutes, leaving him more puzzled.

He ordered dinner to be brought to the room, eating alone when Lily did not awaken. Eventually he stretched out beside her, courting sleep to stifle the swarm of suspicions filling his head.

* * *

Realization woke him out of a sound sleep. His eyes flew open and all of a sudden he simply *knew*.

It was the man from Charolais! The one in the hall—they had nearly collided. His name...his name was Phillip—no! *Phillippe*. Rogan had seen him numerous times while in Cornwall, having taken note of the swarthy complexion and the thick French accent as something out of the ordinary.

Rogan sat up, glancing at Lily curled next to him. Her mood yesterday...could it be the presence of this Phillippe was known to her? It would explain her confused state, her loss for words. Her fear.

Looking at her now, her face in repose appearing angelic and reminding him of her younger sister—she of the cherubic countenance and demonic soul—an old thought burst unbidden and unwelcome into his mind. *Did Lily's beauty hide a similarly corrupt nature?*

Dear God, would this agonizing uncertainty never end!

He swung his legs over the side of the bed and all but leaped out. Restless, irritated, feeling as if his heart were going to burst out of his chest, he clenched and unclenched his fists as he paced.

Bloody hell, where was Andrew? He needed him right now.

Speaking with Alexander on the matter was out of the question. The duke would condemn Lily without a second thought. Rogan needed the *truth*.

Gazing at Lily still asleep, he shook his head silently. She would not give him the answers he sought—her earlier behavior had been proof of that.

This man, this stranger, had come between them, threatening the fragile trust they had begun to build. Had the swarthy knight come to Kensmouth to blackmail Lily over the past, with information she would not wish Rogan to know? Perhaps proof of her duplicity. Or perhaps he was here as her friend, conspiring with her to gain her freedom.

Impossible to know. But he would find out in due time.

Meanwhile, he stayed by his wife as she slumbered deep into the night. His insides felt as if they were shriveling and an ache pressed against the solid wall of his chest, so strong he could scarcely breathe. He prayed. And he thought, with a sinking sense of despair as the hours waned, of what on earth he was going to do if Lily had betrayed him again.

Chapter Twenty-Four

The first ray of sunlight fell across her face, waking Lily all at once. She blinked, smiled and reached her hand out toward the warm presence of her husband lying beside her. Memory hit, freezing her in mid-motion. The babe growing inside her. She had forgotten for a moment. Withdrawing her hand as grief flooded through her, she rolled over and curled herself into a tight ball.

The illness was with her again today. She had heard advice to newly pregnant women about taking dry bread in the morning to still the churning of the stomach. She wished she had some. It seemed that now she knew of her condition, the nausea was stronger.

She was not sure how long she lay there, fighting sickness, before Rogan awoke. She felt him rise from the bed, heard his soft footfalls on the rushes as he headed to the washbasin. The splashing of water signaled his morning ablutions. She could picture him in her mind's eye, rubbing the cold water over his face and through his russet hair. It would drip off his chin, puddling just before his feet as he lathered his face and ran the razor over the whetting stone.

The smell of his soap brought a ripple to her stomach. She tried bravely to fight it, but had to admit defeat in the end and dash for the chamber pot.

Rogan paused, razor hovering over one cheek, and watched her as she emerged from behind the screen.

"If you are still ill, you should stay abed. I will send someone to see to you."

She was about to say it would pass, but caught herself in time. It would surely arouse his suspicions, for the morning sickness was a well-known symptom, one of which even a warrior would be aware. "Thank you," she said weakly, and climbed into bed.

He finished shaving and came to gaze down at her. She raised her eyes, wondering when he had ever looked so hard as now, or sounded as cold as a few moments ago. His eyes were the color of slate as they regarded her.

"I am going to ask you a question, Lily."

Her stomach was heaving again. She swallowed convulsively and nodded.

"Did you have any visitors yesterday?"

What an odd question. Lily thought for a minute, wanting to take care that she hadn't forgotten something. "No," she answered truthfully.

"What of the last few days? Anyone?"

"No. No one."

His eyes seemed to bore into her. "Are you truly ill?"

The question startled her. "Of course." She feared

she was about to demonstrate the fact for him once more.

He gave a curt nod. "Yes, you may be. I have one more question for you. Do you remember a Frenchman in your father's household, a dark fellow. I believe his name was Phillippe."

Lily was aware she was being watched closely. "Yes, I know of him. He was Catherine's man. He served only her, not my father. He was a dreadful man."

A strange look passed over Rogan's features before he abruptly turned away.

"I will send your maid in to check on you from time to time."

He left without another word, leaving behind a void full of question and uncertainty.

Rogan paused, tilted his head back and exhaled a great breath. *She was lying.*

Rubbing the back of his neck, he tried to rein in his thoughts. She was ill. Perhaps that was all there was to this strange behavior she was displaying.

Even while he formed the idea, he rejected it. He had seen Lily face crisis before—one he had served up himself. He had watched as she had confronted the venomous Sybilla and quietly mastered the entire castle, even held her head up in the presence of a duke. Therefore, Rogan found it difficult to believe an illness would so completely undo her.

His hand curled into a fist. He wanted to strike out at something. He heard someone call his name and snapped his head around.

"What?" he snapped.

It was Alyce. Rogan groaned. He did not have time for the woman, and lately her cloying ways were wearing on his nerves.

An excuse to beg off froze on his lips when he saw her expression. He stepped forward, grasping her arm. "Alyce, my God, what is it?"

She was as pale as winter's first snow, her large eyes swimming with a glazed look.

"You shall hate me, I know you shall. But I am so afraid."

"Alyce, tell me." He had known this woman since she was a girl, yet never had he seen her thus. She was plainly terrified.

"I never meant harm. It was a game, to gain favor. I wanted to protect you—you were falling under her witch's spell. You were in danger! There was no one else for me to go to!"

Her panic was contagious, combining with his own knowledge that something devious was afoot. Rogan snapped, *"Tell me!"*

Her shoulders sagged. "I have been receiving messages from Lady Catherine Craven."

Rogan reacted to that name. Alyce saw, and continued in a wheedling voice. "I thought perhaps she could give me some advantage, something with which to use against Lily. But she turned the whole matter about. She wished to kill you." She held her hands out to him in a halfhearted gesture of pleading. "Dorvis was her messenger, but he agreed you should never be harmed. He killed her, to protect you because of my orders, Rogan. So you see, I saved your life.''

She dropped her hands to her side. ''I thought it was over until Dorvis told me he saw her knight here, skulking about the castle, and—''

Rogan interrupted, ''Phillippe. The Frenchman.''

''Yes! How did you know?''

''I saw him.''

''He means you harm, Rogan,'' she said. ''I came forward only because I am terrified for your safety. Dorvis says you are in grave danger.''

''Catherine is dead,'' Rogan muttered, ''and still Phillippe is here. Why?'' He blew out a deep breath and raked his hand through his hair. The one question that plagued him the most, Alyce could not answer: what was Lily's part in all of this?

Or perhaps it was Lily, not himself, who was in danger.

Rogan broke out of his thoughts, infused with a cold pall of apprehension. He shouted to a passing servant, ''Summon my captain.''

He started away when he remembered Alyce.

Rogan looked over his shoulder at the beautiful redhead. His heart was hard, but he had learned the folly of allowing his rage to rule. ''You came forward to warn me, even at risk to yourself. I give you your freedom, but you are no longer welcome in my castle. When the matter of Phillippe is settled, you may leave to take up another life anywhere else but here.''

Alyce gasped a choking cry, though whether of relief or misery, he could not tell.

He found their chamber empty. Asking about, he

was informed his wife was in the garden. He found her seated alone and quite still, hands resting on her lap, back rigid as she watched the play of a pair of sparrows. As he moved closer, he could see she was not watching the birds at all, for her eyes were focused on some faraway point. He paused. Whether it was uncertainty or some primitive flare of instinct, he didn't know, but his delay allowed him the vantage point with which to see danger as it approached.

There! Something dark flitted among the foliage, so quick it was almost undetectable. There again! Advancing. Toward Lily!

He almost shot forward, his impulse to protect Lily overriding seasoned intuition. Then he remembered his advantage, for the archway where he stood gave him anonymity and a clear view of the garden. With a supreme effort of will, he stopped himself, though his every muscle protested this act of reserve.

Flattening his body up against the side of the alcove, he watched the dark shape. Even before it emerged, Rogan knew it was Phillippe.

Lily didn't see the stealthy intruder at first. Then all at once, she sprang to her feet. Her hand flew over her mouth, not quite stifling the scream that tore from her throat before it choked off. Everything, from the horrified look in her eyes to the way she staggered backward, told Rogan what he needed to know.

As much as he wanted to rush forward, Rogan stayed where he was, assessing and planning the most effective means of attack.

They were too far away for their conversation to be audible, but Rogan could see Phillippe was speaking to Lily in a casual manner, not overtly threatening. Yet Lily cringed before him.

Slipping out from under cover, Rogan ran to the nearest line of shrubs. This was infinitely painful, for it meant allowing Lily out of his sight. Every nerve in his taut body screamed in agony as time seemed to suspend forward motion. If she were harmed he would never forgive himself.

Why had he foolishly persisted in casting her the villain, in doubting her character even when he saw her courage and spirit prevail at every turn? Through all he had dealt her, she had remained steadfast.

God help him, he had been so absorbed in his bitterness he had ignored what was so blatantly obvious. Even Andrew had come to see it, but Rogan had refused, clinging to the old hatred because he was a coward. Yes, a coward—too afraid to take the chance again and welcome love.

Gritting his teeth, he crouched and sprinted along the hedge. If Phillippe hurt Lily, Rogan knew his life was over.

He could hear their voices. The oily tone of the Frenchman answered Lily's almost hysterical one. Moving more cautiously now, Rogan inched nearer until he was within reach. Keeping low, he peered at his wife and the dark-skinned man.

"Think of the children, *chérie*," Phillippe was saying. "They could come to great harm if you do not cooperate. I have been watching for some time now. Those urchins are like your own babes. You could never allow anything to happen to them."

Lily's face was ghostly white. Rogan's arms ached to hold her, shelter her, rescue her not only from her present tormentor, but of all the ill he himself had done her. He made himself wait.

"You cannot touch them!" she cried.

"Ah, but I will. I shall find a way. I managed to find you alone, did I not?"

"I shall tell Rogan, he will kill you!"

Gladly, Rogan thought, wanting badly to rush the man. But Phillippe was too close to Lily. There was danger he could grab her and hold her as hostage.

"Ah, *chérie,* but he will have to find me first. And I am not so easy to find. I may even go away for a while and wait for the day when you think I have forgotten all of you. It may be soon, or perhaps not. But I *will* return one day, and you will lose one of those sniveling brats. Who shall it be? The little girl. *Non,* the obnoxious boy, I think."

Rogan's world went red. He struggled for control, squeezing his eyes shut to block out the fury.

"All I am asking of you is a simple favor."

"Simple favor!" Lily exclaimed. "My God, you are mad! You are demanding I kill my husband!"

So, that was Phillippe's plan. *Kill me, and make Lily a murderess!*

"I cannot understand why it is so troubling, after all he has done. He locked you away in that terrible house. We heard of your humiliations. He despises you. Now, I give you a chance to rid yourself of him, and with great benefit. As his widow, you would be rich. And all you need do is empty this vial of poison in his wine."

There was a long silence, then Lily said, "Why are you doing this? Catherine is dead. You told me so yourself. Leave me alone. I could no more harm Rogan than I could one of those children."

"But you must," Phillippe said reasonably, as if they were debating the merits of a walk in the fresh air. "It is so very perfect, do you not see? Ah, Lily, your sister wanted Rogan, but she hated him. I think she despised the power he had over her, for he was her compulsion."

"I shall never know why you encouraged her in such a fruitless quest. Were you not jealous?"

Phillippe laughed. "*Non, chérie,* never jealous. *Ma petite* and I, we had a special understanding. No one knew her like I. No one could calm her, cheer her, read her moods as well as I. Rogan was merely a *possession* she desired. It was her one regret, losing him. As she lay dying, she begged me to send him into death to be with her. Ah, I adored her, you know. She was a goddess. What better justice for my poor *petite* but to send Rogan to her by your hand?"

"I will never do it."

"Then you will lose all you love, one by one, for as long as it takes until you agree. I shall haunt you for years, *chérie.*"

From his vantage point Rogan saw Lily's hands come up and protectively cross over her stomach, and suddenly understanding hit him all at once. His knees went weak and his vision contracted, narrowing to a pinpoint centered on Lily's anguished face.

The moodiness. The withdrawal. The sickness.

She was with child. And he understood. She believed...

He couldn't finish the thought. He remembered his hateful words well enough to know what it was she feared. He had meant to cause her suffering then. And now, now that his child grew within her womb, he found he never regretted anything so deeply in all his life.

Then his advantage came. Phillippe moved away, half turning so his attention was not focused on Lily.

Bending silently, Rogan picked up a fist-sized rock near his foot and tossed it toward the other side of the garden. It hit a tree and made a loud rustle in the shrubbery below.

Phillippe's head snapped up and at the precise moment of distraction, Rogan leaped.

He heard Lily scream. Phillippe stopped talking in midsentence, staring at Lily in confusion until Rogan neared enough to catch his eye. It was too late for the other man to react, and Rogan reached him, had his arms pinned to his back with one hand, the other arm locked around the Frenchman's neck before the villain realized what was happening.

"Lily, get inside!" Rogan shouted.

The urge to kill was strong. Rogan was acutely aware he could snap the cur's neck with a sudden twist done just so. Sweet Lord, he wanted to do it so badly it hurt.

Lily followed his instruction and fled. Rogan concentrated on the man struggling within his grasp. He was not small, but he was thin and soft. Rogan wrestled him down onto the ground until he was supine with his face pressed into the dirt and Rogan's boot planted firmly in the middle of his back.

"Did I hear you threatening my family?" Rogan demanded, leaning on his foot so the man's face was smashed into the dirt, making it difficult for him to breathe. "Did you say you would haunt my wife, killing those she loved until she did your bidding?" More pressure and Phillippe was coughing out the dirt he had inhaled.

Shaking, Rogan reached for him. Shouts and the sound of people rushing toward him snapped him out of his rage. With a parting shove, he whirled and saw his men had arrived. While they took Phillippe in hand, one said, "Thank goodness, my lady found me right off. You are not harmed?"

"By that idiot? He preys on the weak, then skulks away like the cad he is."

Alexander burst out of the doorway, roaring like a lion and demanding to know what was happening. "I will explain later," Rogan supplied. "Suffice to say we had a bit of adventure here today, and I believe my wife is in need of me at the moment."

"Is that all anyone can think about—that blasted woman!" Alexander waved a beefy fist. "All day long, Carina chides me over her, calling her 'sister' and pouting when I refuse to listen to your wife's good qualities. By God, Rogan, has everyone in this castle gone mad? Have they forgotten what she did?"

Rogan grinned at his blustering sibling. "I don't know about others, brother, but I no longer give a damn about what she did. She is my wife. Now, excuse me."

Alexander grabbed Rogan's arm. "What the devil—? You forgive her?" he asked incredulously.

"Aye," Rogan answered without hesitation. "And do not glower so at me. Would you rather I drag myself about in misery to the end of my days, or forgive and live on a happy man?"

"You love her! Do not deny it."

"I do not!" Rogan protested in feigned shock, then cocked a mischievous brow. "Deny it, I mean. Now, excuse me, please, for I think these words are better suited to a prettier set of ears."

Leaving Alexander gaping, Rogan headed toward the door.

Phillippe's voice rang out. "Rogan!"

Rogan turned, facing the prisoner standing amidst several soldiers, all with swords trained on his midsection.

The Frenchman's face twisted in a grimace. "I shall go to her a failure."

His gaze locked with Rogan's for an instant as the latter frowned in confusion. Then, Phillippe lunged toward one of the soldiers with a soul-chilling cry. Realizing what he intended, Rogan called out, "No!" But it was too late. With an expression of blissful satisfaction, Phillippe staggered back. The soldier, dazed by the unexpected assault, looked down at his bloodied sword, then at his master. "I—I am sorry, my lord. I did not realize..."

Rogan gave a quick shake of his head. "He wanted to die."

With a chilling look of rapture on his dark features, Phillippe lifted his eyes to the sky and without another sound, pitched forward and lay still in a spreading puddle of blood.

Rogan was the first to break the shocked silence. "Remove him."

Chapter Twenty-Five

Just inside the doorway, Rogan was brought up short by the terror-stricken face of his wife. He took her by the shoulders and said, "The madman, Phillippe, impaled himself on one of my soldier's swords."

She let out a breath of relief, her eyes wide and unwavering. What an unusual color they were. No matter how many times he gazed into their depths, their beauty always astonished him. Gently he took hold of her hand. "Come."

She flinched at first, but he did not have to drag her through the halls. When he reached their chamber, he said without preamble, "I know about the babe."

Her look of horror tore at his insides.

"How—?" she began, then stopped. "Carina told you."

"No, Lily. I guessed." He drew in a long breath, paused, and blew it out. "I am not mistaken, then?"

"No," she answered softly. Then, something flashed in her eyes and she squared her shoulders. "I would have told you."

He shook his head, smiling sadly. "No, my love.

You were afraid to tell me. You remembered when I said I would keep your children from you.''

Her facade crumpled and her gaze fell away from his. Her teeth caught her bottom lip and tears stole down her cheeks. Rogan took a step forward, grasping her arms and giving her a small shake to make her look at him. "You must forget that, Lily. It was said to hurt you, but I did not mean it. Or maybe I did at the time, but I do not intend such a barbaric thing now. I will not separate you from our child, I promise you.''

She stared at him, frozen, with those fathomless eyes searing his soul. Rogan was surprised to feel the sting of tears at his own eyes. "What a fool I've been,'' he said in a voice gruff with emotion. He smoothed his fingertips along the moist track on her cheek.

Her dainty hands covered his rough, callused ones. "Then you will allow the child to stay with me? At Linden Wood?''

"You will stay with me here at Kensmouth. Always. Do you understand? You and our child. You are never to leave me.''

"Then you forgive me?'' she asked, her voice barely above a whisper.

The truth was that he had a long time ago. He just had not realized it until this very moment.

Drawing a ragged breath, Rogan said, "God help me, Lily, I cannot find it in myself to condemn you anymore. I see before me, every day, your love and kindness and strength, and I cannot believe any longer in my hate.''

She was staring at him in joyous shock, her mouth working slowly as if she wished to tell him something but no words would come. Then, she was his Lily again, holding nothing back as unabashed joy flooded her features and she began to cry and laugh at the same time.

"Shh," he said, holding her tight.

A new voice sounded from the threshold. "And to think I made that whole journey for nothing. You two look like you could scarce be bothered with my most important mission."

Andrew! Rogan's head snapped up and he whirled toward the open doorway. Leaning insolently against the frame was indeed his younger brother, looking smug as a cat.

Rogan remembered he was furious with him. "Where the devil have you been? And what do you mean going off like that without my permission?"

"Permission?" Andrew frowned. "I do not answer to you. I am a priest, remember, not a servant."

"Let me finish for you. You answer only to God."

"Actually, yes. And I daresay our Almighty Creator is quite pleased with me."

"Well, I am not. I want an explanation."

Lily laid her hand on his arm. "Rogan," she cautioned.

He gripped her fingers briefly. Giving her a bracing look, he let her see behind the mask of sternness he wore for Andrew's benefit.

"Let me show you instead," Andrew said. Holding his hand out, he grinned as a small, cloaked figure glided into view.

Rogan frowned, disliking the mystery. "What is this?" he snapped. Then, the gasp of his wife beside him brought realization instantly.

"Elspeth!" Lily cried.

The fragile creature lifted her hood to reveal the familiar cherubic face framed with a short crop of curls.

Pleased with the shocking effect of his guest, Andrew rocked on his heels. Rogan almost growled, but was stopped when Lily took a step toward her sister. Wordlessly he reached out quickly and pulled her back.

"Explain," he demanded in a soft, deceptive voice.

Andrew answered calmly, "Listen to her, Rogan."

Rogan scowled. "Shall she regale us with more lies?"

Breaking away from his grasp, Lily approached Elspeth.

"Tell us the truth, Elspeth," Lily urged. "Do not be afraid. For whatever reason you have come here, you *must* speak only the truth."

"I did not know she wanted to kill him," the girl said in a rush. "Catherine said Father would only send him away."

"Catherine is dead," Rogan said rudely.

Elspeth's eyes widened, her small, perfect mouth forming an *O* of shock. After a moment, she sighed, closing her eyes briefly as her lips moved in silent prayer.

She fell still as everyone awaited her next words. "Then it is over, and she is in God's hands, may He have mercy on her soul." Looking steadily at Lily,

Elspeth explained. "Catherine told me before the wedding that Lord Rogan had...forced her. She wanted me to say it had happened to me because she said no one would believe her."

"On that account she was correct," Lily agreed.

"Of course I refused. She left me alone and I thought it was over." The smooth brow creased as her expression darkened. "On the night you were wed, she came to me again. With that man..."

"Phillippe?" Lily prodded.

"Yes, him. They said if I did not lie, if I did not say...the lie I did, then Phillippe would kill you." She swallowed, her eyes clouded with the depths of her grief. "I knew he would do it. Catherine was mad. Oh, Lily, it was so vile to see her like that, out of her mind with jealousy. I did lie, but I did it to save you."

Rogan was stunned, horrified that even Catherine would be so heartless to force such a thing on a child.

Andrew said, "Elspeth has come to set matters to rights, even before she knew of Catherine's death. Though she lied to keep Lily from harm, she is terribly guilty about her role in the evil done against you, though it was not done out of her own design. I counseled her to come here and make restitution so that the good Lord, who has already forgiven her, will move her so she can forgive herself." Moving closer, he spoke confidentially. "She is fragile, Rogan. For God's sake, do not destroy her now."

Rogan stood silent, stock-still for a long moment as Lily moved to take her little sister in her arms. He heard her say, "Hush, now, sweetling," and he felt a peculiar pressure in his chest. Lily looked at him over

Elspeth's head, which she had laid upon her breast. Her voice was merely a whisper. "Please, Rogan."

He took one step forward and placed his forefinger under the girl's chin. She lifted her gaze to him, her round eyes full of hope and fear. "Worry no more, little one," he murmured. "I have learned that vengeance is best left to God. And those who are responsible for all this evil are dead. Their passing leaves us in peace." Looking at Lily, he felt his face soften. "Besides, for all that was taken away, this day I have been given back twice as much."

"What the devil—?" Alexander's voice boomed, making everyone jump. Ignoring the strange tableau, he advanced on Andrew. "You arrive and do not even have the courtesy to *see me first!*" The last three words were literally shouted.

Andrew only smiled. "Pressing business, brother, I do apologize. Allow me to introduce the Lady Elspeth of Charolais. Our relative, of sorts."

Alexander looked apoplectic.

"You do not know the situation, brother," Andrew began, but was cut off when Alexander lunged forward and lifted him off his feet by two great handfuls of his collar.

"You brought her here?" Alexander thundered.

Andrew cast a helpless look at Rogan. "Ah, well, Rogan, perhaps you should be the one to explain it to him."

Rogan sighed. "Alexander, put him down. He looks ridiculous, dangling like that. In the event that you have not yet noticed, it is I who was slandered by the girl. You do not mind, do you, if I dispense my own judgment? As it turns out, she was as innocent as Lily. She did what she had to, to save her sister's life.''

Alexander looked from Rogan back to Andrew, then to Lily. Slowly he released Andrew, who made a great show of straightening his garments once his feet were firmly planted on the floor.

''And now, if you would,'' Rogan said as he grabbed each brother by an arm and ushered them to the door and shoved them through. That done, he turned and sighed, regarding his sister-in-law, who watched him tentatively.

Lily took Elspeth's hands. ''See, dearling, all is well, now. You must not worry, as Lord Rogan said. Go with Andrew, and he will show you to a comfortable room. I will be in to see you later.'' She smiled, and the sheen in her eyes nearly broke Rogan's heart. ''Oh, Elspeth, I am so happy we are reunited.''

Elspeth offered a shy smile to Rogan before skittering out. At the round of renewed protests from his siblings with the opening of the chamber door, Rogan stalked over and wordlessly slammed it shut.

Casting a look to Lily, he explained, ''Eventually they will go away.''

Her lips twitched. ''You really are a very unusual group.''

''Nobody in the family knows how to mind their own business,'' he muttered.

Lily's mouth curled enchantingly. ''I was rather glad Andrew meddled. And thank you for what you did for Elspeth. The poor child.''

"Yes, she has suffered quite enough. As have we." Rogan grasped her hands and, with a quick pull, brought her into his arms. "So, you will make me a father," he said in a low voice.

Her eyes softened. "Does that please you?"

"You know it does. Against unfathomable odds, you have pleased me well, Lily."

Her teeth caught her bottom lip and she tilted her head to one side. "You will be a wonderful father."

"Shall I? You are far too free with your praise, wife. I would have thought you would have liked to berate me for a cad and a fool. After all, you have been vindicated quite nicely, and I have been shown up as a heartless knave who punished you unfairly."

Her eyes narrowed slightly as she stared back at him. "Are you trying to tell me you are sorry?" she asked.

Rogan squeezed her tighter. "How can I make it up to you?"

Throwing her head back, Lily let out a laugh that was pure music. "You have given me a life I never dreamed possible, and a love restored. And now a child. What more does a wife require?"

"So you will not ask for my prostrate pledge of penance?" he said. "No demands? Nothing?"

"You have forgiven me, Rogan, and you have welcomed my beloved sister. That is all I ask."

His smile was bitter. "You little fool, it is I who am asking you to forgive me."

She thought about this for a moment, then a languid smile stretched her mouth as she looked at him coyly. "Yes, then, there is something I ask."

"Anything."

"I would like to keep the children with us always. Oliver can foster with you, as he has been doing, and Anna and Lizzie will be raised as our babe's sisters."

"That you already have. Though, you must be practical in the matter of their marriages. I cannot give them to men who would expect noble breeding. But something suitable should be easy."

"They shall marry for love," Lily said firmly. "Like me. And our own child, as well."

He toyed with a tendril of hair, watching in fascination as it coiled softly about his fingers. "Do you have any idea how you have turned my life inside and out since the first moment I laid eyes on you?"

"Me?" she asked innocently, but a contented smile curled on her lips. "Tell me, please."

"You little minx, you beguiled me from the first moment when you mistook me for my brother. I was enchanted, and I think I have been so ever since. I always shall be, I suppose. I have resigned myself to it."

Her luscious mouth puckered into a discontented moue. "You do not sound very pleased about it."

"On the contrary, wife." He lowered his head to touch his lips to hers. Meeting his kiss, she then lingered near his mouth as he spoke softly. "I am ecstatic at the prospect. How much you have given me, Lily! Never forget it. I never will, I promise you that. You are my life. And I shall cherish you and honor you—and, yes, *trust,* you evermore."

She sighed, molding against his body in that way she had that set his loins on fire. He gathered her hair in his hands, inhaling deeply of her scent as words deserted him. His kiss descended again, this time filled with all the unsaid promises held in his heart and she answered his message with her own, sealing their souls until the passion was overwhelming, a raging heat yearning to be quenched.

It was much later, when they lay curled together upon the tousled furs, limbs intertwined, that Rogan spoke again.

Taking Lily's chin between his thumb and forefinger, he tilted her face up to his and said simply, "I love you."

* * * * *

Award-winning author

Gayle Wilson

writes timeless historical novels and
cutting-edge contemporary stories.

Watch for her latest releases:

HONOR'S BRIDE—October 1998
(Harlequin Historical, ISBN 29032-2)

*A Regency tale of a viscount who falls for the courageous wife
of a treacherous fellow officer.*

and

NEVER LET HER GO—November 1998
(Harlequin Intrigue, ISBN 22490-7)

*A thriller about a blinded FBI agent and the woman assigned
to protect him who secretly carries his child.*

Available at your favorite retail outlet.

HARLEQUIN®
Makes any time special ™

MEN at WORK

All work and no play?
Not these men!

July 1998
MACKENZIE'S LADY by Dallas Schulze

Undercover agent Mackenzie Donahue's lazy smile and deep blue eyes were his best weapons. But after rescuing—and kissing!— damsel in distress Holly Reynolds, how could he betray her by spying on her brother?

MEN IN UNIFORM

August 1998
MISS LIZ'S PASSION by Sherryl Woods

Todd Lewis could put up a building with ease, but quailed at the sight of a classroom! Still, Liz Gentry, his son's teacher, was no battle-ax, and soon Todd started planning some extracurricular activities of his own....

MEN of STEEL

September 1998
A CLASSIC ENCOUNTER
by Emilie Richards

Doctor Chris Matthews was intelligent, sexy and *very* good with his hands—which made him all the more dangerous to single mom Lizette St. Hilaire. So how long could she resist Chris's special brand of TLC?

DOCTOR, DOCTOR

Available at your favorite retail outlet!

MEN AT WORK™

Look us up on-line at: http://www.romance.net

PMAW2

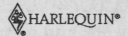

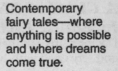

COMING NEXT MONTH FROM

HARLEQUIN HISTORICALS

- **THE WEDDING PROMISE**
  by **Carolyn Davidson**, author of RUNAWAY
  To provide for her young brothers, Rachel Sinclair accepts a
  position as a cook on Cord McPherson's ranch. But will she
  draw the line when the handsome rancher proposes marriage?
  HH #431 ISBN# 29031-4 $4.99 U.S./$5.99 CAN.

- **HONOR'S BRIDE**
  by **Gayle Wilson**, author of HIS SECRET DUCHESS
  A dashing viscount-turned-lieutenant-colonel and the courageous
  wife of a fellow officer must rein in their passion to save their
  honor.
  HH #432 ISBN# 29032-2 $4.99 U.S./$5.99 CAN.

- **A FAMILY FOR CARTER JONES**
  by **Ana Seymour**, author of JEB HUNTER'S BRIDE
  When an upstanding district attorney falls in love with a free-
  spirited woman trying to protect her pregnant, unmarried sister,
  he finds his world turned upside down.
  HH #433 ISBN# 29033-0 $4.99 U.S./$5.99 CAN.

- **LORD OF THE MANOR**
  by **Shari Anton**, author of BY KING'S DECREE
  In this exciting sequel to BY KING'S DECREE, a valiant
  knight must become the protector to the widow and son of the
  man who almost took his life. His thoughts soon turn from
  guardianship to courtship when he falls in love with his
  beautiful ward.
  HH #434 ISBN# 29034-9 $4.99 U.S./$5.99 CAN.

DON'T MISS THESE FOUR GREAT TITLES AVAILABLE NOW!

HH #427 THE LAST ROGUE
Deborah Simmons

HH #428 THE FLOWER AND THE SWORD
Jacqueline Navin

HH #429 THE MISTAKEN WIDOW
Cheryl St.John

HH #430 FLINT HILLS BRIDE
Cassandra Austin